Also by D.A. Graystone

Two Graves

The Schliemann Legacy

D. A. Graystone

Published by
Maaaddy Enterprises Inc.

The Schliemann Legacy

This book is a work of fiction. The characters, locations, and incidents are products of the author's imagination or have been used fictitiously. Any resemblance to actual events, locations or persons, living or dead, is entirely coincidental.

Published by:
Maaaddy Enterprises Inc.
347 Millbank Dirive
London ON N6C 4W6
Canada

ISBN: 978-0-9869341-0-0

http://www.dagraystone.com

Dedication

For my parents who have always believed in me.
None of this would have been possible
without your constant support and love.

For my incredible wife, Yvette, my soul mate and missing half,
who is everything I can only ever hope to be.
Thank you for getting me here.

The Schliemann Legacy

Prologue

THE CITY OF PRIAM WAS FAMOUS
THE WORLD OVER
FOR ITS WEALTH OF GOLD AND BRONZE.

THE ILIAD – BOOK XVII

Prologue

NEW ILIUM, TURKEY
JUNE 1, 1873

The small shovel dug into the dusty earth and rang with a dull metallic clang. The sound reverberated up the handle. Heinrich Schliemann barely stifled the cry welling in his throat. He threw the shovel aside and clawed at the dirt. Slowly, the object emerged; a harsh bright scar marked the shovel's impact. His hand caressed the exposed edge and the rough tarnish flaked off in his gritty fingers.

He squeezed farther into the small hole with the torch held in front of him and squinted at the object concealed in the semi darkness. Schliemann recognized the green cast of tarnished copper. He pulled the artifact aside and could see the unmistakable gleam of rich, brilliant, beautiful gold. "I've found it," screamed aloud.

He immediately clamped a dusty hand over his own mouth. He risked a quick glance out of the mouth of the small tunnel. Blinking against the strong sun, he surveyed the camp. The scorching, mid-day heat had driven the lazy native Turks to the stifling shade of their tents. Relieved that no one had heard his cry, he turned back to the treasure gleaming in the flickering light.

Years of research and months of searching in this god-forsaken country had finally reaped a reward. Scoffed at, called a dreamer, fraud and worse, he had succeeded where others had no belief. His dream was realized, his work validated, his genius proven. Exaggerated tale to some, myth to most – truth only to Heinrich Schliemann.

King Priam's city, which had remained unconquered until it fell to the invading Greeks seeking the return of Helen, was a reality. "I have found *Troy*," he whispered.

Schliemann eased the first piece free – a large copper shield. He brushed it free of the clinging dirt and traced his finger along the smooth edge. He remembered the writings of Homer from the *Iliad.*

On came the Trojans toward the wall with shields uplifted, with a long drawn battle cry.

The sound of clashing metal rang in his ears as he envisioned the two armies engaged on the battlefield. The warrior who had once held this shield had died almost thirty *centuries* before. Still, Schliemann could see the mighty man standing before him. The archaeologist had only to reach out and meet the great man's hand to be transported back to those glorious times.

Schliemann could see it all. The palace, in its prime, surrounded by opulence and grace. Fragrant wine served in golden goblets. Priam holding court, hearing of the approaching invasion of the Greeks. The old king, laughing as he walked along the battlements of his fortified city, confident of its defenses, still ignorant of the Greek treachery to come.

Yes, Schliemann thought, clasping the shield to his chest, *this was Troy*. And, it was his!

PART ONE

DISCOVERY

AMONG THE GODS,
WHO BROUGHT THIS QUARREL ON?
THE ILIAD – BOOK I

Chapter 1

MARDINAUD
JUNE 1981

The man crouched beneath the large low leaves, panting, desperate to fill his aching lungs. He wiped the rain from his face and turned to listen. He barely heard the dogs over the drumming of the rain on the leaves. He prayed it wasn't his imagination and the dogs were moving away from him? Had his ruse worked? He smiled in grim satisfaction. He had wasted time and energy moving in the wrong direction, leading them away and then doubling back, wading along the river to fool the dogs. He shuddered, thinking of the inky black, chest high water.

Distracted by the thought of leeches, he stood and took a step. With a scream, he fell face first onto the muddy ground and passed out.

Minutes later, he came too, the gritty taste of mud in his mouth. Grabbing a tree beside him, he pulled himself to his knees. Disorientated, he fought the nausea and focused on where he was. The violent throbbing in his twisted ankle made it all clear. Shaking his head and spitting out the dirt in his mouth, he checked his watch to see how long he had been out. But more than the glowing hands on his watch, the urgent barking of the dogs gave him his answer.

Not only were they now on his trail again, they were closer, much closer.

Taking more care, he pulled himself upright and hobbled through the jungle, his heart beating faster every time the dogs barked.

* * * * *

The door of the shack banged open and the man fell through the threshold. Grabbing his leg and cursing, he sprawled across the hard floor. His labored breathing sent clouds of dust floating across the floor. It reminded him how long he'd been in Kadner's compound – long enough to deserve a bigger bonus, he told himself. God save him, he had completed his assignment. He was going home. Home was the only thing that mattered. He had one more task and then he could put this jungle and its memories behind him.

Lightning exploded over the trees outside and lit the room through the open door. Almost glowing in the stark light, a white sheet covered several square objects on a table in the center of the room. A thick electrical cord ran from under the sheet and out through the back wall. The man crawled forward and yanked at the sheet. He wrapped it around his wet, shivering body and examined the sophisticated short-wave radio. He flipped switches and waited.

One last transmission. Once he had completed this final transmission, he would start running again. The rain would cover his tracks and fool the dogs.

He thought of his beautiful wife. She would be at home waiting for him. They would use the money to go away. He wouldn't need to work again for at least a year. They would spend the whole year together. This jungle and the dogs would be like a bad dream.

Suddenly, his vision cleared and he realized he was still staring at the radio set. The dead radio. Mentally chastising himself for daydreaming, he flipped a switch on the leg of the table. A generator behind the shack roared and the lights on the radio dials began to glow. The man's fingers trembled as he fine tuned the dials of the radio.

Suddenly, he heard the renewed barking of the excited dogs.

He knew he had little time to escape. If he left now, he might lose the dogs again in the rain. But leaving would delay the message for days and his employer had been specific about the timetable. There would be no bonus if he didn't send the message right away. No bonus. No extended vacation.

He pressed the transmit button.

"Iber calling, please respond. Repeat. Iber calling, please respond. Over."

"Iber, this is Mindpiece. Go ahead. Over."

"Mindpiece, this is Iber. The occupant and possessions are at the location. Be advised . . ."

The man stopped talking and took his finger off the button. He turned and saw them through the open door.

The large man came through in a crouch. His partner stood behind him and fired a controlled burst from his MAC 10.

As the man swung his handgun toward the intruders, the dogs hit him full in the chest, knocking him to the floor. The gun bounced out of his hand and landed three feet away, within sight but out of reach.

Barely held at bay, the two Pit Bulls strained for the man's throat. Their powerful jaws snapped shut, dripping slobber on his exposed neck. The man ignored the gun and desperately fought the dogs. Thrashing his arms, he screamed at the beasts and pleaded with the men who leaned on either side of the door.

The battle was over swiftly. Once released, the dogs chewed through the man's throat and he stopped screaming. His thrashing ceased seconds later.

A ridiculously small and cheap piece of plastic placed behind the triggers turned the MAC 10s into full automatics. At a rate of 1200 rounds per minute, the bullets ripped the radio equipment to shreds. The men fired until the clips were empty and then whistled to the dogs. The Pit Bulls stopped their bloody feeding, padded across the dusty floor, and waited obediently just outside the shack. With a last look around the room, the large man slammed the door and led the way back into the jungle.

"What do you think he said over the radio?" he asked, speaking Spanish. "Bitkowski wouldn't like it if we told him about a message."

"Bitkowski's an asshole," his partner replied.

The large man looked at his partner. They enjoyed working for the drug cartel, but both felt guarding Kadner was beneath them. Each hated protecting the German bastard and they found Kadner's personal bodyguard unbearable. Bitkowski enjoyed giving orders to the Colombian guards and, as long as the Cartel wanted Kadner alive, the men had to obey. Still, why should they care if the guy sent a message?

The large man furrowed his brow in thought. "I don't remember any shack," he said slowly. "We got the bastard in the middle of the jungle and left him for the animals."

* * * * *

Henri Mardinaud reclined on the plush chesterfield and stared at the huge television at the far end of the room. The floor to ceiling screen displayed a simple chessboard from an overhead angle. He turned from the screen and took a king crab leg from the steamer at his right hand, attacking the shell and pulling out the succulent flesh. After immersing the long piece of meat in a pot of melted butter and garlic, Henri held a fine china plate below the dripping leg, crammed the crabmeat into his mouth, and bit down. The juices dribbled over his several chins and onto the brightly colored bib. The size of a large pillowcase, the bib barely covered his immense stomach.

He chewed for several seconds to wring out the last morsel of flavor and then ate half a slice of dry toast to clear his palate. Pulling a cloth napkin from the pile beside him, he carefully wiped his chubby fingers clean. Satisfied he had removed all the butter, Henri reached into a large ice bucket and removed a silver tankard of pink champagne. The ice cold liquid slid smoothly down his throat, quenching his thirst.

As he pressed the tankard back into the shaved ice, he leaned forward, his brow knotted with concentration. He consulted the screen once more before speaking into the small microphone on the table.

"Knight to King's Bishop three."

The screen immediately responded.

The computer animated picture tightened down to a blowup of Henri's white knight sitting atop a tall warhorse. The knight spurred his mount and they galloped across the checkered playing field. Gaining speed, the knight moved across three squares and made a wide, graceful arc to the left. There, he faced another knight in black armor. They saluted each other, presenting their colors. The black knight's steed snorted and moved forward as the visored defender dipped his lance in challenge. The two raced toward each other, weapons at the ready.

The collision knocked both to the ground. The knights faced each other, then pulled two handed broadswords from their saddles and raised their voices in battle cries. The skirmish continued for half a minute before Henri's knight finally dispatched its foe. As the bloodied black knight magically faded from view, the white knight wearily climbed back on his steed.

"Excuse me, Monsieur Mardinaud. I did not mean to startle you. I knocked, but you could not hear me over the battle." Martin Erhart pushed up his glasses and nodded at the screen, which once again displayed the entire chessboard. "You appear to have the advantage. My congratulations."

Mardinaud looked at his assistant. "Merci, Martin. I may have him this time." Henri began another crab leg as he continued to speak. "Quickly, why do you interrupt me?"

"We have received word from Colombia," the assistant said.

Henri suddenly clapped his hands together and sent butter spraying in all directions. He cursed, grabbed a napkin, and dabbed at the greasy splatters on his fat cheeks. "I trust all is well and the report is satisfactory. What does our man in Colombia have to report?"

"Unfortunately, all is far from well." Martin hesitated before continuing. "One of your listening stations received a message from him. He was in some kind of trouble."

"Trouble?"

"The operative confirmed his earlier communications, but something interrupted the transmission before the message was complete."

"Meaning?"

"We suspect he is dead," Martin replied, dabbing his upper lip with a handkerchief. He always felt a little nauseous when he had to discuss the death of an employee.

"No confirmation?"

"No. We did not want to arouse further suspicion by investigating."

"Is there anything to link the body to me?"

"No."

"Then forget about it. What of his mission?" asked Mardinaud.

Martin bristled at his employer's effortless dismissal of the death but hid his feelings. "Ulrich Kadner is an alias for Friedrich Heiden, as you suspected. We think it is the only alias he has used since his escape. He's living in a well guarded compound in the Colombian jungle fifteen kilometers upriver from a small village. Viktor Bitkowski, another German, also lives there along with a young woman Kadner claims is his granddaughter. A lovely girl. Unfortunately, her less-than lovely reputation has kept her moving from school to school. She is currently attending a school in America."

"Interesting. I would like to know more of her and her schedule. Particularly, when she will return to Colombia. What of the treasure?"

"Again you were correct in your assumptions. Everything points to the artifacts being at Ulrich Kadner's compound. Our man did not actually see them; his information comes from observing Kadner's activities. The German has a habit of disappearing into the basement area of the main house every night for some unknown purpose. The plans of the house show a vault located in a subterranean room where we assume Kadner stores the treasure. Unfortunately, because of the circumstances of the final transmission, we were unable to learn more."

Henri chewed thoughtfully on his crabmeat. For a moment, he watched the large television screen. The Black Queen moved regally forward five squares and confronted one of Henri's bishops. A thickly muscled man appeared wearing a black hood and carrying a wicked looking ax. The Bishop bowed to the Queen with a flourish of his robes before turning to the executioner and kneeling in front of a chipped, stained stump. The Bishop laid his head down on the bloody piece of wood and the man in the black hood raised the ax. Seconds later, the executioner placed the Bishop's head in a basket. Then, both he and the remains of the Bishop faded from the screen.

"Unfortunate, Monsieur," Erhart said, his eyes on the screen.

"Alas, there must be sacrifices." Henri paused a moment before continuing. "Does Kadner suspect he is in danger?"

"Not as far as we can tell," Martin said. "He's still at the compound and the Medellín Cartel remains on guard."

"Unusual for the drug merchants to take such an interest in one person," Henri said. As Colombia's current main drug smuggling organization, the Cartel controlled the drug trade throughout North and South America. "I wonder what Kadner is giving them in exchange for their protection?"

"He has the necessary funds," Martin pointed out. "I will obtain the girl's schedule, as you requested."

Henri removed his bib and leaned back into the soft couch. The steamer beside him was empty, only the pile of shells hinting at its original condition. As he sat staring into space, Mardinaud considered his options.

The Frenchman had made a considerable fortune as an Information Broker – a well deserved fortune as Henri was the master of his profession.

Not aligned with any government, group, or individual, he independently gathered data he thought governments, businesses, and freelance operatives would find useful. He brokered this information to anyone who could pay. The reasons for his success were twofold. Not only did he gather useful information, he also knew how to price and distribute the intelligence. The most important reason for his success, however, was the speed at which he became bored.

With a body so overweight as to be almost incapable of movement, he had forsaken everything physical and become a passionate player of mental games. Ordinary parlor games bored him. Dealing with world-shaping events spoiled him for such mundane pursuits. Henri began using his information to play out complicated games with real people, learning to mold the gathered intelligence and create authentic predicaments for his players. He employed unsuspecting players to amuse him as they traveled his playing board – the shadowy world of international espionage. The skills and abilities of the players brought uncertainty and excitement to the game. Once he had assembled the players, Henri could sit back and watch the progress. The game invigorated him and he played as often as an opportunity presented itself.

"Martin, a scenario begins to unfold. The players introduce themselves. I see many different paths converging in Colombia. We will have great sport."

Erhart grimaced and waited for the standard lecture from his pompous employer. It always began . . .

"Who deserves to amuse me by accepting this morsel of information?" The fat man struggled to his feet and paced across the suite. After several steps, he began to wheeze. He stopped and lowered himself into the creaking desk chair. "We will ignore the so-called "Superpowers". They offer so little enjoyment. Instead, we limit ourselves to the smaller organizations," Mardinaud continued. "Those directly involved with the treasure or the Nazis. We must invite the Israelis to our little game. Obviously, they do not know of Kadner's whereabouts or Assi Levy would have sent a team after him. I am sure he will be ecstatic to hear about this old acquaintance. Yes, Assi Levy will pursue the matter."

"Who else would you suggest?" asked Martin, scribbling on his pad.

Mardinaud examined his fingers for residue butter as he spoke. "The next most obvious would be the Greeks. The treasure substantiates much of their civilization's ancient history. At the very least, the Greeks could goad Turkey with the artifacts. I look forward to seeing who they send after them. Contact Nikolas Stefandis."

Martin frowned at the mention of the head of Greek Intelligence. "Stefandis opposes Greece's preoccupation with antiquities. He wants the Greeks to abandon the past and create an even greater present. Surely, he is not the man to contact."

Henri chuckled. "Yes, he's rather vocal about his countrymen resting on the laurels of their ancestors, isn't he? Which is exactly why you *must* contact him. No matter how much he may wish to, Stefandis won't be able to ignore this task. The news of the treasure will destroy his weekend. Contact him at his home on Saturday afternoon."

"Very good, Monsieur," the assistant sighed. "Will there be anyone else?"

"One other. Contact Duman."

Erhart nearly dropped his notepad. "Are you sure it would be wise to bother Duman?" he asked weakly.

Henri looked at Erhart's pale face and understood the fear he saw there. Mardinaud, himself, felt uncomfortable around Duman. However, Henri had his reasons for wanting this particular terrorist. "Duman is important to the game. Someone must represent the Turks if the Greeks have a player. He's as good a representative as any. Besides, Duman will add the missing spice to the game. A measure of danger – especially for the Greek player." Mardinaud chuckled once more.

"I . . . I just don't like the man," Erhart said. "He's a sadistic killer, a psychotic, a maniac…"

"Nonsense. There is no reason to distrust him. He's not psychotic. He's simply a man with a passionate dream. It just happens he believes violence is the key to realizing his dream. He is a killer, but he has integrity and honor. The only danger is in betraying him. Believe me, I have no intention of doing that. Try Paris," Mardinaud suggested.

"I still don't know about him," Erhart persisted. "He's uncontrollable."

"Nonsense!" Mardinaud roared. "I control the information. Through the information, I manipulate him. I am control. Besides, without uncertainty, what is the value of the game?"

Erhart did not look convinced but made a note on his paper. Remembering a tidbit of information he had received several weeks ago about Duman, a plan flitted across the landscape of his mind. Unbidden, a smile tugged at the corner of his mouth. He dismissed the thoughts as foolish – dangerously foolish. But enticing, so enticing. Handled properly, with finesse, bravado, and intelligence... "If that is all, Monsieur, I will begin immediately."

As Erhart left, Henri painfully waddled back to the chesterfield. With the thoughts of the coming adventure, the fat man had lost interest in the chess game.

He would enjoy setting his players in motion and watching their progress. They would fight and claw to attain their goal and, in the end, only the best would survive. All because of him.

He felt like a god.

Chapter 2

GREECE

"With the mood he's in today," the secretary said, "you'd think it was Tuesday."

George Stamatakes smiled at middle aged woman. Since the Ottoman Turks took Constantinople on May 29, 1453, a Tuesday, the Greeks had considered it the unluckiest day of the week. George paused with his hand on the office door.

"Mr. Stefandis wanted you to go right in," the woman urged, not wanting her boss further annoyed.

George ignored the secretary and collected his thoughts. When the Director's summons had arrived, George had made several hurried telephone calls. After the third call, he was cursing aloud. Mardinaud's communications always meant problems and this latest information was no exception. However, his outlook had quickly adjusted when a new thought occurred to him. This mission presented a perfect opportunity to bring Katrina back to active duty. All he had to do was convince Stefandis to acquiesce – something he'd been trying to do for three years.

George knocked once and pushed open the door to the Director's office.

* * * * *

"It's ridiculous," Nikolas Stefandis repeated for the eighth or ninth time in the past fifteen minutes. "Why should I waste time and money on something as unimportant as this? We don't have enough to deal with? But what choice do I have? I *have* to send someone after it. If I don't, and the damn artifacts turn up... Stupid, damn stupidity!"

Stefandis kicked at the small wastepaper basket beside his desk. The can soared across the room and crashed into the wall. A portrait of President Sartzetakis slid along the paneling and landed face down on the blue carpeting. The revolving can slowed and came to a stop as Stefandis sank into his chair.

George Stamatakes walked across the room and scanned the dark paneling for the nail that had held up the large, gold framed portrait. Unable to find it, he leaned the portrait against the wall before retrieving the trashcan. He ran his fingers along the several large dents in the sides. Hiding his smile, he set the can in its place, then lowered himself back into one of the two leather chairs in front of the Director's desk.

He sat silently, watching the red slowly drain from his boss's face and neck. As Operations Chief, George had seen many such outbursts from the ill tempered Director of Greek intelligence but today's was special – a masterpiece of rage. George had been listening to Stefandis rave for over fifteen minutes but had been told little.

All he'd gleaned from Stefandis' ranting was that a message had arrived from Mardinaud at the Director's home yesterday afternoon. The message had ruined Stefandis' weekend. In return, Stefandis seemed determined to ruin everyone else's week. Of course, prior knowledge via his own sources did give George the advantage of understanding the rage.

In the past, information had frequently come unbidden from the grotesquely fat man. In fact, the choicest bits usually arrived unsolicited. Unfortunately, according to the Director, this latest intelligence was both unwelcome and distressing. Mardinaud had dredged up a morsel, which was contrary to everything Stefandis believed the Greek people should be.

"That French bastard had it delivered to *me* on purpose," the Director said. "He knows how I feel about our history. He has no right to do this. Why couldn't he just keep the information to himself? With everything going on right now, I don't need this!"

Stefandis stopped talking and sat motionless with his eyes closed.

George imagined Stefandis was thinking about last week's meeting with the Minister of Finance. The Minister had announced a twelve-percent cut in funding. The shortage of funds had forced Stefandis to cancel several operations. Operations that the Director considered critical to monitoring the continuing tensions with Turkey.

"It just isn't possible to do it all. Don't they understand?" By the sudden calm in his voice, George realized the Director had accepted his fate and was beginning to address the logistics of the operation. "God, but I hate that Frenchman," Stefandis continued. "Still, we have to take the good with the bad. His information has been welcome in the past. The treasure might even bring us some needed funds."

"What was Mardinaud's message?" George asked. He didn't want the Director to suspect how deep his sources were within the agency.

With a sigh of resignation, Stefandis sank back in his chair. A heavy paunch protruded over his belt and strained the buttons of his shirt. He scratched his hairless head and then kneaded the muscles in the back of his neck.

"Mardinaud claims to have located Schliemann's treasure. That is, the golden treasure discovered at the site of Troy."

"Sorry, sir. I'm not up on ancient history." The lie came easily to George. "Never had much of an interest. Not very patriotic of me, I guess."

For the first time that morning, Stefandis smiled at his Chief of Operations. "Congratulations, George. This country would be better off with more people like you. Our countrymen spend too much time reveling in the past instead of creating a future."

George relaxed. Stefandis was in a better mood now and thinking less emotionally. "Yes, sir. I couldn't agree with you more. Still, remember Lord Elgin. When the Turks sold him one of the caryatids from the Acropolis, all of Greece mourned. Schliemann's treasure belongs in Greece."

"Of course, you're right. However, I can think of much better ways to spend my manpower and dwindling budget than chasing after bits of metal, ancient or not."

"Where is the treasure?"

Stefandis sighed. "The Frenchman doesn't say. All I know is, he located the treasure and wants a meeting."

"Where?"

Stefandis leaned forward and looked at a sheet of paper. "Don't ask me why, but Mardinaud wants to meet in Munich."

George laughed. "The fat slob must have suddenly got a craving for Wiener Schnitzel. Either that or life is too hot for him in Paris. Too much terrorist activity. Have you thought about who you would like to send on the mission, sir?"

"No, but obviously you have."

George paused and took a deep breath. "I think, sir, it's time we gave Katrina Kontoravdis another chance."

Stefandis slammed his fist down on the desk. "I don't have enough problems with this damn mission?" he cried. "You want to send her out? Christ, she screwed up the last time and it cost her partner's life. Some mistakes are unforgivable. She shouldn't even be in the service."

George glanced down to see if the blow had cracked the glass desktop and resisted the temptation to reply immediately. The predictable refrain about past mistakes concealed the Director's discriminatory nature. Centuries of conditioning had ingrained his sexism and George had long ago abandoned any effort to change the attitude of his boss. To Stefandis, the male was God and the female was little more than a slave.

Stefandis used the failure, no matter how unfairly, to justify keeping yet another woman away from field duty. Regardless of the past, Katrina was still one of the best agents they had. George knew her work in the previous years had been exemplary. That was why he had fought so hard to keep her in the Service. A fight he had barely won. George knew the only reason she was still in the Service as Stefandis' perverse nature. He enjoyed dangling the possibility of reinstatement in front of the woman. Assuming time had not eroded her confidence completely, she would be perfect for this assignment.

"With all due respect, sir," he began, "our investigation showed Katrina was not at fault. She only…"

"She only fucked up and got her partner killed," Stefandis interrupted. "If she'd done her job, Alex would still be alive. There are no ifs or buts. Plain and simple – she fucked up. She can stay down in Records where she won't kill anybody."

Despite the Director's flashing eyes, George tried again. "I realize Alex was a friend, but he was looking for glory. He wanted Duman for his own and didn't wait for assistance. Alex was the senior operative and the decision to proceed was his. He got himself killed trying to be a hero. Katrina deserves another operation. Three years is long enough for her to pay for Alex's error."

"Well, maybe you're right at that." George looked up in surprise and saw Stefandis was grinning widely. Too widely, George thought. "You're the Operations Chief, George, and this should be your decision. Maybe it's time she had another chance. Yes, this could solve all my problems. Go tell *Miss* Kontoravdis that she has an assignment."

Something was wrong, George thought. The Director was submitting too easily. "As for her partner, sir, I would like to..."

"No partner," Stefandis said. "She's a good agent? Isn't that what you keep telling me? She's capable? She's not the screw up I think she is? No? Good, then, she doesn't need a partner for so simple an assignment."

George met the Director's challenging gaze. "With all due respect, sir, we don't even know who has the treasure. Wait until she gets word from Munich before you decide if she gets a partner. You know how Mardinaud arranges his little games."

Stefandis shook his head. "I'm not going to risk another man with her. I can't afford it. If she gets the treasure back, I'll admit I'm wrong. I'm a big man, I have broad shoulders. If she screws up, she risks only herself. Then, you'll have to get off my back about her. She's on her own for this one."

George looked across the desk and knew he had no choice. The Director had won this round. Stefandis cared little for the operation and less for Katrina. The perfect combination to get Katrina killed.

George rose from the chair and snatched the piece of paper off the desk. At that moment, he would have given his pension to knock the grin off Stefandis' face. Instead, he turned and left the office, heading directly for the basement sports complex.

Since Stefandis had retired her from active duty, Katrina had been spending more and more time at both the gym and the firing range. For the past three years, she had been sharpening her skills in preparation for a return to active duty. Now, George was finally able to give her the opportunity.

Katrina was working on the Nautilus equipment. George stood and watched her for a time – acutely aware of his aging body. He found himself admiring her figure clad in the tight blue leotard. Katrina's short hair, almost black, was combed back in the latest style. (George missed her long hair and wished she had never cut it off.) Her dark eyes shone brightly as she strained against the weights. Well proportioned curves softened her lean and tightly muscled body. As she did her arm flies, her breasts pressing against the thin cloth, George found himself wishing that his new *twenty-four-year-old* wife had the body of this *thirty-four-year-old*.

Finished with her workout for the day, Katrina grabbed her towel and walked across the mats. When she saw George, she stopped in midstride and stared at him as though she dared not step any closer. The Operations Chief held his thumb up to her and she began to smile. Then, to the amazement of the others in the room, she let out a loud cry, took three steps, and executed a perfect midair somersault.

Katrina Kontoravdis landed with her legs split and her arms stretched skyward.

Chapter 3

ISRAEL

Morning came to the desert.

The large, orange sun slowly rose, brightening the low sand dunes that stretched far into the distance. The temperature had already risen ten degrees. Most of the wildlife had long since returned to their dens in preparation for yet another day of scorching, dry heat. The remaining few worked feverishly to retrieve the last drops of dew deposited in the leaves of the stunted growth. Only the slight shift of the red sand betrayed the movements of the small creatures. A hawk circled, seeking the sparse prey before resting for the day.

The village was as silent as the surrounding desert. Laid out in habitual Arab fashion, the mud and straw brick huts were lifeless. The normally early rising laborers were absent and even the small square, home of the village's single spring, was empty. No stooped, black-robed widows came to draw water for their families. No chickens or goats gathered for their morning feeding; the stalls were empty of animals. No children ran in play before their day of labor. The dirt streets, normally teeming with activity, were desolate, as though visited by a plague.

The silence spread out from the village in ever widening circles, like the hawk high in the sky. There were no groups of men bickering among themselves as they watched their women prepare the morning meal. Even the bell in the makeshift mosque had not called the faithful to morning prayers.

In the quiet, the hawk's high pitched cry was deafening. With all its God given grace, the bird sped off to the west, frightened by a sound still beyond human ears.

Suddenly, the scream of two jets shattered the silence.

Two F 16s emerged out of the blinding sun on the eastern horizon and flew directly at the village, skimming the desert floor at 200 feet to defeat the radar. As they reached their predefined initial point, they pushed their noses up and climbed to 2000 feet. The noise increased to a frenzied pitch as the two planes rolled to acquire their target and flipped back over. Suddenly, death fell from the planes.

Each pilot released two 750 pound M117 bombs and throttled into a steep dive. By the time the four bombs exploded, the jets were back below the radar, employing terrain masking. Seconds after the blast, the F 16s had disappeared from sight.

Frail huts burst apart, their hard bricks shattering into thousands of projectiles that punched fist sized holes in the few remaining walls. The spring sustained a direct hit. Water and debris showered down on a third of the compact village. The stables caught fire and the straw erupted into flames.

A volley of bullets kicked up the dust as two attack helicopters rose under full power from behind a nearby dune. A sixty eight millimeter rocket flattened the uncompleted mosque and four incendiary rockets exploded at the edge of the village. Each helicopter continued the barrage from its single, front mounted machine gun while skidding to a stop.

Before the helicopters could settle to the ground, commandos jumped from the two craft. The double lion insignia of the elite Israeli squad gleamed prominently on the shoulder of their desert camouflage jumpsuits. Each commando carried an ARM assault rifle. Grenades swung from their webbed belts. A knife sheathed on the outside right calf and a holstered Beretta completed the uniform. Every third man also carried a pickax.

The soldiers began firing as their feet touched the ground and they headed for the closest cover. The pilots delivered another hail of machine gun fire above the heads of the running men as the transports took off. Lifting to two hundred feet, the craft hovered like huge dragonflies.

As the sun obliterated the shadows, the commandos formed a jagged line along the border of the town. At a signal, they moved into the village, splitting into groups of three soldiers. The teams broke into the remaining buildings and searched for survivors or snipers, using the pickax to check for trap doors. When they heard the dull thud of the wooden cover, the men surrounded the entryway, pried open the door, and lobbed a flash grenade down the hole. A team member risked a cave in and checked the tunnel. After completing each search, the team marked the hut with green paint and moved on.

The men reached the far end of the village within ten minutes and a blue smoke flare exploded in the air. Seconds later, the signal repeated. A loud air horn sounded as the helicopters settled to the ground. The commandos relaxed and broke formation, trying to escape the scorching sun by sitting against the partial wall at the rear edge of the village. Drinking from their canteens, they laughed and talked, oblivious to the destruction behind them.

* * * * *

As the rotors of the helicopters slowed and stopped, the silence of the desert settled back over the village. Only the crackle of fires and the low murmur of the men broke the eerie calm.

Behind the soldiers, the village lay in ruin. No building had escaped the onslaught of bombs, artillery and commandos. Huts were missing roofs and walls or totally reduced to heaps of rubble. Deep craters pitted the roads. Fires continued to burn, fuelled by wood and straw. All the visions of war were complete, save one.

No bodies littered the battlefield.

The village was deserted.

David Morritt stood on the low wall and scanned the destroyed buildings. The barrel of the rifle he held was still hot from the rapid firing only minutes before. The ammunition pouches of his jumpsuit were empty, as was the final clip he had discarded. His web belt held no grenades. As David surveyed the ruins, another commando, sporting the rank of a *Rav Seren*, came up behind him.

David, sensing the other's presence, turned and gave a mock salute. "Major Sigura. How did we do on this most important mission? I trust we did not lose any men."

Yaacov Sigura ignored the older man's sarcasm, but the obvious boredom in David's voice concerned the major. "The timing was a little off," he said. "We were almost twenty-five seconds behind."

"I hope this old body didn't hold *you* back."

Yaacov watched David remove his helmet and scrub his sweat drenched head. Gray was heavy at the temples and sprinkled throughout the short dark hair. At fifty, Morritt stood out among the young men of the elite squad. Even Yaacov, the commander of the unit, was over twenty years his junior. However, David possessed a commodity none of the younger men did – experience. Each commando considered it an honor to have David Morritt present. In many ways, David was a legend in their eyes, though most would never know reality from legend. And even the legends paled against the reality that would never be known by more than a few select individuals.

"Hold us back? We needed someone to hold you back." Yaacov pointed at David's empty ammunition pouches. "Have you forgotten the most important rule?"

"I know. *Don't use all your ammunition unless absolutely necessary,*" David quoted.

"It could save your life one day," Yaacov said.

"Maybe, but I never get to feel the kick of a gun or smell the powder." Morritt's voice trailed off.

Yaacov glanced back to check his men and then sat down on the wall. "Do you want to talk, David?"

David turned back to the view of the village. "What's to say?" he asked.

Yaacov laid a hand on the older man's shoulder. "David? I've never seen you this bad before."

Morritt sighed and sat down on the wall. These exercises challenged the boredom, but he was becoming anaesthetized to the thrill. "I haven't felt this bad before. I suffer the curse of Bilbo Baggins."

Yaacov avoided David's eyes. "I'm sorry, I'm not familiar with this Baggins fellow," he said. "Was he also in the Service?"

David threw his head back and laughed. "Yaacov, you must vary your reading. Put down your manuals and histories. You can learn much from fiction. This 'Baggins fellow' is a character in Tolkien's *The Hobbit.* After many great adventures, Bilbo couldn't settle into his old life so he wanders from home at every opportunity. His life bores him and he prays for adventure. That's me. I can't settle into the routine. All my life, any type of routine could be fatal. Now, they expect me to sit back with my feet up. I can't do it."

Yaacov knew much of David's past, although he did not know even a third of the truth. His security clearance was too low to allow for such knowledge. "You have served your country in the field for many years," he said. "The time has come for you to sit back and give others the benefit of your experience. You deserve a rest."

"I don't want to rest. I don't want to *teach*."

David had been semi-retired from the field. Politics had interfered yet again in the Mossad and many of the longer-term agents were considered a liability – or more likely a possible embarrassment. Supposedly, times were changing and the Mossad had to change with them. David hoped his was a temporary problem that his friend and head of the Mossad, Assi Levy, would solve. But until that time, David was forced to leave the field and instruct the new soldiers with their new technology.

"Look at me. I'm in excellent shape. As good as I was ten years ago. Maybe better, since I stopped smoking. My reflexes are still good. If I was a soldier, I'd still be able to fight in a war. I just want to be useful. I'm only fifty. I'm not dead, yet. You should understand how I feel."

Yaacov smiled at the man sitting beside him. He did feel for David. In less than a year, regulations would prevent the major himself from leading commando missions. The elite squad was a young man's unit. Strategy meetings and lectures would soon occupy Yaacov's time.

"Yes, I will soon be a Bilbo Baggins," Yaacov agreed. "But what can you do? Regulations are regulations. You can only make the best of your life."

"Sounds good," David said. "We'll talk again in a few years. Then you can tell me all about the wisdom of the regulations."

David shaded his eyes to watch a white and red Ecureuil II helicopter land near the two heavily armored craft. He raised his eyebrows at Yaacov. Both men rose and headed toward the sleek craft as the pilot jumped out and ran to the nearest commando. The soldier pointed at David and the pilot trotted to meet them.

The pilot saluted sharply. "Colonel Morritt?"

David returned the salute. "Yes."

"If you would come with me please, Colonel. I have orders to bring you to Tel Aviv."

David looked at Yaacov. The major shook his head and shrugged.

"Assi Levy told me to bring you immediately, Colonel," the pilot said.

At the mention of Levy's name, David's face brightened. "Then, by all means, we shall leave immediately," he said, handing Yaacov his ARM rifle and helmet.

Once in the air, David could see bulldozers heading for the destroyed village. The machines would plow the remains of the buildings under and redo the roadwork, then the construction crews would move in. By this time next week, another mockup of the Arab village would stand on the same spot, ready for the next training mission.

Turning away from the window, David wondered why Assi Levy, the *Memuneh* of the Mossad, had called him back to Tel Aviv.

Chapter 4

PROFESSOR MILNER

George Stamatakes expertly guided the open convertible around the many curves of the coastal road. Katrina Kontoravdis sat beside him, watching the scenery through the wisps of her windswept hair. She knew even the short style would be a mess by the time they arrived at their destination, but it was worth the irritation. The sea air and warm sun were relaxing and she desperately needed relaxation. She could feel the excitement and tension knotting the back of her neck. The acid content of her stomach would melt lead.

Following George's appearance at the gym, he had suggested they take a short drive down the coast. Katrina had hurried off to make herself presentable. After a quick shower, she rushed into the midday sun. Instead of the leotard and sport shoes, she now wore a simple shift of white cotton and open sandals. Her tan was dark against the bright cloth. With George in his open necked shirt, they looked like tourists heading out of Athens for an afternoon at the sea.

George evaded any mention of her reactivation and said little about their destination or the actual mission. Katrina hated to press him for information. He was the only friend she had in the higher echelon of the service. Because of Stefandis' obvious hatred, most treated her as a pariah.

All the same, she was becoming impatient with the silence.

"Can you tell me what's going on?" she asked, finally.

"What?" George glanced at her and the car veered toward the shoulder of the road. Looking to her right, Katrina swallowed hard. There *was* no shoulder – only a fifty foot drop to the rocks and water below.

"I said," she shouted, "can you tell me what's going on? Why are we going wherever it is we're going?"

George looked over again and Katrina grabbed the steering wheel. George smiled and turned his attention back to the road. "Relax," he said. "You shouldn't be so tense."

"Just watch the road. I can hear you without you looking at me."

"All right," George laughed. "Our destination is a small, unimportant dig in the southwest. The dig itself is inconsequential, but the archaeologist working the site is important to us. Do you know anything about Heinrich Schliemann and his discovery of Troy?"

"Naturally. Every school child knows about him."

"Yes, well, be that as it may, I think you might need a little brushing up for this mission. Since I'd rather be outside today than in a library, we'll visit the professor." George reduced his speed and steered the car down a road that was little more that a wide cart track. The suspension protested at each rut and Katrina's voice vibrated as they bounced along.

"Why do I need to brush up on some man who's been dead for, what, almost a hundred years?"

"Let's just hear what this professor has to say first, shall we?" George suggested, pulling off to the side. "The dig is right up here."

George shut off the engine and got out. He was several paces away before Katrina, exasperated, got out to follow him. She trotted up beside him and together they walked through the large gates marking the entrance of the excavation. Two huge dolphins, remarkably well preserved, adorned the top of the arch. Katrina recognized the stone carvings as dedications to Poseidon, the god of the sea.

Just inside the gates, two local men wearing side arms ordered them to stop. The rusted pistols, dating back to the Italian invasions of World War Two, were useless. George flashed his identification, which did little to impress the illiterate guards. After several minutes of fruitless arguing, George handed each guard several folded bills. "Just tell the professor we would like to speak with him," he said. "I'm sure he'll see us."

With the money in their hands, all sense of duty disappeared. The guards immediately dispatched a runner who returned moments later.

After relaying a message to the guards, the boy motioned for Katrina and George to follow him and they wound their way through the ruins. Almost reverently, Katrina passed the partial walls and fallen buildings, lightly dragging her fingertips along the worn stonework crafted by artisans dead for thousands of years.

The creations were exquisite examples of Greek capabilities, she thought as she walked along. At one time, Greece had led the civilized world in all aspects of life. Could the Greek people ever be that great again? Katrina doubted her countrymen were up to the challenge, but the solution was not to deny the past.

Unlike Stefandis, Katrina considered the ancient past important. Instead of worshipping or completely forsaking the past, the country needed a balance, a delicate and difficult balance between past and present, she thought. The Greeks must surround themselves with the art and traditions of their ancestors without denying the advantages of progress. Progress without a past was unfulfilling and sad. An illustrious and celebrated past without a progressive drive leads to death and decay. In Katrina's opinion, the latter was the current direction of Greek society.

"Welcome!" Katrina jumped. The accented voice seemed to come from nowhere.

Switching effortlessly to English, George addressed the Englishman standing on the wall above him. "Professor Michael Milner?"

The man climbed down a ladder, showing an agility that denied his advanced age. He wiped his dusty palms on his pants before shaking hands with George. "The very man," he said.

"My name is George Stamatakes, Professor. This is Katrina Kontoravdis."

Milner's hand lingered momentarily as he shook with Katrina. The professor did not receive many female visitors at the site. She could feel his eyes run over the thin white material of her dress, but she was neither embarrassed nor angered. Amused, she toyed with the old man, following his gaze and shaming him into keeping eye contact. Her dark brown eyes burrowed deep into his lecherous soul. Soon, he was blushing and turning back to George.

"So, how can I help a member of the Greek government?" he asked. "I trust I am not in some violation."

"Far from it, Professor," George assured him. "The Ministry informs me you are most welcome in our country. We need information about Heinrich Schliemann and, apparently, you are an authority on the man and his work."

The professor's stooped shoulders straightened as he puffed with pride. "You flatter me, sir. I would not call myself an authority, but Schliemann's work has always been a passion of mine. Please, join me in my tent for a drink. We'll be more comfortable out of this heat. I'm sure you're thirsty after your long drive."

Milner led the way to the tent where he poured them glasses of lemonade. He pointed at two uncomfortable chairs while he went through a complicated ritual of making a cup of tea. The tent was hot, almost as hot as the outdoors, and the odor of the canvas was overpowering. Katrina felt a trickle of perspiration run down the length of her spine. She took a long drink that temporarily choked off the urge to be sick. The professor immediately refilled her glass and then remembered to turn on the exhaust fan. The large blades stirred the air, creating a small breeze, and the smell and the heat lost some of their intensity.

Sitting heavily in a small chair in the corner, the professor brought his fingertips together in what Katrina suspected was his standard *lecture* pose. "Schliemann's critics have written many unkind statements about him," Professor Milner began. "There are even those who consider him a thief. Imagine, a thief! I suppose he wasn't entirely honest, but neither were those he dealt with. A man has to protect himself, don't you think? Of course," he hastened to add, "I've never had any problems with your countrymen, Mr. Stamatakes. But then one can't compare the Greeks to the Turks, now can one! I only say this so you will understand my position on Schliemann. He was a great man. Is there anything in particular you wish to know?"

"Just background information," George replied. Experience told Katrina her boss was trying to sound nonchalant. George had specifics in mind and was hiding something. "What the man was like, his major discoveries," he said. "His life in general. Of course, we would like to hear about Troy."

The professor nodded. "Yes, Troy, naturally. Well, as I said, Heinrich Schliemann was a great man. He was born a German in 1822, but also became an American citizen. By the time of his death, he spoke eighteen languages. He made a considerable fortune in the import business before starting his hunt for Troy. You see, he believed Homer was recounting actual history when he wrote about the Trojan War in the *Iliad*.

"Schliemann researched for years and became convinced Troy was in Turkey. After quite a bother with the Turks, he received permission to dig.

He located the city and found several inconclusive pieces those first years. In 1873, he discovered a cache of treasures which proved his theories."

Milner leaned forward and lowered his voice. "Quite the legend has developed around the discovery of those artifacts. Several different versions of the story have surfaced. Schliemann, always the businessman, promoted the legend to increase the value of the exhibits."

"Can you give us the facts of the discovery?" George asked.

"Facts? No. Nobody knows anything for certain. You see, Schliemann had to sign a *firman* stating that all artifacts would remain in Turkey, but he never intended to honor it."

As the professor spoke, Katrina looked out the tent flap at the ancient dig. Schliemann's Troy excavation would have looked much like this. She could envision him working at the bottom of his trench.

* * * * *

Schliemann backed out of the hole holding the shield. He looked up and saw his wife, Sophia, gracefully descending the ladder. Gathering up her skirts, she kneeled at the mouth of the hole beside her husband. She did not cry out or gasp. Instead, she turned to the excited man beside her. She gently brushed the loose earth from his dirt streaked cheek and spoke. "Again, as my husband predicted. And now?"

Sophia understood what the archeologist faced. Not a concern of conscience – he had always known, long before he signed the *firman*, that he would keep all the treasure to himself, if humanly possible. God knows what the Turks would do with them. His was a problem of logistics. He had to sneak the treasure past the government watchdog on the site and then smuggle the artifacts out of Turkey to his home in Athens.

Sophia took the shield from him and he reluctantly let it slip from his grasp. Ever the pragmatist, she took the artifact and slipped it under her skirt. Smiling, she stood and presented herself. Only a slight bulge showed under the loose folds of cloth. Schliemann jumped to his feet and grasped her shoulders. He kissed her full on the mouth and then pulled back to look at her.

"My sweet wife. No man could ask for a wiser, more dedicated assistant. You will save my treasure for me. Together, no one, not even a legion of Turks armed with reams of *firmans*, shall stop us."

＊ ＊ ＊ ＊ ＊

The professor's movements brought Katrina came back to the present.

"Gold and silver," Milner was saying. "Vases, goblets, shields, rings. Schliemann filled three or four crates that day. He then duped an unsuspecting acquaintance into smuggling the boxes back to Greece.

"However, I have my own theory on that . . ."

Katrina stopped paying attention to what the man was saying. Watching the professor fascinated her more than listening to his words. The small, gray haired man had become more and more animated as he warmed to his audience. Unable to remain seated, Milner stalked about the tent, his hands flying in all directions as he spoke. His cultured English accent was at odds with the wide eyed expression and elaborate gestures. Perspiration ran down the man's cheeks and into his bushy beard. As he paced briskly across the canvas floor, loose dust floated from his hair and stuck to his face like pancake makeup. The professor looked like a comical silent film star as he described the man he had deified.

"And what happened to the treasure after Schliemann smuggled it into Greece?" George asked.

The question broke the logical stream of the lecture, leaving the professor mildly flustered. Deflated for the moment, he returned to his chair. "Well, this does jump ahead several years, you understand. The treasure remained hidden in Greece for a time. Schliemann distributed the various pieces to his wife's relatives for safekeeping. She was Greek, you know. When the Turks finally agreed to a price for the artifacts, Schliemann paid them five times the contracted price. Fully five times! That was the kind of man he was. And yet, people still call him a thief. Generous, I call him. I'd like to see what the Turks would have done in his place."

Milner sat quietly for a second and then shook his head. Looking embarrassed, he hurriedly continued. "In any case, Schliemann was now free to display the treasure. He took the collection to several places around the world, but eventually he became dissatisfied with its promotion. A feeling which, by all accounts, was justified. He decided to return to Germany.

"All the time the treasure was on display, Schliemann was trying to get back into the good graces of the German government. He wanted the recognition that had always eluded him in that country. As a bribe to the government, he donated the entire collection of artifacts to Germany. Schliemann brought the treasure to Berlin in 1881 and displayed it in the Berlin Ethnological Museum. The treasure remained in the city until the war. The Second World War, that is."

Milner again stood and paced about the tent. The mysterious look on his face made Katrina smile.

"The treasure disappeared during the war. Just vanished," the professor said, snapping his fingers. "Of course, there are many theories about where it went. The Russians were the first to arrive at the museum's underground bunkers. They may have secreted the treasure away to avoid splitting it with the Allies. Most believe the Berlin bombings buried the collection. Personally, I think the Russians took it and melted it down. Either way, it seems to be gone forever."

The professor droned on for another twenty minutes before George finally rose and shook the professor's hand. "Well, thank you, Professor. You've been very helpful."

Milner sat down in his chair and stared at George. Once again, he put his fingertips together. "I ask myself," he said, "why would an official of the Greek government come all the way out here to discuss Schliemann and the treasure of Troy? You had a long, hot drive from Athens – too long and too hot. I have heard that Greek Intelligence prefers an oral report from a so called 'authority' over more pedestrian forms of research. You Greeks always have enjoyed a good tale, haven't you? And yet, why would Schliemann and the artifacts from Troy – a treasure that disappeared forty years ago – interest Greek Intelligence? Has someone rediscovered the treasure?"

"As I said, thank you, Professor. We have taken up enough of your valuable time." George motioned at the activity through the tent door. "I wouldn't want to be responsible for keeping you from your dig. I will mention your consideration and *continued cooperation* to the proper officials."

Milner looked from the smiling man to the ruins. He had dealt with foreign governments long enough to recognize a threat when he heard it. Even one so veiled in niceties. Continued cooperation! British law required him to report anything such as this to the government. However, as a dedicated archaeologist, he had to consider his personal future in Greece.

Professor Milner nodded at George and smiled.

* * * * *

George stopped at a seaside café on the way back to Athens. Following the accepted Greek tradition, Katrina and he ignored the menus and wandered into the kitchen. The chef greeted them like relatives and beamed as George circled the huge tub of hot water. Peering through the steam at the various pots sitting in the water, George complimented each dish. The chef devoured the praise. George sampled the contents of several pots and ordered his meal. By the time he led Katrina out of the kitchen, he and the chef were fast friends.

The waitress placed the obligatory glasses of water and small cups of Turkish coffee on their table. After she left, Katrina cursed at George. "Damn you, that old professor was right. You do know where the treasure is."

George just shrugged and smiled. Katrina glanced off into space, dreaming about finding the treasure. Lord, to bring those artifacts back to Greece. The history they represented, the history they substantiated. They represented Greece at its best. How could anyone resist such an opportunity? "Where are the artifacts?" Katrina demanded.

" *We* don't know, but Henri Mardinaud does. Or so he says."

"That fat bastard? I've heard of him. Will I have to deal with him?" Katrina asked.

"I'm afraid so. But don't rely on rumors. In person, he is much worse. Your meeting is tomorrow. You fly to Munich tonight."

The waitress brought the food and George quickly sampled everything. He clasped his hands together and held them to his heart. The grinning chef gave the waitress a loving shove and pointed at George. The white clad man looked elated as he walked back into his hot kitchen.

"How did I get this job?" Katrina asked.

"You deserve the chance. I know Alex's death was not your fault – even if Stefandis won't admit it. Katrina, you have done excellent work in analysis. You deserve another chance in the field. I'm just glad you stayed with us."

Katrina looked down at her food. "Your confidence means a lot to me. I must admit, I considered quitting. Possibly even emigrating somewhere if they'd let me." She was silent for a moment before looking back up at George. "Who am I working with?"

George told her through a mouthful of food. When she asked him to repeat himself, he swallowed and said, "Nobody."

"What? I'm going out alone?"

George heard the catch in her voice and again worried about her confidence. "That's the only way Stefandis would agree to your reactivation," he said. "He doesn't care if you find the treasure. And, frankly, he would be overjoyed if you failed." George patted her hand and looked into her eyes. "Prove him wrong, will you?"

Chapter 5

PARIS

Duman loved wearing leather-soled shoes in Paris. Nothing compared with their slap on wet cobblestones. The rain had stopped early in the afternoon, but the pavement was still damp. Small puddles, scattered here and there, added a faint splash to the slap. The sound relaxed him and added to his excellent disposition. Today was sure to be profitable.

Less than two hours ago, he had received a carefully routed communiqué from Henri Mardinaud. The fat Frenchman had used a network usually reserved for emergencies. Apparently, the information broker thought he had something of importance. What Mardinaud was doing in Germany, Duman could not guess, but he would fly to Munich this evening to find out. That left time to run a small errand for Chanda before leaving for the airport.

Duman paused in front of a small shop and examined his reflection in the window. His complexion, unusually light for a Turk, blended well with the tinted hair. However, the bearded jaw made him look older than his thirty one years. He would be happy to leave Paris and discard the identity, even if it meant leaving Chanda behind. Until then, Charles Davoust wore a beard and today, Duman was Davoust. Requiring many identities was just one of the prices he paid for his vision of a free world.

Duman stepped away from the window, continued along Rue de la Ferronnerie, and stopped in front of number eleven. Although the building looked ordinary, it was special to Duman. For him, this visit was almost a religious experience. He had several such personal shrines throughout the world. He gazed at the structure and remembered its history.

In 1610, François Ravaillac, a schoolmaster and mystic, had assassinated King Henri IV in this small home, committing one of the most significant acts in the history of the common people. Alone, the small man had demonstrated the way of the people – violence. It was the same course Duman continued to tread, walking in the footsteps of the great men in history.

Duman believed in the common people and their right to rule their own destiny. But he knew the common people could not achieve this goal without help. Oppression kept them weak, too consumed with daily survival to fight. They needed the strength only he could provide. He would seed the way to victory.

The Turk had dedicated his life to the struggle for universal freedom – his every action designed to rid the world of its oppressors. In small nations like Haiti and Jamaica, he supplied the political gangs with weapons and expertise. In the streets of the so-called superpowers, his hidden armies spread hatred and bitterness, massing for the final revolt. The battle would be long and required violence and shock. *Terror!* Someday, Duman knew, he would be a hero of the people, just like François Ravaillac. He possessed the drive, the skill and the patience.

Reluctantly, he continued down the street. Although this area north of Ravaillac's home was unfamiliar to him, Duman enjoyed the peaceful quiet of the pedestrian only streets. He didn't really mind running this errand for Chanda. He knew she was busy with school right now, her studies proceeding faster than even she had hoped. Duman enjoyed doing little things for her. He was proud of his young beauty and she gave him the pleasure he could not easily find.

Not that Duman ever allowed himself the luxury of falling in love. What he felt for Chanda fell far short of love. Love required too much trust. Chanda was a convenience. He provided her with an apartment and lived with her whenever he was in Paris. He considered the relationship a worthwhile and acceptable risk.

Duman skirted the crowds at the main entrance of the Square des Innocents. His dislike of crowds and persistent caution sent him around to one of the smaller alleys. He stopped himself as he started to step into the crowded square. A sudden unease crept along his spine and his hand sought the reassuring bulk of the Mauser under his coat.

Church bells tolled the hour. Duman jumped. Every nerve in his body screamed in warning. Duman remembered his unfamiliarity with the streets – the unfamiliar *pedestrian* streets. He edged into the shadows of the alley and scanned the square.

Chanda had sent him here, he reminded himself. He had come willingly, as a favor to her. But now, he could see the men who did not belong to the street, neither tourists nor locals. Like him, they wore coats on this warm summer day. Beneath those coats, Duman was certain they carried Model D MAB pistols, the preferred gun of the DST, the group responsible for antiterrorist activity within France. He spotted five agents.

Duman cursed himself for not suspecting Chanda or this location. Had the conspirators sent him to a deserted area, he would have fled immediately. Instead, the DST had risked many innocent lives to capture him. Was the French government that desperate to quell the anger of a panicking public? The plan was frightening in its audacity. Only Alain, the director of the DST, would have the nerve to order such a move.

They had played him expertly and he had almost stepped into their trap.

He started to edge back down the alley. Suddenly, a DST agent stepped out of the bright sunshine of the square into the alley. He noticed Duman's movement and squinted into the shadows. Duman yanked the Mauser from its holster and fired twice. The noise was deafening. The first bullet shattered the man's skull, killing him instantly. The second bullet hit his right shoulder and sent him twirling back into the square.

Women began to scream. In seconds, panic spread through the square. People scattered, trying to escape. The screaming masses blocked the DST men. Their urgently shouted commands and brandished guns only added to the frenzy. By the time they reached their fallen comrade, Duman was emerging onto Boulevard de Sebastopol.

Sprinting to the edge of the busy street, the terrorist looked for a car to steal. He knew the DST men were close behind, but the bumper-to-bumper traffic left him no escape. Sirens wailed in the nearby streets. Vaulting the hoods of the stopped cars, Duman crossed the road in seconds. Just down Aubry le Boucher, the Turk could see the Beaubourg and salvation. Hundreds of people wandered on the front lawn of the art gallery, watching the varied entertainment. Duman holstered his gun. He did not want panic, not yet.

The terrorist worked his way into the throng and watched the DST agents fall in behind him. Protected by the crowd, he searched for his target. He moved in front of two young street musicians and stopped behind a homely woman dressed in a bulging, white pantsuit.

The musicians were playing Claude Bolling's *Picnic Suite*, one of Duman's favorite pieces. Moving to the fluid music, he slipped a knife from under his pant leg, turned, and smiled at the DST. Frantically, they worked toward him through the milling crowd.

Duman grabbed the woman in front of him, wrapped his left hand around the woman's forehead, and drew the blade across her throat. Bright red blood gushed from the gaping wound and soaked into the white cloth. Duman held the woman by her hair and displayed her to the crowd.

The earlier hysteria in the square was mild compared with the bedlam created on the lawn. People ran in all directions, trampling others in their haste. The DST lost Duman in the crush.

The killer used his elbows, shoulders, and several lethal blows to make his way to the edge of the crowd, then ran to Rue Renard and jumped into an out of service taxi. A substantial number of 100-Franc bills thrown into the front seat convinced the driver to ignore his lunch. Tossing a sandwich aside, the man guided the taxi across the Seine at Pont de Sully. The driver registered no surprise when his fare jumped out unannounced at Quai Saint Bernard. He pulled the taxi to the curb, counted the bills, and ate his sandwich.

Duman hurried along the street to the Gare d'Austerlitz. At the rail station, Duman used the washroom to clean up. His beard was miraculously still in place. He combed his hair and washed his hands. As he approached the ticket window, the terrorist resembled any one of the many businessmen in the station. He bought a ticket to Madrid. "You will have to hurry, Monsieur," the man behind the counter said. "The train leaves in ten minutes."

Duman hoped the ticket seller had a good memory. Once the agent's attention was elsewhere, Duman left the station. He took his time, walking with the lazy pace of the tourists. At the "Yawning Lion" gates, he turned into the Jardin des Plantes.

* * * * *

The uniformed policeman crossed the floor of the Gare d'Austerlitz and walked up to a tall man smoking a cigar. "The ticket agent says a man answering Duman's description bought a ticket to Madrid. The train left a half hour ago."

Claude Alain, director of the DST, considered the tip of his cigar for a moment. "Did the agent see Duman get on the train?"

"He said he was busy at the time and would not have noticed. Should I alert the Prefects along the line?"

Alain stared out the large windows and down the tracks that led to Madrid. "Yes. Have the train stopped and searched." He turned away in disgust. "Not that we will find him," he added.

Chapter 6

DAVID

David Morritt watched the beautiful scenery pass below and wondered why Assi Levy had summoned him to Tel Aviv. Assi's order concerned him, but David forced himself to enjoy the flight. He loved flying over Israel, especially the desert. No matter how far he traveled, Israel would always be the most beautiful country in the world to him. It was home.

The flight path had taken the helicopter over the red desert surrounding Beersheba, an area that might appear desolate to the casual observer. But the sand and rock teemed with life. David knew his people would use their advanced agriculture to renew the desert wastes. The settlements would swell and the desert would support a more varied life than ever before in the history of man. Such was the drive and desire of the special breed of Israeli who followed Ben Gurion's wisdom.

At David's request, the pilot had reluctantly veered off course to fly over the Palmach Brigade Memorial, Dani Karavan's enormous sculpture. The huge dome, split and riddled with shell holes, reminded David of his life. As Dani himself had said, the creation evoked "the memory of the dead at the same time as the fight for life." David understood and appreciated the words. He had fought in the wars – though not behind a gun or mortar. David's battle was within the enemy's camp. He used cunning and craft rather than artillery and armor. The Israelis had never underestimated the value of intelligence although even they were using technology over human intelligence all too often.

David felt the helicopter tip as they began a gentle arc into Tel Aviv. Following flight regulations, the pilot approached from the Mediterranean Sea. David studied the rough surface below. Small swells dotted the waves with foamy caps and a near black patch of water marked a school of feeding fish. Commercial fishing vessels surrounded the area and prepared their nets. Over fifty small sailboats raced through the water near the shore, their colored sails swelled by the brisk wind. The tourists were taking full advantage of the early summer heat.

As always, David's first sight of the sprawling city both warmed and depressed him. The skyline stretched back for miles from the sandy coast and reminded him of a miniature Manhattan. Tel Aviv represented the development of Israeli commerce and the abandonment of the desert communities. As in so many countries, urbanization had consumed much of Israel's population.

Made up almost exclusively of white cement buildings, Tel Aviv might look sterile if not for the thick haze of pollution that hung over the hot metropolis. Tall, haphazardly placed complexes broke the monotony of the squat buildings. As they neared the rooftop heliport, David's eyes traced the narrow streets leading to the wider, modern avenues carefully planned by urban developers. This combination of roads illustrated the essence of the Israeli people; a lack of fear of the high technological present set beside a love and respect of the ancient past.

※ ※ ※ ※ ※

Still wondering if he was about to have his butt kicked, David knocked on the plain wooden door and heard a familiar voice tell him to enter.

Assi Levy sat behind his desk, a stack of papers in front of him. He ignored David while he finished reading a report from one of the Mossad stations. A quick glance told Morritt the report was from a base in Southeast Asia – a small grocer in Saigon, if his memory served. He avoided the secret documents and walked to the large picture window to gaze at the spectacular view of the Mediterranean. The bulletproof glass gave an added blue tinge to the glaring water. Leaning on the sill, David felt slight vibrations in his fingertips and glanced down. Since listening devices could translate the minute window vibrations into recognizable speech, this wall was equipped with speakers to vibrate the glass and distort the reception of any bugging equipment. A simple but effective precaution.

Floor to ceiling bookshelves lined the remaining three walls of the office. Assi was a voracious reader and an avid collector of both ancient and modern books. One entire row of the east shelf displayed religious texts of dozens of religions in various languages. The shelf below held books on major historical battles. An ancient copy of the Talmud occupied a position of honor on the north wall. Across the room was a collection of manuals on exotic poisons, weapons, and hand to hand combat techniques, many written by Levy. This was Assi Levy. He was devoted to both religion and to the defense of his country. To him, they were the same.

The sound of shuffling papers brought David around to face the desk. The Director had completed his reading and was carefully locking the files in his desk drawer. In the enclosed space, Morritt noticed the acrid smell of cordite, smoke, and sweat that permeated the material of his jumpsuit. Acutely aware of his filthy uniform, David stood straighter and formally addressed the older man. "*Hamefaked.*"

Assi rose. He was short but powerfully built with broad shoulders. He limped around the desk and thrust out his thick arm to shake David's hand. "None of that nonsense," he said. "*Hamefaked,* my ass. I am only your Commander outside this office – and when you do stupid things. Like this practice raid."

David winced. Now he knew why Assi had forced him to return. The Director returned to his seat and David gently lowered himself into a chair. "Assi, I'm only trying to fight the boredom. I should be in the field, not stuck behind some desk. Retiring to a desk at my age is ridiculous."

"Relax, David. I didn't call you here to discuss this indiscretion of yours. Not that you don't deserve a reprimand. I was unhappy to hear you were in the desert again. I thought I scheduled you for the classroom." When David tried to reply, Assi interrupted him. "But this is not why you are here. I have important news which may solve several problems for both of us."

David leaned forward, recognizing the tone in his old friend's voice. "Go ahead, I'm listening."

Assi pulled a single sheet of paper from a drawer and placed it face down on his desk. "I wanted to see you at your home," he said. "This meeting should have been private, but time would not permit it. Instead, this conversation never took place."

David looked puzzled and pointed toward the roof. "But the flight? Not exactly a quiet way of getting me here."

"I've taken care of that. You will have an official reprimand on your record." Assi waved down David's protest. "You went on the exercise without my permission. You were away without leave. You are deep in it, old friend."

Then, the Director lightened his tone. "Naturally, we don't want to embarrass such a well respected man. We will ignore your childish behavior. However, I have granted your request for a vacation – so you can consider your tenuous position."

David slumped back in his chair at the mention of the unwanted holiday. "Thank you, *old friend.* I deeply appreciate your consideration. Now, what the hell does all this mean?"

"Early today, I received a message from Henri Mardinaud. He has come across some information he thought might interest me." Assi took a deep breath. "He has located Friedrich Heiden."

David flinched. A chill passed through his body. Vivid memories assaulted his senses. The stench of urine, blood, and sweat filled his nostrils. Bile rose in his throat. He fought to breathe. Noises battered him. The clang of the bell. The deep rumble of the locomotive. The moans of thousands, the scream of one.

His chest constricted and he felt the cold glass of a window pressed against his face. Inside, he could see Heiden, the Nazi's pants down around his ankles and an ugly gash dripping blood from below his left eye. David watched Heiden's club, rise and fall, spraying blood across the wall and window. A woman lay across the table. She had stopped screaming, stopped moving. Still, he bludgeoned her with the stick. He beat her until his arm fell limp and her face was an unrecognizable mass of torn flesh and broken bone.

David opened his eyes, fighting to escape the memories. He shook uncontrollably as he fought the hands pinning his arms. Then his vision focused and David realized Assi held him. His heartbeat slowed and returned to normal as Assi gently lowered him back into the chair.

"I'm sorry, Assi," he said in a weak voice. He coughed and wiped his forehead with the back of his hand. "It's been a long time since I remembered that day in so much...detail."

Assi gave David a glass of water. "I'm the one who should apologize," Assi said. "I could've broken it to you better. Forgive me. God knows, when I read Mardinaud's message, I thought I'd have a stroke. Heiden's name has always caused grief, pain, and revulsion. We have dreamed of vengeance for many years, my friend."

Assi made his way back around the desk, his limp accenting his personal reason for revenge. The *Memuneh* also had frightening memories of Heiden. Heiden and Majdanek.

"Where is Heiden?" David's voice cracked as he spoke the name.

"Mardinaud doesn't say. He wants a meeting in Munich."

"When do I leave?"

"Wait, David. We have to get things straight before you go." Assi was self consciously playing with the pen on his desk. "I can't sanction this mission. I am sending you alone."

"Alone?" David asked. He had worked alone in the past, gathering intelligence while on a deep cover operation. But no Mossad agent worked alone while after a Nazi. The targets were too important to risk to one operative. They always used a team of at least five men, often more. David could not understand a one-man operation.

"I have used all my *protektsia* to get you on this mission," Assi confessed. "It was not an easy task. Your name brought strong resistance. Even my most loyal supporters are hesitant. Your personal involvement disqualified you in many eyes, but not mine. I trust you more than any of our agents. I trust you to deliver justice. In the end, the arguments against you turned into the logical justification for your assignment."

David did not understand the comment, but he could imagine the pull it would take to put him in the field again. "I still don't understand. Why alone? Why not send a team?"

"Publicity, mainly," Assi said. "In recent years, a negative bias against Israel has been building in the press. The botched missions. Innocent people dying. Many view us as heavy handed."

"But we have justification."

"In our eyes, but not in other's. The war was long ago for most. A concerted effort by the Arabs has turned world opinion against us. To many, we have become as bad as those we hunt. And we have harmed ourselves. That book and movie about Avner. The continuing problems on the West Bank. The military film leaked to the press. The Iran arms deal. Izat Napsu here and Pollard in America. There's been too much. We can't afford another mistake. You know what we have faced. Too many scandals."

David grimaced at the thought of each scandal. Though he could justify in his own mind the methods of the Mossad, he knew the rest of the world often could not. Even in Israel, support for the military and the Mossad was declining. And, David knew, in the end they were still just a bunch of *Jews.*

"But this is Friedrich Heiden," he protested. "He's on the list."

"Exactly," Assi said. "I put him on that list. I can order the mission. I can have him brought to Israel. I can testify against Heiden. I can get the death penalty. What would it get us? Too many forget the camps, David. They only see pitiful old men. They don't see the monsters beneath. The action would become *Levy and his personal crusade.*"

David nodded, avoiding the Director's eyes. He knew Assi was under pressure, even from within Israel. Those who sought control of the Mossad saw Assi Levy as a major hurdle. They thought he had been in office too long. Without Assi, they could shape the Mossad to their vision.

As David began to understand his mission, he agreed with the strategy. Any exposure would give Assi's enemies the ammunition they needed to force the *Memuneh's* resignation. That would be disastrous for Israel. "So, I go in alone," he said. "If it folds, I'm still on my own. No official backing – I'll be a rogue. A man out for revenge."

Assi didn't answer immediately. Finally, he looked up from his pen. "I can't offer you much support, but funding won't be a problem. Most of our accounts are still active."

He was referring to bank accounts he had opened to hide money for operations unable to get official allocation. Like many agents, including David, Assi diverted part of the operational budget into these accounts. David had used the system many times.

"You'll still have certain resources available to you," Assi continued. "We can supply documents. You can obtain them on your authority from any station, unless someone begins to ask questions. Regardless, the networks are out of bounds."

"I won't need them. I'll use my own contacts." David was already thinking about the relays he would rig in his apartment before leaving for Munich.

Assi nodded. "I thought as much. Just remember, don't make too much noise. You have a tendency to create an awful commotion."

"You won't even know I'm out there," David promised.

Chapter 7

DUMAN

Duman wandered past *le cedre de Jussieu*. During the early 1700s, Jussieu had brought the seedling for the huge cedar tree from England in his tri cornered hat. Today, three old men dressed in dark suits and black berets sat under it playing backgammon in the fading light. They played daily in this same spot beside the tree. As Duman passed, he wondered how the elderly eyes could make out the difference between the pieces. Years of practice or, possibly, they no longer cared who won. Their final years spent reliving past victories and past loves. Duman despised them and their complacency.

He knew when his time to die arrived, it would be exceptional. He would not merely fade from existence. The death of the greatest assassin and terrorist ever known would further the struggle of the people. His death would change the world. Those fools in the Middle East with their Jihads were puppets, controlled by those only slightly higher on the evolutionary scale. They replaced one domination with another. Their shortsighted plans limited their journey. But his path to greatness would be long and glorious. He would mirror his father's success, with one exception.

Duman traded in death.

* * * * *

Duman's father, Cahil, had been a minor merchant with a brilliant mind for business. He had built his fortune without the aid of a formal education, teaching himself by studying the biographies of past successes and learning the world markets by observation. Working from a detailed, long term plan, he nurtured his contacts throughout the international markets. By his thirtieth birthday, Cahil had stretched his empire throughout Europe and Britain.

During one business trip to England, he met and courted Elizabeth Estair. Much to her wealthy father's distaste, she ran away with the love struck Turk. The couple returned to Turkey where, less than eight months later, Elizabeth presented Cahil with a son, Hasad.

The boy was small for his age, which displeased his father. Cahil ignored the child while continuing to build his empire. The other children tormented Hasad because of his English mother and told him he did not belong in their country. Hasad loved Turkey and this insult hurt deeply.

As the years passed, he made up for his slow start in life and grew tall and strong. Soon none of the other children dared cross the boy. Years of repression had turned him sadistic and cruel. When one of his early tormentors was found dead at the bottom of a deep pit, most of the townspeople suspected Hasad but had no proof. However, the suspicion just further ostracized Hasad from the community.

Cahil died of a heart attack the following year. Because of her British heritage, the Turkish government denied Elizabeth and Hasad all rights of inheritance and the state took possession of Cahil's business interests. Although Hasad understood how his mother had been cheated, he still loved Turkey. He blamed the corrupt government, not the people, for stripping them of the family fortune and Hasad swore he would see justice done.

Elizabeth and Hasad returned to her late father's home in England. Suitors arrived to court his mother amid the luxury of the ancestral home. These men left a deep impression on the boy. Hasad hated the upper class. Those who had no skills of their own and nothing to offer that wasn't given to them by the accident of their birth. They took from the world and rarely gave back anything. He quickly equated them with those who had stolen his father's fortune – insipid takers who lived off the work and emotions of others. While attending Oxford University, he refined his ideas about the struggle of the people.

Through his interest in Marxism, Hasad's feelings about the ruling class became well known. His keen intelligence and ability in languages attracted the attention of KGB recruiters. Hasad was receptive but was afraid his mother would marry one of the upper class snobs if he left. The Russians accepted his decision, leaving the offer open.

The following month, Elizabeth died in a fire at the estate. The last tears he would ever shed during his life spilled over at her graveside. Three days later, he sought out the recruiters and transferred to the Patrice Lumumba University in Moscow. Supposedly a place of higher learning, the stately buildings actually housed the training center for non Russian KGB agents. Here, Hasad learned of Carlos.

Though Carlos had already completed his training, Hasad sought to compete with the international terrorist. The Turk's instructors capitalized on this one sided rivalry and drove Hasad to exceed all expectations. While the newcomer studied, Carlos forged a reputation for himself. This notoriety only spurred Hasad to work harder. Upon graduation, he sought to fulfill his dream for the people. He took "Duman", Turkish for mist or smoke, as his professional name. As he appeared, struck, and disappeared, the name became more and more apt.

Duman became a freelance killer and worked for the KGB as required to repay the debt of his schooling. When his KGB masters called, Duman was forced to respond. However, he was determined to see the end of that servitude. The day would soon be at hand when he would no longer work for the Russians. An expert with guns, knives, and poisons, his specialty was unusual and inventive bombings. Interpol attributed many key assassinations and devastating bombings to the young terrorist. His services were in high demand and he inflated his reputation by carefully picking his operations. Rather than attempt the more numerous but less significant kills as Carlos had, Duman chose a more selective route. Each execution was high risk and high profile with the added advantage of large financial returns. Also unlike Carlos in the early years, Duman never worked without a client.

His reliability became well known and that reputation brought abundant job opportunities. Rumors credited the terrorist with a chilling one hundred percent kill rate. And as his reputation grew, his need for more spectacular assassinations increased. As time passed, the collateral damage from the assassinations ballooned. Dozens of people often died along with the intended victim. With this notoriety, he became a target himself, sought by every major anti-terrorist force in the world.

Then Duman disappeared. For nearly four months, talk spread of his capture and death. Many suspected Carlos of having killed his young rival.

When speculation reached a peak, Duman struck. With the speed and precision of a surgeon, he eliminated eight men in less than twenty four hours. Duman served notice to the intelligence organizations of the world. He intended to lead the people in an international revolution to insure their inherent right to self rule. Anyone who stood in his way would meet with the same fate as the eight men – the Turkish officials who had orchestrated the theft of his father's fortune.

Duman claimed justice for the world.

* * * * *

Watchful of all activity on the street, Duman left the *Jardin des Plantes* and walked along the Seine. As night approached, this quarter of Paris came alive with the people he loved. The people of the night. Everywhere, they moved with the rhythm of the shadows. He could see prostitutes in scant clothing trying to make enough to pacify their pimps. The pickpockets, con men, and shills trying for the big score. All slaved for a better life, yet never had enough to satisfy themselves. They played the game the Overlords had created to subjugate the masses. Someday, Duman knew, the people would see their folly. They would be free and he would be the man who freed them. He would not be a leader, for the people did not need a leader.

He was their Savior.

Duman had seen the truth in Russia. There, he had discovered the possibilities open to the people although the perverted socialism of Russia was not the solution. The Russian Revolution had been a valiant attempt, but the course had fouled. The new rulers were no better than those of the past. The Tsars still reigned with bureaucratic titles and military uniforms. The current leaders, with their political machinations, replaced the rich and noble as the privileged class while ordinary people lined up for bread, meat, and toilet paper. Like flies on rancid meat, the scavengers had settled on the system, consuming the choicest morsels for themselves. In the end, even the leaders of the Politburo must die. Only another revolution – a world revolution – would reform the system.

Duman's burning desire was for world revolution. For years, he relentlessly pursued his dream, fighting, killing, and plotting. He created cells throughout the world, training the faithful, arming them, showing them how to disrupt their respective countries, governments, and religions. He guided them through demonstrations, strikes, and uprisings. The unrest fuelled* the revolution. Next came riots, burnings, and assassinations.

Like a sea crashing against the shore, the demoralizing violence eroded the foundations of the governments. The revolution spread slowly, forcing governments into submission. The small countries would crumble first because they were the least stable. The democratic governments would fall next. Their free rule provided ample opportunity for disruption and subsequent escape. In time, however, the revolution would touch everyone. Then, the people would take over. The people would enjoy self rule and true freedom.

Duman glanced across the river at Notre Dame. The sight of the exquisite structure bathed in light helped to bring his racing mind under control. Although he despised what the church represented, he could still appreciate the beauty of its architecture.

* * * * *

Located in a seventeenth century building on Rue St Julien le Pauvre, the inn was both discreet and moderately priced. Duman ignored the front desk and ran up the small staircase, taking the steps two at a time. He stopped at the landing in front of room number three. He'd paid the rent for another two months and knew Chanda, whore that she was, would be incapable of resisting the free lodgings. The DST wouldn't bother to inform her of his escape and, unless she had seen a news report, she would imagine herself safe.

He knocked once.

"Just a second, please."

Duman felt elated at the sound of her voice. He could hear rustling from inside the room and knew what she would be wearing.

"Yes, what..." Chanda froze with the door half open. She stared at him, fear leaping into her eyes as they locked with his deep blue ones. She said nothing, but the ancient doorknob rattled from the force of her trembling.

Her expression was all Duman needed to convince himself of the truth. He smiled, his eyes becoming soft and inviting.

"Aren't you going to let me in?"

After a moment, Chanda threw the door open wide, giggling nervously as it banged against the wall. "Sure, come in. I...I didn't expect to see you. When you didn't come back, I mean, I thought... Would you like a drink?"

Duman eased the door shut, locked it, and quietly slid the dead bolt into place. He leaned against the frame and watched as Chanda turned to pour him a Scotch. As he suspected, she was wearing the short silk kimono he had bought for her in Hong Kong. It clung to her young figure and, when she bent over, he could see the pink curve of her naked buttocks. Turning, her breasts swung freely beneath the thin material. He felt himself begin to harden as she walked toward him.

Chanda's hand was steady as she passed him the drink. She had recovered. The fear had left her eyes and was replaced by the confidence he had always admired. She cleared her books and papers from the bed, positioning herself so he could see her cleavage. Her nipples stood out hard, aroused by the cool, smooth material. Finally, she leaned back against the headboard and loosened the tie of her gown.

"I missed you," she pouted. "Why don't you bring your drink over here? You can show me how much you love me."

Duman tossed his clothing on a chair in the corner of the small room and turned to face her. He was fully erect.

She smiled seductively and slipped the kimono off her shoulders. "Bring that over here. I want you."

Once on the bed, he began to work on her. With each touch, she relaxed more, content in her deception. Tender caresses, gentle bites, and strategic kisses had her moaning in minutes. Not allowing her to touch him, Duman stroked her breasts, sucking on the hard, dark nipples. When he finally slid his hand between her legs, he knew she was ready. He gently entered her.

With increasing speed, Chanda moved with him, her hips coming up to meet his. She uttered small sounds, her mouth wide. Her eyes fluttered shut and she tilted her head back. He sensed she was close to climaxing. As their tempo worked to a feverish pitch, he grabbed the kimono and, without breaking the rhythm, brutally shoved the silk material into her open mouth.

She stared at him in surprise. He wrapped his hands around her neck.

Desperately, she fought him, beating at his arms and shoulders with her small fists. He squeezed tighter, the muscles of his forearms bulging. Her face took on a flattering red color and Duman could feel her rapid carotid pulse beating fruitlessly against his fingers. Still inside her, he matched the bucking motions as she tried to throw him off. Her face turned a beautiful blue gray color.

As the life drained from her terrified eyes, Duman felt himself climax. The thrashings of her body ceased. After one final thrust, he collapsed on top of her.

Gently, he removed the gag and closed her staring eyes. He kissed her slack mouth. For some time, he stared down at her full, youthful body. Unable to feel remorse, he stood and began to search the pockets of his clothes.

He carefully burned all Charles Davoust's identity cards and flushed them down the toilet. He had discarded the beard and mustache earlier. After dressing, he looked again at the body on the bed. He could see the dark marks on Chanda's neck. Having exacted his revenge, he found he could almost forgive her. She had paid her penance. He pulled up the sheet to cover the bruises. With something resembling love, he arranged her dark hair on the pillow. Her slack face looked innocent and peaceful now. Duman thought she looked like a sleeping angel. He stepped back to observe the results. This was how he wanted to remember her, not as the deceitful whore slut he knew she was.

* * * * *

After retrieving another set of identification papers, Duman took half an hour to get to the Nova Park Elysees hotel where he registered as Richard Wakefield, British businessman. He enjoyed a leisurely dinner at the Paris Match restaurant and then had two drinks in the bar. Several young ladies presented themselves, but he decided none could surpass the night's earlier encounter. He returned to his room alone and used the telephone.

"This is Mr. Wakefield in suite 6009. Could you tell me when the first plane leaves for Munich at a civilized hour?"

"Please hold, Monsieur." Duman heard the quiet tap of the computer terminal keys. Seconds later, the voice was back. "Would ten forty five in the morning be satisfactory, Monsieur?"

"Yes, that would be excellent. Could you book me on the flight – one way, first class? And wake me at seven thirty for breakfast in my room at eight."

"Oui, Monsieur. Good evening."

After a long, hot shower, Duman slid between the soft sheets. He was asleep in seconds.

PART TWO

MUNICH

TELL ME NOW, MUSES...
AS YOU ARE HEAVENLY,
AND ARE EVERYWHERE,
AND EVERYTHING IS KNOWN TO YOU
THE ILIAD-BOOK II

Chapter 8

LEBERKÄSE AT THE MARIENPLATZ

The sun approached its zenith and Katrina Kontoravdis' anger rose with it. Since seven o'clock that morning, she had been going from place to place throughout Munich. Her journey had begun at a locker in the central train station. The supplied key unlocked the door to reveal a typed note. Following the scant instructions, she worked her way out to the Olympic Village. At the Pool Building, a small man folding towels sent her to the zoo.

Amid beautiful, multicolored creatures at the tropical bird exhibit, she received another note from the handler. This message directed her to a small shop specializing in Pre-Columbian art. After convincing the persistent owner she did not want to purchase anything, he delivered a cryptic message. Mystified, Katrina left to discover a man selling small dolls under a wide umbrella. During his sales pitch, he pressed a slip of paper into her hand. This note clarified the previous message from the art dealer. She proceeded north toward a bakery where she received a *roscon*, a sugar sprinkled bun with guava jelly, and another piece of paper. Finally, she found herself walking through the Marienplatz.

She had followed the obtuse instructions for over three and a half hours but was no closer to Henri Mardinaud. The fat information broker was playing his childish games, she thought. Warnings about the man fell short of the truth. Her feet ached and she was tired. The late flight from Athens had been a horror. She had been unable to sleep on the plane because of the turbulence. Then the call to her hotel room woke her at five thirty this morning. The entire episode seemed designed to keep her off balance and the effort was succeeding. She was in no mood for this nonsense.

One of the most popular spots in Munich, the Marienplatz was thick with tourists. As Katrina passed the many outdoor restaurants, the smells of the warm German delicacies made her empty stomach growl. She realized she had eaten nothing but the *roscon* for the past several hours and considered stopping for a light snack before continuing. Eyeing one particularly crowded restaurant, she recognized the unmistakable bulk of one of the patrons sitting behind a steaming platter of Leberkäse. Henri Mardinaud smiled at her and motioned with his fork to an empty chair across from him.

"Katrina Kontoravdis," he said as she walked toward him. "It is so good to meet you. You will excuse me if I don't get up. The effort is hardly worth the result." Mardinaud smothered a sausage in mustard and forked the tube of meat into his mouth. A chunk of black bread followed. The display of gluttony fascinated Katrina.

"Where is the information I paid for?" she asked.

Mardinaud ignored her question and continued talking between mouthfuls of food. "Would you like something to eat? A small salad to start, perhaps? You must be hungry after your travels."

"No, nothing. I just want the information. Your game bores me. Just tell me what you know."

Mardinaud laughed. "To tell you all I know could take quite some time. And you don't seem to have the patience. I don't understand you women nowadays. Always in such a hurry. You should learn to relax. Learn to take your time and enjoy the sights around you. Smell the roses, as it were. I think this 'biological clock' one hears so much about is responsible for your inability to slow down. Possibly, you women are taking on more than you are capable of handling."

Katrina's brown eyes seared Mardinaud with a devastating look. He coughed self consciously before continuing.

"Yes, well, possibly not. Regardless, Munich is an elegant city and I researched your tour with care. I endeavored to show you the major points of interest, while giving you a clue about where you are going. And what thanks do I receive? After this morning, *you* should be able to tell *me* where the treasure is located. I thought you were smart enough to solve the puzzle. You disappoint me. Possibly, I overestimated you?"

Katrina stared at the man in front of her as she remembered her vague and seemingly unconnected wanderings. A pattern began to emerge from the twisted route. She'd been so frustrated with the delay that she had paid no attention to what she was doing. Mardinaud could see the dawning realization in her eyes.

"You did not understand, did you?" the Frenchman asked. "Extremely dangerous for one in your profession. Did you learn no lesson from the death of your partner?" Mardinaud's smile widened as Katrina exhaled a small sound of surprise. "Did you think I would not know of that? Give me more credit."

Pudgy fingers opened a manila file folder and thumbed through the sheets. "Yes, here it is. New York. A little over three years ago."

"Don't bother. I know the details," Katrina said coldly.

"Yes, I imagine you know them all too well. I also see you haven't been active since the...incident." Mardinaud shut the folder and looked up at her. "I should think you're a bit rusty. Nikolas Stefandis doesn't give a damn about this mission, does he? He might even find it preferable if you failed." The information broker shrugged. "Stefandis never did believe women should be in his organization. Personally, I can't understand his attitude. But to each his own."

"Could we get on with this? Just give me the information."

Mardinaud finished chewing a mouthful before he answered. "Don't you want to display your superior intelligence and feminine intuition by guessing where you are going? It shouldn't be too hard."

Katrina watched him fork more food into his mouth. His habit of chewing with his mouth open was beginning to nauseate her. "If it will hurry you up, I'll go along with your..."

Katrina broke off suddenly as she realized Mardinaud was staring past her. She tensed and laid her hand on the closest weapon – a serrated table knife. She turned and scanned the crowd behind her, but could see nothing amiss. Most people were staring in the same direction as Mardinaud. She followed their gaze to the Glockenspiel above the town hall across the street. The dancing figures had begun to move.

Mardinaud watched as one of the figures moved slowly around the circle. The jester's bright outfit shone in the summer sun while the tune played flawlessly. Necks craned throughout the square as young and old watched with rapt attention. Except Katrina. Mardinaud glanced at the bright brown eyes glowing with impatience.

"Is it not magnificent?" asked Mardinaud. "I never tire of hearing its clear tones or watching the regal promenade. I find it difficult to believe the object is not French. Do you know its history?"

"No, I don't. Does it involve my mission?"

"No, I suppose it doesn't," he admitted. "You have come to hear of Ulrich Kadner and his ill got possessions."

Katrina waited while the fat man continued. "I'll start you out, shall I? I sent you to the train station first. Obviously, you must travel. Not by train, though. You have to go over water, as you did at the Olympic pool. I wanted to be sure you saw that building. A true treasure demonstrating nature's mix of strength and beauty. Such an architectural vision. But I digress. Just be glad I didn't send you to your departure point, the airport in Frankfurt."

Katrina glared at him. "I assume from the trip to the zoo, I'll be going to a tropical zone."

"Yes, yes. Very good. You see? You can enjoy the game. All you have to do is try. Can you narrow it down even further?"

"You sent me to the shop specializing in Pre-Columbian art. The bakery. Clumsy reference with the art but everything leads to Colombia, so I assume that is my destination. However, nothing tells me who has the treasure."

"My dear, you continue to disappoint me," he said. "You have stopped short of the answer. Where did you go before you came here?"

Katrina was again growing impatient with the Frenchman. "The cemetery," she said.

"And the inscription above the gates to the cemetery?"

"I never noticed."

"Exactly!" Mardinaud's voice was suddenly serious. "And that is why you may not live to see the end of this game. The clues abound if you can find them. Clues to both the treasure and to the dangers. You must sharpen your powers of observation. You have, once again, entered the real world. You are no longer hidden among your files and forms. You must prepare for the consequences of your chosen life. I had hoped for a better player."

Katrina bristled at the admonishment. "The inscription?" she asked.

"Yes. Well, in short, it is a prayer dedicated to the dead of the Second World War. More specifically, to those slaughtered by the Nazis. That leads us to the current owner of the artifacts – a member of Hitler's elite SS. One Ulrich Kadner, known as Friedrich Heiden during the war. This file contains all his personal data and where to find him. It also details where he keeps the treasure. You should have no trouble, once you get into his compound."

"What about security?"

"Surprisingly good – considering where he is. The stress is on human, rather than electronic, surveillance. The tropical weather plays havoc with the equipment. Apparently, the plants grow quickly and can block the sensors in a matter of days. Also, the weather...I'm sorry," Mardinaud held up his hands. "I digress again. Regardless, I have included full details of the precautions Kadner has taken, including the number and placement of personnel. You should have no trouble getting in – with the proper equipment. Of course," he added with a smile, "getting out with the treasure is another issue."

Katrina stood and picked up the file. The information broker reached out and grasped her arm with surprising speed and strength. "Remember. You are in the real world now."

Katrina shook the plump, greasy hand from her arm and turned away.

* * * * *

Katrina replaced the telephone and reclined on the thick comforter. A late night flight or a flight the next morning, those were her choices. She closed her eyes and massaged her temples. If Mardinaud had not played his foolish game, she could have caught a flight this morning and already be on her way to Colombia.

Her hand shook as she reached for a glass of water and she felt a wave of dizziness. My blood sugar is low, she thought. That's the problem. She knew she should have picked up something to eat. Once she ate, she would recover.

Her best course of action was to get into her rental car and drive to Frankfurt. The sooner she arrived in Colombia, the better off she would be. Sitting in this cramped hotel room would do nothing to build her confidence.

She glanced at the open file beside her on the bed. One look at the sheet of security specifications and she flopped back against the headboard.

Kadner's compound was a fortress. A small army of experienced, well armed men guarded him constantly. Getting in was impossible, getting out was slightly more difficult. Why rush to Colombia with no plan in mind?

She would spend another night in Munich. Spend the time sleeping and studying the file. With food and rest, she could overcome her nervousness at being in the field again. All she needed was some time to build herself up, to acclimate herself. Once she could think without the distraction of nerves, she could analyze the defenses of the compound. The weakness was there and she would find it.

Chapter 9

BEER GARDENS AND BRIEFINGS

Duman walked slowly along the pathway beside the Isar River. The night was warm and fragrant, almost as sweet smelling as the large breasted *Fraülein* walking beside him. He slipped his arm around her thick waist, letting his hand ride up to her breast. She smiled wickedly at him as she tossed back her flaming red hair. Duman had been sitting in the bar at the Munich Hilton when she walked up to him. At first glance, she looked like a professional. Instead, she was just horny. In ten minutes, they were lying naked in his hotel suite. She had been...inventive. They had coupled there until just before his scheduled meeting with Mardinaud.

As they approached the entrance of the Gastatte zum Flaucher, Duman allowed the woman to walk ahead. Her ample figure would absorb any initial gunfire from the front leaving him free to concentrate on any attack mounted from the rear. Though he doubted the Frenchman would risk selling him out, Duman lived with precaution – especially after the trap in Paris yesterday.

Pretending to enjoy the view of the river, he casually allowed the girl to lead him through the flower strewn trellis arch over the entrance. The heavy German music pounded in his ears as they rounded the building and walked into the outdoor beer garden. True to tradition, the first sight was a buxom blonde carrying no less than a dozen *mass* of beer. Other beer maids were in constant motion, squeezing around the huge chestnut trees that gave shade to the underground cellars during the hot summer days.

The pair wound their way through the heavy wooden tables and Duman watched for any sign of trouble. His nerves were on edge, his senses tingling. But nothing seemed out of place. By the time he was halfway to the information broker, the terrorist felt he was safe. An attack in the densely packed garden would cost too many innocent lives – even more than in Paris. Duman relaxed slightly.

Mardinaud sat alone, though the number of empty plates gave the table an atmosphere of a riotous party of diners. Drinking heartily from a *mass* of beer, the Frenchman motioned for the couple to join him. Duman turned to the redhead.

"*Liebste*, go find us a table and order whatever you want. Don't wait for me. Enjoy yourself and eat your fill. You have to keep up your strength for later tonight."

The girl gave him another wicked smile and started away. Duman watched her walk, her buttocks moving provocatively beneath the tight, leather miniskirt. Sheer stockings and high heels accented her heavily muscled legs. If this afternoon was any indication, he thought, tonight was sure to be an exciting occasion.

"A most lovely woman, Monsieur...?"

"Wakefield, Richard Wakefield." Duman supplied the name for Mardinaud in a flawless British accent. "Yes, she is rather fulfilling. Thank you for seeing me on such short notice."

"I would not have it any other way." Mardinaud blinked rapidly and looked down at his plate to avoid the piercing blue eyes. He used the side of his fork to scrape the last remnants from the dish. The confidence he'd demonstrated with Katrina had dissolved. He happily played games with most of his other clients but not with Duman. Mardinaud would never make the terrorist tour Munich as the Greek had this morning. The girl was impatient by the end; Duman would be deadly. "You have been well, I trust," he said.

"A small bit of trouble, yesterday. I imagine you heard about it."

Henri had indeed heard about it. A DST agent shot and a woman's throat cut in full view of hundreds of people. Several others killed or injured in the ensuing panic. The inevitable last corpse – that of Duman's betrayer – remained undiscovered. When the authorities found the informant's body, it would serve as a clear warning to all. The news discouraged Mardinaud – another reason he had not toyed with the terrorist. "*L'incommodite?*" he asked, lightly.

Duman laughed, enjoying the understatement. "Yes, an inconvenience."

A waitress set down a foaming brew to replace the empty mug on the table and placed a plate of *weisswurst* with sweet Munich mustard in front of the Frenchman. After pouring the mustard over the plateful, he forked one of the small, white sausages into his mouth, smiled at the barmaid, and began talking while he chewed. "Bring my friend something."

Duman had endured other meals with Mardinaud. In fact, whenever he'd met the man there had been some type of food between them. Like Katrina, he lost his appetite quickly around the information broker. "Nothing for me," he replied.

They both watched the waitress move through the maze of tables. "Nothing like the ass of a healthy German girl," Mardinaud said approvingly.

Duman doubted the Frenchman had been with a woman in years – unless she was an excellent cook or dipped in chocolate. "What is it you have for me, Henri?" he asked. "I trust it is important or at least interesting."

"It might be, if you have not severed all your ties with Turkey."

Duman bristled at the mention of his birthplace. "Those in power forced me from the country, but my heart and allegiance will remain forever with Turkey. If you give me something that aids Turkey in its struggles, I will thank you many times over."

Henri pushed the empty plate aside and drained his beer mug. The waitress was at the table immediately. Only Henri warranted such service. "That was delicious." Mardinaud looked at his watch and then added, "I suppose it was a little early for them."

"I beg your pardon?" Duman had lost track of Henri's quick shifts of thought.

"The *weisswurst*. The dish is to be eaten between midnight and noon. Especially therapeutic after a night of revelry. Or so the superstition has it. If you will indulge me, I believe I will order another plate and risk the misfortune."

After the barmaid left, Henri slapped his hands together. "To business."

Duman listened as Mardinaud recounted the treasure's history from

Priam's Troy to Hitler's Berlin. Though he knew the story, Duman could not resist hearing it retold -especially by such an expert storyteller as Henri. He'd always been fascinated by the history of his country. He longed to live in those ancient times. A time when one man, a common man, could make a difference in the world. An age when an individual could shape history and leave his mark, as he, Duman, was destined to do.

"I have discovered where the treasure has been all these long years," the Frenchman boasted.

"Not my usual employment, but this could prove to be interesting." Duman's smile made Henri shudder involuntarily. "I would like to return the artifacts to their rightful place in Turkey. That should strike a particularly satisfying blow to the Greeks. Where is the treasure?"

Mardinaud slid a file folder across the table. The blue folder itself was a duplicate of the one he had given to Katrina. However, Mardinaud had tailored the information inside for Duman. As Henri was fond of saying, *control* of information was power. "Everything you need to know is in this file," he said. "Ulrich Kadner has the treasure. He's an ex Nazi who stole the artifacts during the war. Now he keeps them hidden in his home in Colombia. Actually, his home is more of a fortress."

Duman raised his eyebrows, becoming more interested as the challenge mounted. "I assume you detail his security and any presumed weaknesses?"

"That and more. It may not be necessary to use force to get into Kadner's home. Pay particular attention to the section on Helene Kadner. She could be useful to you."

Duman thumbed through the pages until he came to a color photograph of a beautiful, blonde girl dressed in a school uniform and trying unsuccessfully to use makeup to look older. Her stance offered her body to the camera, or the photographer. The open blazer revealed a white blouse with small buttons straining under the pressure of her well developed breasts. The short skirt displayed two exquisitely shaped legs, accented by high-heeled shoes that could not have been part of the uniform. Duman smiled at the photograph. The combination of innocence and lust excited him. Helene Kadner definitely interested him.

"The picture is a year old," Mardinaud said. "She's nineteen now. I have included her school schedule. She will arrive in Bogotá sometime in the next two days to spend time in the city before she goes to Kadner's. Her grandfather is unaware of this change in her plans."

"Looks like quite a girl," Duman commented.

"She has a rather sordid past. Three schools in Europe expelled her before she went to the States. Certain indiscretions unbecoming a young lady." Henri leaned forward and whispered. "She is apparently free in her selection of partners. I have it on good authority that one expulsion was for seducing one of her teachers. The teacher's husband, the headmaster, took exception to his wife's choice of recreation. Don't worry," he added when he saw the Turk's frown. "She enjoys men much more than women."

Duman laughed and nodded. "I think I'll meet her plane. If nothing else, she might be a pleasant diversion. Is that everything?"

"No, I have one more bit of information for you. I hope you won't think me presumptuous, but there is someone here you should see."

Duman's hand immediately slid beneath his coat. He glanced once around the perimeter of the gardens.

Henri rapidly held both fat palms out to placate him. "Please, there is no need for that."

"What games are you playing?" Duman still had his hand under his jacket.

"Do you remember a Greek?"

"You have told the Greeks about the treasure?"

"Naturally. You know how I operate. The information is for sale. The only condition placed on purchasing my product involves money. Besides, this Greek is special. They reinstated her to active duty for this mission. A beautiful girl by the name of Katrina Kontoravdis."

Duman thought for a moment. "The name means nothing to me."

"She was one of the two agents who found you in New York three years ago."

Duman looked off into the distance, his hand coming out from under his coat. "Yes, I remember. Her partner died, shot through the head by one of my bullets. Fools. They both deserved to die. I only caught a glimpse of her at the time. Long, dark hair."

"She has restyled it. Short. Quite charming."

"I'm sure it is," Duman said impatiently. "What does all this have to do with me?"

"From what I understand, the episode in New York caused you some difficulties. Loss of face? I assumed you would appreciate the opportunity to eliminate her. Take care of her before you go to Colombia?"

"The 'loss of face', as you call it, is inconsequential. If anything, it proved they cannot capture me easily. The death of her partner made my adversaries nervous and hesitant. As in Paris, they learned a valuable lesson. However, I have never passed up an opportunity to see a Greek agent dead. Tell me about her."

* * * * *

An hour later, Duman was alone on a dark street. Having had time to digest Mardinaud's information about the Greek, Duman had decided he had neither the time nor the inclination to dispose of Katrina Kontoravdis himself. The kill made him nervous. Duman's survival was based on a policy of maximizing his safety. An unprepared, rushed attack was unacceptable – even dangerous. His ego was huge, deservedly so, but he was not blinded by his own reputation. And besides, this was a lowly Greet agent and a woman at that. Hardly deserving of personal attention.

Mardinaud understood that. The Frenchman was playing his childish games again. Knowing Duman was the better player, the fool was evening the odds. Duman preferred having the odds in his favor. That was how he survived. Kontoravdis was unworthy of his time. Bigger game was available. He needed to get to Bogotá to prepare for Helene's arrival. Therefore, he had decided to make other arrangements for the Greek and fly to Bogotá that night.

Duman located the address he was looking for. Avoiding a streetlight, he walked around to the side of the building and knocked. A small man with a pockmarked face peered out. Surprised to see Duman, the man almost slammed the door but stopped himself. His left cheek twitched repeatedly, a nervous condition which had earned him the nickname of *the Mouse* years before. Only Duman and the Mouse's mother ever called him by his Christian name.

"I have a little job for you, Joseph," Duman said. "Won't take much of your time."

"Sure, whatever you want."

An American expatriate, the Mouse had come to Germany in 1980. With two crime families and the FBI looking for him, the heat was too intense for him in the States. Now, he worked as a freelance operator, doing anything from penny ante shakedowns to murder. The Mouse was an idiot but knew more than capable of killing Katrina Kontoravdis.

Duman enjoyed the pungent odor of fear emanating from the man as he explained what he wanted the Mouse to do. This was power, he thought, the power over life and death. A weaker man than he might fall prey to the sense of power, let it overcome him and take control. A weaker man might stray from the chosen path and seek the materialistic rewards such domination offered. Duman preferred the spiritual rewards the *true course* would provide him. All the same, he allowed himself to bask in the Mouse's fear for a time.

"She might be taking a flight tonight," he cautioned. "If she doesn't, you can do the job at her hotel."

"Sounds like a breeze. What does it pay?" The Mouse suddenly realized his mistake. "I hope you don't mind me asking. I...I just wondered, you know. I mean, like, a guy needs money, right? Not that I'd argue the price or anything like that. You know me. I wouldn't do anything like that."

"I know you wouldn't, Joseph. What do you think the job is worth?"

The Mouse thought carefully before he answered. "How about a thousand marks? Give me enough to impress one of the ladies."

Duman counted out five bills and handed them to the Mouse. "Pick up the rest from the usual place," he said. Then he turned away without another word.

If that was the value one of the people put on life, Duman thought, it was no wonder the rulers thought so little of the people.

Chapter 10

DINNER IN A FISHBOWL

David Morritt had arrived at the Frankfurt airport while Mardinaud was meeting with Katrina in the Marienplatz. His instructions were to remain in his hotel room until contacted. Standard practice for Mardinaud. David spent the time watching the television and refreshing his German. After two hours, he could follow even the most rapid dialogue.

When the phone rang at 7 p.m., David caught it on the first ring. He detected a slight Oriental accent in the female voice that told him to go to the *Hauptbahnhof.*

As usual, the train station was busy when David arrived. Since the caller had not directed him to any specific area, he positioned himself under the central departure board. A sickly looking man in a three piece suit appeared at his side. The personal service surprised David, but the message did not.

He left the station with no intention of following the directions to the Olympic Village. He had seen the complex, in 1972. David ignored the message and began his own search for Mardinaud by activating his old network. He started by trying to find Dieter Treliert.

Early in his career with the Mossad, David had discovered the perfect operatives. The idea arose from a conversation with Assi Levy about his crippled foot. The prominent limp and ugly deformity of the poorly healed bones led some people to shun the Mossad director or make him the target of ridicule and prejudice. They seemed to look upon him as less than a man – as though the foot governed his masculinity and virility.

Assi had seen even the most liberal of thinkers incapable of separating the physical deformity from his mental ability. Assi proved his superior intelligence repeatedly, moving higher in the bureaucracy of the Mossad, but the misguided thinking persisted.

As David traveled the world, he saw the consistency of this prejudicial attitude and decided to test a theory. He created a physical "handicap" and gauged the response of those he encountered. People spoke more slowly when he had an exaggerated limp. People spoke louder when he posed as a blind man. Most important for his purposes, when he posed with some impairment, people ignored him if possible. He existed on the edge of society.

David decided he could employ these nonexistent people.

Like most organizations of its kind, the Mossad's intelligence network operated mainly on the upper level of society, its agents working out of embassies, military establishments, and government offices. But that was the world of James Bond and not where Israel's real enemies lived. David operated among the undesirable segment of the population. Deals for munitions and terrorist strikes took place in the quiet, rubbish strewn back streets and alleys, not in five star hotels. The deeper David penetrated the terrorist organizations, the greater the need for a local network familiar with the streets. Not trusting the criminal element, he turned to the ignored legions of the street.

In every city David visited, he recruited his own underground network. He made contact with the street people – those whose physical problems gave them nowhere else to turn. David treated them with the respect they deserved and soon gathered a loyal group. As he listened with genuine interest to their often-exciting reminiscences, he realized how much these people had to offer not just him, but society as well. David supplied them with the money they needed to survive and used them to gather information.

Dieter Treliert had been an engineer on the railroad until an accident with two coupling boxcars severed his legs below the hip. When David finally found him again on the streets of Munich, Dieter was using his gloved hands to push a small, four wheeled dolly along the sidewalk. Though they had not seen one another for years, Dieter waved with instant recognition. He waited until David was standing over him before he spoke their ritual greeting.

"Jew. Why do you bother me? Tonight, I was to taste the delights of many women."

"Forgive me, old friend," David replied. "I could see you later if it would better suit your busy schedule."

"No. Now is always best. There is a ceaseless stream of women who hunger to experience the man whose middle leg is longer than the other two!"

Dieter burst into hearty laughter and grasped David's hand firmly. David winced; he had forgotten the old man's strength. "Can we go somewhere?" he asked, flexing his fingers.

"We *are* somewhere." Dieter slapped the pavement with his hand. "This is as good as anywhere." He lowered his voice as he pushed the dolly into a doorway. "Why are you here?" he asked. "I thought you'd retired. Surely the Mossad is not so desperate that they would send an old bastard like you out to do battle with the world?"

"I'm looking for Henri Mardinaud, the information broker."

Dieter laughed. "Excuse me, David. It strikes me as humorous. You wish information about a man who sells information. He's a little out of my usual sphere of influence, but I think I can help you. He has not exactly been hiding. Luckily, the man has certain perversions. So do some of his staff."

"Such as?"

"With Mardinaud, it's food. I heard about him when I was working the rear doors of some of the better restaurants. A few of my friends heard the same stories. The man just eats and eats. Doesn't even leave us any scraps. He'd chew the bones if he could but he satisfies himself by sucking the marrow out. An absolute pig. All the best restaurants are catering to the fat slob and competing for his patronage."

"That's Mardinaud," David said with a smile. "What about his staff?"

"Do you remember Susie?"

"Used to work the hotel about a block from here?"

"That's the one. Well, she has a son who has followed in his mother's footsteps. Might even be servicing his mother's clients, if you catch my meaning. For the past month, he's had a standing appointment with Mardinaud's second in command. A little shit named Erhart."

"Martin Erhart?"

"That's the fag. Anyhow, your best bet is Susie." He gave David's leg a gentle pat. "Be kind. She doesn't know what her son is doing."

"Thanks, Dieter." David gave the man several bills. "Why haven't you got yourself a wheelchair yet?"

Treliert rubbed the bills before stuffing them in his pocket. "A wheelchair? Won't work. Looks like I'm doing too well. Really cuts down on the sympathy."

David shook hands with Dieter. "Thank you, old friend."

"I am here whenever you need me, David." David started to release his hand, but the beggar held fast for a moment longer. "Be careful, Jew."

David nodded and turned away. Behind him, he could hear Dieter's trolley rolling down the sidewalk.

He walked over to Susie's small apartment. The retired prostitute did not recognize him as quickly as Dieter had. David's shoulders slumped when he saw how time and multiple beatings had ravaged the woman. Earlier in her career, her beauty had commanded a high price. This was no fairy tale of the prostitute retiring to a privileged life. Now she looked wasted and used, with a haunted look about her eyes. From the way she patted her skirt and posed herself, David realized she was still living in the past. Her rose perfume was suffocating and clung to everything in the room. But in her mind, she was still the young girl working the up-scale bars, admired and desired by all men.

After several minutes of conversation, David decided that Dieter was right; Susie had no idea about her son's profession. When he asked about Stephen's acquaintances, she told him the boy was meeting his "friend" tonight at the *Yellow Submarine* in the Hotel Holiday Inn.

David knew the bar and headed across town. He hoped Martin Erhart still stayed close to his boss.

* * * * *

The disco was as crowded as in its earlier days although the name had changed. The *Yellow Submarine* was now the *Aquarius*. Loud music bounced off the glass walls and bodies careened off each other on the dance floor. The imaginative decor brought many tourists to the disco. Built in a huge steel tank, the name suited the bar – either name. The thick glass windows gave the patrons an unobstructed view of an aquarium full of fish.

The previous owners of the *Yellow Submarine* had stocked the aquarium with forty sharks imported from Florida. At the posted feeding times, the crowds cheered as the sharks attacked and devoured entire sides of beef. Now, tropical fish had replaced the sharks. David missed the frightening predators and a familiar depression crept over him as he moved through the bar. Time continued to pass.

Henri Mardinaud was sitting on one of the risers near the largest window. In keeping with the Frenchman's warped sense of humor, he had a dinner of fish in front of him.

The change in Mardinaud shocked David. In just three years, the man appeared to have almost doubled in size. David thought Mardinaud must weigh close to 500 pounds.

When David sat down opposite the grotesque man, Henri almost choked. "Watch the bones," David warned. "You get one caught in your throat and it's all over. The Heimlich Maneuver is out. Unless we could find a gorilla, nobody could get their arms around you."

Henri downed the last of his beer and used a linen napkin to delicately wipe his lips and chins. "My contact at the hotel said Assi Levy had sent you, but I wouldn't believe them," he said, after clearing his throat. "What are you doing here? You didn't follow my instructions."

"Have forgotten how much I hate your childish games? I have no time to play so I cheated."

David's unexpected arrival upset Henri so much, he ignored his meal for a moment. The Frenchman thanked the fates that Morritt had not found him at the beer garden with Duman. That would surely have caused a premature end to the game for one of the two players and possibly the game master himself. "My information has you retired," he said. "I didn't expect Levy to send you. I hate surprises."

"I have personal reasons for wanting this particular mission." David dangled the morsel of information and the Frenchman snapped at the hook like a huge grouper.

"Interesting," Henri commented. "Would you care to elaborate?"

"Find out yourself. You're the expert." David smiled carefully as frustration clouded the fat man's face. Only one other person knew of Majdanek. Mardinaud's obsession for knowledge of other people's affairs was nearly as strong as his preoccupation with food. Any lack of information caused Mardinaud an almost physical pain. No matter how inconsequential, the knowledge increased in importance simply because it was unknown. "For now, I just want the information you have for me," David said.

Mardinaud handed him a folder, squeezed a lemon slice into a fresh mug of *weissbier,* and spoke through a mouthful of fish. "You're lucky I had the file with me. You are two hours early. I only arrived here myself." He smiled as David looked at the empty plates on the table. "I keep the empty plates to remind me of my diet," he said. "Aren't you going to read the file?"

David rested his hand on the folder, deliberately ignoring it. "Heiden has the artifacts from Troy?" he asked.

"An added bonus. I hesitated to mention it since I knew the treasure would not sway Levy one way or the other."

Mardinaud finished his food and stared as David drummed his fingers on the file. "It truly amazes me that you would come out again, Morritt," he said. "You do realize you're a hunted man? There is still a price on your head, several in fact. All tolled, they present a substantial sum. Your whereabouts would definitely interest certain parties."

David leaned across the table, picked up a napkin, and gently wiped a speck of food off Mardinaud's cheek. His eyes narrowed and took on a glassy chill. "Like you, I hate surprises," he said in a low voice. "Fortunately, I can count on your discretion in the matter. You know how easily I can locate you. I am old, it's true. But not so old that I can be taken *that* easily. If you are sure someone can take me, send them. Be sure they get me the first time, though. If they miss, I'll take the opportunity to look you up. Then, we can have a proper visit. You look like you might enjoy a couple weeks in the desert at one of the Mossad's special spas. I imagine the weight would just drop off you."

Mardinaud blinked rapidly. Sweat appeared on his forehead. He prided himself on his ability to control his players, but like Duman, David Morritt frightened him. The Mossad agent was too good to disregard. Morritt had survived countless attempts on his life in the past. Even one by Duman, if memory served. Henri knew he would not – could not – take the risk of exposing the Jew. "I would never consider telling anyone. However, now that you are out of Israel, anyone could see you. You might have been observed leaving Israel, for God's sake. If something happened..."

"Then make sure nothing happens. Use your network. I could be anywhere you want me to be."

Mardinaud nodded and smiled at him. "You have not been away so long, have you? It will be done. Possibly somewhere in Saudi Arabia or maybe Lebanon?"

David smiled at the thought of them tearing Lebanon apart looking for him. He tapped the file in front of him. "Who else knows about this?"

"Part of the fun is discovering the other players. I would hate to spoil the game for you."

"Spoil it."

Not for the first time, Mardinaud noticed David's gray eyes. Cold and hard as slate. In this world, there were no *good guys.* Morritt killed when necessary, with chilling efficiency. Mardinaud could see the years had not softened the Jew. "I informed the Greeks and someone representing the Turks," he told him. "Their interest, obviously, is with the treasure."

"Who are the representatives?"

"The Greeks have sent an enchanting woman, Katrina Kontoravdis. She may be of interest – unless you still mourn your wife."

At the mention of Shana, David glared at the Frenchman. "And the Turk?"

Mardinaud realized he had gone too far with the mention of Shana. "Duman," he answered immediately.

David stared at Mardinaud for a moment longer, then gathered up the file folder and left. Henri recognized the look on the other's face; he had seen it in the mirror on many occasions.

A plan was forming in the Jew's mind.

Chapter 11

ROOM SERVICE

Katrina stepped back and let the pock faced bellhop enter. "About time," she said, looking at her watch. She barely had time to eat breakfast before catching her flight to Bogotá. "Sorry, I guess it isn't your fault," she admitted with a sheepish grin. She turned and grabbed some money off the bedside table. The bellhop's left cheek twitched as he slid his hand under a napkin on the tray.

"Here," Katrina said, half turned toward him. She froze as the double edged knife blurred across her vision.

Katrina stepped back into the wooden wardrobe. The tip of the knife caught her blouse and sliced through it, revealing her lace bra. A small trickle of blood seeped from the thin cut above her left breast.

Overbalanced, the Mouse took a step, then stopped himself and reversed the direction of his swing. He jammed his elbow into Katrina's ribs and she stumbled backwards over the corner of the bed. She landed sitting down with her legs spread in front of her. The Mouse's greedy eyes looked down at her, focusing on her torn blouse.

Katrina made no move to cover herself. She knew that without a weapon, she was dangerously outmatched. With little effort, she allowed fear to creep into her eyes and the Mouse's confidence grew. In his mind, he held his knife on a helpless woman. Katrina watched as he took a step toward her, studying his weight distribution and the way he held the knife.

When the man stepped forward again, she smoothly regained her feet. A clear view of her almost bare breast shifted his gaze. Katrina moved. She feinted a punch to his left. As the Mouse slashed upward at her arm, Katrina kicked out and connected with his exposed right knee. A pop sounded as the joint dislocated.

The Mouse slashed again, the blade's tip catching the inside of Katrina's upper left arm. Blood quickly soaked her blouse. She retreated and he scurried back, dragging his injured leg. He slipped his foot under the wardrobe, and pulled, snapping his knee joint back into place.

The Mouse's face was drenched with sweat. Knowing he was close to passing out, he rushed at her, but his hurried thrust was high. Katrina stepped hard on the top of his left foot and could feel the fragile bones splinter.

The Mouse turned sideways and thrust the knife up, but his injured foot could not support the weight. Katrina jabbed the heel of her hand upward to push his ribs into his lungs. She connected with his diaphragm instead. The Mouse let out a rush of air and sank to his knees, moaning as his right knee hit the ground.

Katrina moved behind him, grasped his head, and placed her leg along the right side of his back. She heard a sickening snap as she twisted his head with a rapid turn.

* * * * *

Katrina stripped off her blood-drenched blouse and bra and carefully washed her wounds. Although the cut on her breast was a scratch, the slash in her arm was serious. It needed stitches, but she could not afford the time or the questions. Pressure was doing little to stop the flow. Remembering a favorite remedy of her grandmother's, she risked infection and used pepper from her room service tray to aid the clotting. The pain was slight and the bleeding stopped quickly.

She hurriedly dressed and went back into the bedroom. The Mouse was still on the floor where he had fallen. Katrina did not have time to dispose of the body and still make her flight. The body would have to stay where it was. And she'd have to get out of the country before the maid discovered the corpse.

PART THREE

COLOMBIA

THE WHIPPING STRING SANG,
AND THE ARROW WHIZZED AWAY,
NEEDLESHARP, VICIOUS,
FLASHING THROUGH THE CROWD.
THE ILIAD-BOOK IV

Chapter 12

IN FLIGHT MEMORIES

When psychologists reasoned that a professional impression gave passengers more confidence, *Avianca* had discarded the "fly me" look of previous years and updated their employee uniforms to light brown business suits. Now, as the seat belt sign blinked out, the stewardesses began to make their way along the aisle. David Morritt rose and started toward the back of the plane, but a beverage cart blocked his way. He returned to his seat unperturbed. He'd completed his desired task; Katrina Kontoravdis sat eight rows behind him on the other side of the 747.

Following his visit with Mardinaud, David had contacted the Mossad station in Athens. He'd placed the call from Munich, using the system of phone relays he'd set up in his Tel Aviv apartment. Moshe, an old acquaintance and the station head in the Greek capital, promised to gather whatever information he had on Kontoravdis. Because of the relays, Moshe assumed the call originated from Israel and thought the request was part of a training exercise. He gave David better than usual service. David had the information within four hours and studied it on the train from Munich to the Frankfurt airport.

Initially, he'd planned to find Kontoravdis in Bogotá and follow her. He knew Duman would be unable to resist a Greek target and would eventually move against her. When he did, David would move against him. Morritt wanted to capture Duman alive, if possible. If not, he would kill the fanatic with little remorse.

But when he arrived at the departure area, Katrina Kontoravdis was standing just ahead of him. He immediately sensed something was wrong. The Greek woman appeared nervous and agitated. She relaxed slightly once she passed through the metal detector, but continued to watch the other passengers.

Then, David noticed a small spot of blood on her blouse and a bulky bandage beneath. Her manner, combined with an apparently fresh wound, led him to suspect Duman had already attacked. If so, Katrina Kontoravdis' survival attested to her ability.

She favored her left arm and massaged her ribs. Watching her, David felt a surge of protectiveness that made him cringe. He knew such a macho attitude directed toward a woman with much the same training as he was ridiculous. The file from Moshe made her accomplishments clear.

Moshe had implied that Kontoravdis' work in intelligence compilation and extrapolation over the last three years was nothing less than brilliant. But the Station Head had said nothing about her beauty. As she moved to the boarding gate, her graceful movement attracted him. Now, sitting on the plane, he knew he was experiencing dangerous feelings.

He would try to ignore her, he thought, pulling out the file Mardinaud had given him the night before. He placed the blue folder on the tray in front of his seat. Until now, he had avoided reading it — reluctant, almost afraid, to even open the cover. As he removed the enclosed papers and saw the picture attached to the front page, he felt the terror and the anger seize him.

Sweat stood out on his forehead. Staring at him from the grainy black and white photograph were the strange, penetrating eyes and evil face of Friedrich Heiden as he had been in 1941; a Nazi standing at attention in his black SS uniform. The demon's presence emanated from the photo and surrounded David. He felt the familiar dizziness. The smells came first. Always the smells, he thought. He fought the sensation, but the horror grew, engulfing him.

For years, David had tried to remember every sight, every sound, every detail. He needed those memories to kindle the fires of revenge. He would lie awake for hours on his wooden sleeping pallet, preparing for the vengeance he desperately sought. In a hundred different ways, he had imagined himself killing Friedrich Heiden.

Later, forced to accept that revenge was beyond his reach, David had prayed for the memories to leave him. Night after night, his own screams had awakened him while during the day every woman's tortured cry reminded him of another's.

Then God, in His compassion, created a block for the pain. The memories faded, becoming a blur of the past.

Now, confronted with the returned evil, David faced his past to relive the darkest time of his life.

✻ ✻ ✻ ✻ ✻

The train stopped suddenly. The people in the cattle car were tossed to the front only to be thrown backward when the train resumed its course with a lurch. David slipped to the floor and an old lady fell on top of him. He struggled to get out from under her. She was asleep and he couldn't rouse her, no matter how hard he tried. Though big and strong for a ten-year-old, he could not move the woman and soon gave up his exhausted effort.

David had lost track of time during the journey. He remembered the loading of the trains in Warsaw. Although all the Jews on the platform wore the bright yellow star on their drab, dirty clothes, the talk had been of relocation and new hope. Now, David could hear the passengers mumbling about *Majdanek*. He didn't know what *Majdanek* was, but the tone of their voices frightened him.

The doors of the car slid open and the cold winter air rushed in. David watched through the forest of legs as several elderly people collapsed from the abrupt change in temperature. He felt warm and protected under the sleeping lady.

Three men dressed in coveralls pushed their way onto the car as the Jews shuffled out. Without the crush of people, David found he could move. About to crawl from under the old woman, he froze when he saw what the workers were doing. The oldest man carried a clipboard. The other two each carried a great hook, similar to the ones his uncle used in the butcher shop. As the older man made marks on his clipboard, the others used the enormous hooks to drag the sleeping Jews from the car. A chilling realization seeped into David's consciousness and a wetness soaked his trousers. These people, including the old lady on top of him, were not asleep. They were dead.

In shock, David watched as the sharp hooks plunged into the chests of the still warm bodies. The hooks made plopping sounds as they broke the skin and then grated against bone. Steam rose from the gaping wounds. Some were not dead but merely unconscious. Still, the hooks dug deep into these pitiful souls. They screamed as they were dragged out.

David struggled under the old woman, startling the man with the clipboard. A hook came at him and David, his legs crippled with cramps, stumbled outside. He landed amid the dead and dying bodies on a wagon beside the door. He squirmed frantically and plummeted over the edge, puncturing his hands when he hit the ice-covered gravel. Two guards grabbed his arms and dragged him to the group that had exited from the car moments before. Covered in blood and urine, he desperately searched for his mother.

What would his father want him to do? David thought. He could feel the light touch of his father's massive hands on his shoulders and smell the familiar odor of flour and yeast. The gentle baker had discussed much with his son before leaving with the Polish Army to defend the country. Though David knew the Germans had killed his father, the man's spirit lived on in him. "You must be a man," his father had said. "Be strong and look after your mother. You've got a good head, David. Remember to use it. Don't act rashly. We face dangerous times. Stop and think."

As he remembered his father's words, his panic eased somewhat. David saw his mother ahead of him. A tall man dressed in the black uniform of the *Schutzstaffel* led her away. In his limited dealings them, David had grown to hate the sadistic Germans, especially the dread SS. His mother should not be with one of those creatures, he thought. She should be with him, not with the Germans. David moved carefully through the frightened people.

Before the Germans invaded Warsaw, David had spent many hours playing a combination of tag and hide and seek, soon learning to throw small pebbles and twigs to distract the other children. He used natural cover and always watched for any convenient diversions. The other players never saw him until it was too late.

Now, as he watched the Nazi push his mother into a small shack, he began to play the game. His instincts told him the stakes were much higher this time.

The guards were busy playing sadistic jokes on the older Jews so they ignored the boy. Suddenly, David heard a shout about two hundred feet away. Three shots followed. David took advantage of the disruption and ran to a jumbled pile of scrap wood by the shack where he crouched and edged his way toward the shack's misted window.

He could hear his mother's voice through the thin walls as she pleaded with the soldier. The soldier laughed an evil laugh that chilled David's soul. A vicious slap rang out, followed by a sound like a sack of flour hitting the floor.

David stretched to peer through the high window and heard a noise behind him. Before he could turn, a powerful arm encircled him. A voice spoke to him in broken Polish.

"Want to see inside the shack, boy? Want to see what it is to be a man?"

"My mother..." David began.

When the big arm twisted him around, David saw Horst Dausel for the first time. Dausel looked so deeply into David's frightened, angry eyes that for an instant, David thought the man would save his mother. But then Dausel began to laugh and twisted him back to the window, pressing his face against the glass. "Your mother?" the guard sneered. "You must watch what happens to dirty Jew whore mothers."

His mother was lying on her back on a filthy, wooden table inside the shack. Her skirts were bunched up around her waist, her blouse and undergarments in tatters. Blood – bright red on her bare, white breasts – dribbled down from the deep scratches in her skin. Her face was bruised below one eye. She seemed to be unconscious.

David squeezed his eyes shut but then heard his mother scream as she swung at her attacker. Beating at Heiden's face, his mother landed two blows before the Nazi backed off. A broken button on her sleeve slashed the left side of his face. Blood ran freely from the ragged gash and dripped onto his uniform. Heiden grabbed a thick piece of firewood and stood over her, cursing in German.

The club rose and fell, spraying blood across the wall and window. His mother stopped screaming, stopped moving. Still, Heiden bludgeoned her with the stick. He beat her until his arm fell limp and her face was an unrecognizable mass of torn flesh and broken bone.

Then, he breathlessly began to laugh.

David heard Dausel's hoarse voice in his ear. "Be proud of your mother. She has just serviced the Third Reich!"

* * * * *

David was sweating when the stewardess tapped his arm. "Are you all right, sir?"

His eyes snapped open and he gave her a weak smile. "Yes, just a bad dream," he said.

"You'll have to put your seat belt on. We'll be landing shortly."

David looked out the window and saw Bogotá in the distance.

Friedrich Heiden was Ulrich Kadner. Horst Dausel still served his friend, but now as Viktor Bitkowski.

David vowed to send both to hell.

After they taxied to the terminal, David followed the other passengers off the plane. He stopped and pretended to read a sign as Katrina Kontoravdis walked past him. He glanced at her occasionally as they went through customs.

She had lost her tenseness during the flight and, with her features relaxed, she was even lovelier. David felt desire as he had not felt in years. He shook his head to return his thoughts to business.

Once through customs, Katrina went straight to the line of rusty taxis parked outside the terminal. David followed and took the taxi behind hers. He tossed some bills into the front seat and told the driver to follow the car ahead. Lounging back, he tried to forget Heiden and the painful memories that always left him so emotionally exhausted.

Chapter 13

NEWS FROM MUNICH

Duman cursed at the television and turned up the sound. The German satellite news report was about a bizarre murder in Munich. A maid had discovered a body in a hotel room. Someone had snapped the man's neck. Although the police had not yet identified the corpse, Duman recognized the description of the small man and immediately made several calls to Germany.

His suspicions were confirmed. The Mouse had not been seen. Contacts in the police department itself said they were still searching for the woman who had been occupying the room. Their leads were few and they feared she had fled the country. The description of the unknown woman left no doubt in Duman's mind; Katrina Kontoravdis and the mystery woman were the same.

Obviously, he thought, the Greek agent was better than he had anticipated. To have broken the Mouse's neck was a surprising feat. Duman knew he should have killed the Greek himself and vowed not pass up the next opportunity. Next time, he told himself, he would not underestimate the woman.

The pledge did little to quell the terrorist's anger at his own miscalculation. He arranged to have a man watch all flights arriving from

Germany. The police might not know where she was, but Duman was sure the Greek would waste no time leaving Germany. She would eventually appear in Colombia and he would be waiting. As soon as possible, he also took up a position in the parking lot opposite the airport entrance.

When the Greek walked out of the terminal a short time later, Duman crouched down in his car and watched her. She was even more beautiful in person than in her photograph. She moved across the sidewalk with a dancer's grace and confidence. He could imagine her tall, well proportioned body engaged in the deadly battle with the Mouse. Duman thought it almost sad to destroy something that added such beauty to the world, especially without the opportunity to taste her delights. However, he took more pleasure in the act of killing than any act of sex.

She walked straight to a taxi and Duman started to straighten up behind the steering wheel. He stopped short when he saw a man slip out of the terminal after her. For a moment, he could not believe whom he was seeing, but his mind reluctantly accepted the truth. The man was grayer, older, but the same man. *The* man. Unexpectedly, the Mouse's failure thrilled the terrorist.

Duman watched as David Morritt climbed into the taxi behind the Greek's. Still reeling from the apparition, Duman pulled out of the parking lot, keeping several cars between himself and the taxis ahead of him. He followed them to the Bacata hotel and made certain his operative was in position. Then, he turned the car around and hurried back to the airport.

Duman could not believe his luck. At the time of their meeting, he had been sure Mardinaud was withholding information. While tossing in the tidbit of the Greek, the Frenchman had not mentioned the Mossad. Duman should have expected Israel's involvement, considering Kadner's past. Still, even if Henri had told him of the Jews, Duman would not have expected David Morritt.

For years, the terrorist's life had been tied to the Mossad agent's. Either Morritt had been frustrating him or Duman had been trying to eliminate the agent. The Israelis, particularly Morritt, were responsible for thwarting several of Duman's important operations. The stubborn Jew foolishly viewed all terrorist acts as equal, Duman thought. Morritt did not understand that, unlike the Arabs and their Jihad, Duman labored for the good of all people. The killing done in his name would benefit everyone.

As far as Duman knew, David Morritt had retired years ago. The Jew was well over fifty. Too old to be in the field, Morritt should have given up years ago and stayed in Israel. Duman promised himself to teach the Jew not to allow an over inflated ego to cloud better judgment. In one fell swoop, he would kill his two birds.

And Henri Mardinaud, Duman thought as he sat down in the airport waiting area. He should have told him about the Israelis and David Morritt. The Frenchman would regret that minor omission. Though not a mistake worthy of death, Duman would consider breaking the man's jaw. Duman grinned at the thought of the huge man with his gluttonous mouth wired shut. Drinking his dinners through a straw was just the diet the obscene man needed.

✻ ✻ ✻ ✻ ✻

An announcement erupted from the crackling speaker and Duman turned toward the arrival gate to watch the passengers arriving on the flight from Miami. He compared the small picture in his hand to one of the female passengers and smiled.

The young blonde clad in a T shirt and unbelievably tight jeans stood in line waiting to go through customs. In the chill of the air-conditioned terminal, Duman could see her large nipples protruding through the thin material of her top. Her intricately strapped sandals with their two inch heels accented her shapely legs that met in a fleshy, inverted "V" between her thighs. Turning to face the customs worker, she presented a profile that was as impressive as the front view. Her pert, round ass stuck out invitingly and balanced the firm breasts bulging in front. Straightening the tie of his immaculate white suit, Duman rose to his full six feet one inch and walked toward her.

He stood half-hidden behind a pillar, listening as she used her abundant charms on the customs official. The overwhelmed man returned her stamped passport without searching her luggage and with only a cursory look at her papers. She gave him a devastating smile of thanks, then turned and dragged her large suitcase across the tiled floor while she struggled with her carry on and purse. Duman fell in step behind the girl. A young man she had graced with a glance started to help her but disappeared after taking one look at Duman's cold eyes. Sensing someone behind her, Helene angrily whirled to face him.

"Please, allow me." Duman reached down and grasped the handle of her large bag, his hand gently covering hers.

Helene stared at him, her anger replaced with blatant interest. She looked longingly, without shame, into the deep blue eyes of the most debonair man she thought she had ever seen.

Duman returned the stare. Her tanned skin was smooth and her freckled, pug nose gave her the look of a little girl. A look that belied the body beneath. The overdone makeup of the file picture was gone, replaced by a sexier, more mature application.

She smiled, showing even white teeth. Never had Duman experienced such a combination of innocence and brazen lust in a single smile. He wondered how long she had practiced the look, and how many unsuspecting men – and women, apparently – had fallen prey to it.

"That would be very kind," she said, slipping her hand from under his. "Thank you. My name is Helene Kadner."

"Richard Wakefield," he replied in his cultured British accent. "Are you going into the city?"

"Yes, I am. Would you care to share a taxi?"

"I have a car. May I drive you in?"

"Please."

Duman motioned toward the door. "After you," he said.

Helene nervously scanned the area as they stepped onto the sidewalk and he led her to his car. She glanced over her shoulder before getting in.

As soon as she sat in the car, Helene removed her sandals and slumped in the passenger seat with her bare feet on the dashboard. As she flexed her tiny toes, Duman pulled out of the parking area, silently blessing Mardinaud for his information about the horny young girl. An animated speaker, she was also a toucher. She emphasized every sentence by placing her hand on Duman's leg and giving him a sensuous squeeze. As they drove into Bogotá, her hand moved farther up his leg. The gentle touch had the desired effect as he felt himself becoming aroused.

Halfway through the trip, she complained about being hot. Duman turned up the ineffective air conditioning, but she was not satisfied. She reached into her bag in the back seat and pulled out a pair of cutoff shorts.

"Do you want me to pull over?" he asked.

"Don't be silly."

With that, she wiggled and squirmed out of her tight jeans and directed the air conditioner vent between her legs. Duman could see the tuft of blonde hair crushed beneath the lace of her bikini panties. Then she pulled the cutoffs up, glancing slyly at him. "Eyes on the road. You can look at me later," she promised.

Duman allowed himself to be seduced. He talked sparingly of himself, claiming to be on a business trip from London. Helene, on the other hand, kept up a steady stream of chatter, mostly about herself.

"I was due to arrive in another day. At least, that's what my grandfather thinks. He'd never let me to stay in the city alone. He's a strict old bastard. Thinks I can't look after myself. He always sends Viktor, his main asshole, to look after me. When you came up behind me in the airport, that's who I thought you were – Viktor, I mean. My grandfather still thinks I'm a child. You don't think I'm a child, do you?"

Almost breathless from listening, Duman replied slowly. "Not at all. In fact, you strike me as a very mature woman. I would trust your judgment."

Helene cooed her thanks and ran her fingers down the crease between his thigh and groin. As he turned into the driveway of the Bogotá Hilton, she pulled her hand away and sat up straight in the seat. "You're staying here?" she asked.

"I always stay here. Do you want to have a dinner with me?"

"I'll have to change first." Helene looked down at her T shirt and cutoffs, wishing she had worn something more dignified. "Can I use your room?"

"Of course."

"For as long as I want?" she asked, smiling her sweetly lustful smile.

* * * * *

An hour later, they sat close together at a booth in the hotel restaurant. Helene had changed into an off the shoulder red dress that fell in ruffles to just above the knees. A lace crinoline, the latest style at her school, finished the effect. In a sudden burst of modesty, she had not allowed Duman to watch her change. He had used the time to check the hiding places of the weapons he had purchased earlier. As Duman finished a cryptic telephone call, Helene proudly presented herself. She twirled to flare the skirt, reminding Duman of a child dressing for her first day at school. They had left for dinner hand in hand.

During the meal, Helene chewed each mouthful sensuously. They talked little and looked down at the swimmers through the glass roof of the pool. A tropical conservatory surrounded the clear water. Beautiful men and women in colorful bathing suits lounged in the green jungle terrain or dove into the warm water.

Duman refilled his wineglass and turned to Helene. She stroked the gray at his temples. Though Richard Wakefield, supposedly a man in his late twenties, was not gray in his passport picture, Helene's file had told of her penchant for older men. Duman was now an indistinguishable thirty to forty years old.

"Would you like to have dessert sent to the room?" Helene asked with a hopeful look on her face.

Duman considered his schedule. He had already contacted the man watching the Greek. According to the latest report, Katrina Kontoravdis had settled for the night at the Bacata. Morritt was not at the hotel. The Jew's absence meant that Kontoravdis would not move until morning. Duman knew Morritt did not make mistakes in surveillance. He was confident he had time to solidify his relationship with the girl before the Greek left for Kadner's compound.

At a wave from Helene, their waiter approached the table. "Would you care for dessert?"

Duman nodded and Helene turned to the waiter. "Please have whipped cream, honey, chocolate sauce, marshmallow sauce, and cherries sent to Suite 1470."

"The makings for the ice cream sundae. And the flavors of ice cream?" asked the waiter.

"No ice cream," she said firmly.

The waiter allowed himself the slightest raised eyebrow at Duman before turning away.

* * * * *

"Come in. Come in, my dear Martin. A glorious day."

Martin Erhart looked past Henri Mardinaud to the window of the hotel suite. A cold rain swept across Munich, as it had for the past day. Nothing about the day was glorious.

Mardinaud saw his assistant's doubtful look. "Ignore the weather," the fat man said. "The rain is not important. True happiness comes from the heart, not the weather."

Erhart handed him a file folder. Mardinaud set the papers aside without looking at them. "Talk to me, Martin. I want to the words. Let the joyous news tickle my ears with delight. Tell me, how fare my players across the sea?"

"They have all arrived in Bogotá, Monsieur."

"So bland, Martin. Give me details. Give me nuances. Paint portraits with your words. Explain the fears and doubts of the players. It is all so exciting. Speak to me of my young lady. She has arrived in Bogotá after her daring brush with death?"

"Duman's operative was unsuccessful," Martin said.

Henri ignored his assistant's displeasure, taking his words as an amusing understatement instead. "Unsuccessful! Very good, Martin. I like that. She dispatched Duman's thug with such finesse. I am as proud of my dear lady as I am surprised."

"The local police have issued a warrant for her arrest," Erhart pointed out.

"Not to worry. The police know nothing about her. She is only a name and a false one at that. They have been convinced she is unimportant, for now. I worry about our pretty Greek, though. She remains at the Bacata?"

"According to our latest intelligence, she has settled for the night."

Henri clucked his tongue. "A careless move. I thought she would have learned something from her ordeal. What about our eager Jew?"

"Morritt is following her. Your assessment seems to be correct. He's using her to get to Duman."

"Exactly what I would do. Don't judge that one by his age," Mardinaud cautioned. "Or, rather, do judge him by his age. He has survived much longer than most. Duman knows how good Morritt is. How good do you think they are? Who do you think will win?"

"I couldn't begin to guess, Monsieur."

"You aren't much fun today." The information broker thrust a fat hand toward the computer console. "Set up that program, the one that works such miracles with odds. Give me the best prediction of the outcome from your miracle machine. Then I'll tell you what is really going to happen."

Martin leaned over the keyboard and called up the handicapping program. He wondered if he should mention the report he had received just before entering Mardinaud's inner sanctum. He knew the fat man had resources Martin had no control over. Should he mention the shadowy inquiries being made about Kadner? Would revealing the message throw off suspicion or accentuate it? Best to remain true to form.

"There have been inquiries made regarding Kadner," Martin said slowly.

"Inquiries?"

"By persons unknown."

"I do not enjoy hearing the word 'unknown' uttered in my presence."

"We are investigating."

"See to it. I do not appreciate uninvited guests. Find them and eliminate them."

Martin jumped and glanced nervously out the window as a bolt of lightening brightened the sky.

Mardinaud sat back in his chair, a huge smile creasing his fat cheeks. "Forget this storm, Martin. The true storm is gathering in Colombia."

Chapter 14

SUNDAES AND SNIPERS

Duman stepped from the shower and vigorously dried himself with one of the oversized blue towels. He padded back into the bedroom of the suite and sat on the edge of the rumpled bed. He lightly ran his fingers down Helene's naked back and over the swell of her buttocks. Even asleep, she raised her hips when he slipped his fingers between her legs. Like the night before, she was incredibly sensitive.

When they had returned to the room last night, Helene had showered and changed into a tight pink teddy. The lacey transparent material clung to every curve of her body. She strolled over to him and gave him a deep kiss while her hands roamed over his body. Soon she'd removed his clothes and he was lying on the bed with strict instructions not to touch her. She answered the discreet knock on the door without bothering to put on a robe. She took the tray of sweet sauces from the waiter, smiling her thanks.

"Good evening, Miss," the waiter nodded. From the strained sound of his voice, the outfit had the same effect on the waiter as it had Duman.

Helene set the tray on a bedside table and smiled at Duman. She began by covering his lips with honey, then passionately kissing the sweet, sticky material off, poured honey over his nipples and licked his chest clean. Then she announced the *piece d' resistance*. Leaving a trail of chocolate down his abdomen, she had covered him with chocolate and marshmallow sauce, whipped cream, and a cherry. Finally, she had devoured her "sundae." Unable to resist, Duman had grabbed her and, ripped the teddy down the middle. For the next two hours, they had feasted on one another.

Duman was surprised at his stamina, but he understood how much Helene was responsible. Her acrobatics and imagination were unbelievable. Unafraid to try anything, her single desire was to please. When total exhaustion forced Duman to rest, the insatiable girl brought herself to multiple orgasms with a variety of methods – including three pieces of furniture in the suite. Then, before he thought it possible, she had aroused him again and they continued. Finally, they had fallen asleep in each other's arms.

Now, her nubile body beckoned to him again. He considered waking her, but knew he would not escape the room until late afternoon if he did. He gently removed his hand, slipped from the bedroom, and dressed in the outer room.

The front desk had a message for him from the man watching the Greek. Kontoravdis was on the move once again. Duman went to a pay phone down the street from the hotel and called a relay number. A woman with a heavy accent answered.

"Harry told me you'd be calling," she said.

Originally from Australia, Harry was now a member of M19, the most spectacular of Colombia's half dozen terrorist groups. The organization of white collar professionals had formed after General Rojas Pinilla lost the 1970 elections, supposedly due to the combined pressure and deceit from both the conservative and liberal parties. They christened themselves Movement of April 19 after the date of the election but shortened the name to M19 for publicity reasons. So much was about the sound bite on the evening news.

At first Duman had infiltrated the group by providing weapons. Soon he became more entrenched and involved himself in the planning stages of operations. Once the terrorists fully appreciated his expertise, he used his influence to tailor their activities around his personal dream.

Now, M19 spent more time battling Colombia's drug smuggling organization than harassing the government. The Medellín Cartel controlled the government more and more every day. Though Duman supported the drug trade in smaller countries like Jamaica, he despised the Cartel, which fed off the weaknesses of the people. He would be happy to see the business end in Colombia.

"Has Harry called?" Duman asked the woman on the phone.

"About a half hour ago. She spent the night at the Bacata."

"She didn't change hotels in the night?"

"No."

Duman could not understand why the Greek had not tried to cover her tracks. Still, it was good for him. Kontoravdis would not change her plans this late in the game. She would remain at the Bacata. "Is she there now?" he asked.

"No," the woman replied. "She's been out shopping all day. Leading my Harry a wild chase that one is. He said she's been stopping at outdoor stores. Seems as though she is going on a little trip of some sort. She bought maps for an area in the jungle about fifty miles north of here."

"And the other man?" Duman asked.

"Still following along."

"Has the other man seen Harry?"

"My Harry? You must be joking. If Harry doesn't wanna be seen, you better bloody well believe he ain't gonna be seen. The cheek! Harry said he'll call in every half hour, if he can."

"Tell him to break off surveillance when the Greek is within two blocks of the Bacata."

"Within two blocks. Sure."

Duman replaced the receiver. Regardless of what Harry's wife had said, he suspected the Jew had seen the operative. Morritt still had a price on his head and was too professional not to be checking for a tail, if only out of habit. Therefore, the Jew was obviously content to let the man follow or he would have disposed of Harry long ago. All of which was logical. The Jew preferred a known enemy. That would only help Duman.

* * * * *

Duman headed along *Avenida* 19 into the south end of Bogotá, an area comprised of industrial plants and blue-collar neighborhoods. It was also the home of Bogotá's criminal element. He pulled his car through an open gate in a chain link fence surrounding a group of privately owned warehouses and slowly drove along the row of narrow, cement block buildings. The fourth building displayed no name and looked deserted.

Parking his car and locking it, Duman crunched across the gravel to the small entrance. A middle aged man with spectacles answered the door and stepped back to let him enter. The man's eyes blinked behind his lenses as he nervously peered out and checked to the right and left. Seeing no one, he quickly closed and bolted the door.

Lathes and drill presses crowded the front half of the shop. On the right wall hung an empty gun rack. A vise on the workbench held the barrel of a disassembled rifle. Duman breathed deeply. He loved the heavy odor of oil and cordite.

"Gunther, I trust you are well?" he asked.

The small, precise man nodded his head and shook hands with Duman. His Belgian accent was heavy, even years after leaving Europe. "I am well," he replied.

Duman turned immediately to business. "I need your special services."

The gunsmith led him through a doorway on the left and into a small office. He always enjoyed working with Duman. As an expert marksman, Duman could appreciate Gunther's skill, his craftsmanship, his art. Most of his customers here in Colombia simply required a gun altered to full automatic or the serial numbers removed. The drug dealers and thugs possessed no class, no style. They sprayed bullets, hoping to hit something. But Duman! An artist himself, Duman understood the devotion the gunsmith poured into each of his creations.

Duman sat in a creaking chair but refused the offered drink of *Aguardiente.* "I don't have much time," he said. "I need a rifle with a sniper scope."

"What are the specifications?" Gunther pulled a pad and pencil in front of him.

"No more than a three hundred yard shot, I think. Has to break down into a compact case. I may have to leave it, as well."

"Daylight?"

"Yes."

"I only have a bolt action available. In a day or two..." Gunther shrugged.

Duman considered for a moment. A bolt-action rifle dismantled into a smaller package, but the first shot would warn the second target. That would require speed. He could load a bolt action and aim with deadly accuracy in under two seconds. He calculated the average reaction time of an agent with Morritt's experience and the time required to find cover.

Two seconds was enough. With the ensuing panic, the Jew would not have time. Duman was confident he could still guarantee two kills. "Yes, that should suffice," he said. "I'll need it immediately."

Gunther raised his eyebrows. Duman usually requested a personal fitting which entailed a return visit. "I do have the one. Untraceable and it has a scope. Not top of the line. Nothing I would normally consider for you. However, given your skill, I would guarantee the accuracy up to five hundred yards. That will give you the leeway you might require."

The gunsmith got up and walked into the main work area where he removed a long cloth wrapped package. He untied a ribbon and slid off the cloth to reveal a rifle fitted with a telescopic sight. With another rag, he lovingly wiped the gun down and handed it to Duman. The Turk quickly broke it down into its constituent parts. After checking each piece, he reassembled the rifle, loaded it, and sighted through the scope at the far end of the warehouse where a man sized target leaned against bales of hay.

Duman stepped up to a line marking a hundred and fifty feet from the target and fired. The first shot was wide of the heart by four inches. Gunther looked at the target through binoculars, took the rifle from him, and used a small screwdriver to adjust the anchor screws on the sight. Duman's second shot was wide by an inch. After another adjustment, the third bullet struck squarely in the center of the heart.

Loading one bullet and setting another on the bench, Duman took a deep breath and sighted. He shot, reloaded, and shot again – in less than two seconds. Then he gently laid the rifle down.

He and Gunther walked the length of the room to the bales of hay. Two jagged bullet holes marked the target's eyes. Duman smiled and clapped the gunsmith on his back.

* * * * *

The Turk parked his car in an underground garage on *Calle* 19 and strolled down the narrow street. After walking down both sides twice, he stood at the corner and determined his best angle. Paying particular attention to a tall office building on the left side, he watched the movements along the street. Traffic into the building was light and erratic. With no doorman or reception desk, he was certain he could enter without being noticed. After familiarizing himself with the various shops and alleys, he returned to the car for the gun case and a pair of binoculars.

He walked back to the six-story building and casually entered. He toured the ground floor, noting the exits and memorizing his escape routes. Satisfied, he trotted up the steps to the roof, picked the padlock on the door, and stepped onto the searing pebble and tar surface. Crouching, he ran to a low wall at the street side edge. He sat on his heels with his back against the wall as he unpacked and assembled the rifle.

Something wet dribbled down his neck and under his shirt. Looking behind him, he saw pigeons sidestepping along the wall, their heads bobbing with every step. He pulled a knife from his pocket, reached up, and snatched a pigeon from the wall. A dozen birds scattered as he slit its throat and rubbed the dead bird's blood along the top of the wall. He grabbed another bird and repeated the process. He set the two dead pigeons on the wall, one at each end of the three-foot smear of blood. The remaining birds instinctively avoided the area.

Once he finished with the pigeons, the terrorist rocked on the balls of his feet and watched the entrance of the Bacata Hotel.

Chapter 15

DEATH IN NEW YORK

Katrina was beginning to think she would spend her first mission in years touring foreign cities. She had spent most of the morning shopping in Bogotá, not for the usual tourist bargains, but for the equipment necessary to infiltrate Kadner's compound. The inventory, printed only in her memory, read like a prop list from a Hollywood war movie.

Unfortunately, the Greek Intelligence Service did not have a station in Bogotá. Before this operation, the Greeks had never operated in Colombia. The embassy had been no help, no doubt because of Stefandis' influence. Katrina had to locate her own equipment and her absence from the field had left her lacking practical ideas. The supplies for the hike through the jungle had been easy to attain and were now safely locked in the trunk of her rental car. The firearms were another matter.

She had drafted a plan during the flight and decided on the weapons necessary for breaching Kadner's security. A frontal attack was suicidal for one person. Her plan entailed stealth and concealment, thus requiring weapons that were compact, high caliber, and silenced. Precisely the type of weapons outlawed in a country determined to wipe out illicit drug and emerald smuggling.

Without the usual intelligence contacts, Katrina turned to the criminal element. She had visited a wealthy Greek in the northern edge of town where, amid the large homes and state residences, they had discussed the *attirail de la guerre* in an excruciatingly civilized manner. Other than information, his practical contribution had been a single automatic. For the rest of her list, he had recommended an acquaintance, a member of the most well connected criminals in the country – the Medellín Cartel.

She had spent the rest of the morning working through several middlemen to set up the purchase. The trail eventually led to an abandoned factory at the western edge of *Carrera* 3.

Now, Katrina paused just outside the factory to examine the Heckler & Koch automatic the Greek had given her. She slipped it into her purse and shoved a satchel of American cash into a stack of wood. If the contacts checked out, she would return for the money. She slipped through the partially open door into the darkness.

Grease and grime covered the high windows of the factory, allowing little light to filter into the interior. Decrepit machines, vandalized for useful parts, lined both walls and created a wide walkway down the middle. She could make out three separate sets of footprints in the dusty floor; two turned to the left into a small, dimly lit room and the third branched off to the right and disappeared into the darkness. She heard muted voices coming from the small room and headed toward it, calling out in Spanish.

The two men in the middle of the room stopped talking when she entered. She could feel their eyes work over her body. Their crooked, yellow teeth showed when they smiled at her. The shorter of the pair approached her and ran his fingers through his greasy hair. Needle marks dotted his arms. The pupils of his bloodshot eyes were dilated and when he spoke, his voice had the careless tone of a dedicated addict. Katrina thought he may have shot up just before she arrived.

"Beautiful lady," he said. "You come to buy something from us?"

He tried to caress her face, laughing when she batted his hand away.

"Where is the merchandise?" Katrina asked.

"Where is the money?" he mimicked, openly leering at her. "Or do you plan to pay with something else?"

Katrina glanced over at the second man whose stare had not left her breasts. "My partner has it, outside. When I see the merchandise, he'll bring it in."

"So, you have a partner," said the first man. "Just outside is he? Is that the truth?"

Suddenly, someone snatched her purse from her shoulder and threw it across the room. Two strong arms wrapped around her, pinning her arms to her sides and crossing her stomach just below her breasts. Her captor pulled her back and lifted her off the floor. She was helpless. As he squeezed tighter, she could barely breathe. Dangling from one massive hand was her satchel of money.

The other set of footprints, Katrina thought. She had ignored the third person and kept her back to the open door. She struggled but the arms only tightened. She could feel the man grind his pelvis against her.

The first man approached and caressed her face again. His hand traced a path to her left breast and he squeezed viciously. "We have you. We have your money. Now, we'll have some fun."

Katrina brought her right knee up and connected with his groin. The force of the blow almost lifted the small man off his feet. He moaned and sank to the floor.

The second man made a move toward her, pulling an eight-inch knife from a sheath in his belt. Before he took half a step, Katrina slumped in her captor's arms and lowered her chin to her chest. The arms around her tightened, but she felt the man's body straighten.

Instantly, she brought her head back and snapped it up into the third man's chin. His jawbone pushed into the soft tissue of his lower brain, knocking him unconscious. His arms went slack. Katrina used the big man's arms to pivot and propel him into the second man and the outstretched knife. The two men collided and fell to the floor, the second man pinned beneath the dead weight of his partner.

Katrina snatched up her bag and ran between the machines and scrambled through the outer door. Once outside, she blocked the entrance with a length of wood and sprinted for her car. Gravel sprayed from the tires as she sped from the lot. Looking through the rearview mirror, she saw the second man emerge from the factory with a Cobray M11 in his hands. She instinctively ducked, expecting a spray of bullets from the powerful gun. Surprisingly, only a single shot rang out. She was moving too quickly to consider the implications of that shot.

Now, as she walked toward her hotel, she wondered if Stefandis was right. Considering her recent failures, maybe she shouldn't be in the field. She had a talent for analyzing intelligence, but was she effective away from the safety of her basement office? First the attack in the hotel room and now a nearly fatal mistake with the gun dealers.

She had no excuse for falling into such a blatant trap, she told herself, other than pure stupidity. She should still be buried in the records department. She couldn't even attain her weapons. What hope did she have of getting into Kadner's compound and escaping with the treasure? The doubts that had mired her in fear and self pity for so long following the death of Alex returned with vengeance. Even after three years, the memory of that day remained sharp and clear.

* * * * *

Although they were by far not his *exclusive* target, Duman had acted against the Greeks several times. These attacks, combined with his Turkish descent, goaded Greek Intelligence, who desperately wanted credit for ending the terrorist's career. By capturing Duman, they hoped to restore some of their country's lost pride. Eight Greek intelligence teams tracked down all leads regarding the terrorist and unearthed information that placed him in New York City. Katrina and her partner, Alex, did the initial surveillance work.

The gods had graced the pair on their arrival in New York. They found Duman and tracked him to his hole – the second floor of a crumbling hotel. The front door of his room led into a narrow hallway and the single window opened onto the fire escape. Alex decided to wait until Duman was alone. Then Katrina and he would make their move.

"We can't go in with just these," Katrina argued, holding up her handgun. "And how can we coordinate an assault without radios?"

"We have him trapped. We can't wait any longer. He could leave any second and we'll lose him."

Katrina saw Alex's eyes gleam with the thought of capturing Duman. He was her partner, but she hated him for his single minded ambition. He was always ready to risk anyone's life, including his own, if it might mean his advancement. He knew the Turk's capture would propel him into the circle of his idol, Nikolas Stefandis. When Alex mentioned his seniority, Katrina knew she had lost the argument.

According to his plan, Alex would storm the front door of the room while Katrina entered through the window. By cutting off his only exits, they hoped to surprise and eliminate Duman. They would shoot to kill. Alex had witnessed the death of eight children when one of Duman's cleverly disguised bombs had detonated a school bus. He had no intention of taking Duman alive.

They synchronized their digital watches and separated.

Katrina encountered her first obstacle when the heavy padlock on the door leading to the roof would not come free. She worked quickly and carefully with a tire iron, but she still used most of her five minutes. She knew Alex would be preparing to batter down the door of the room below and debated whether to risk going back to warn him. At any moment, Duman could leave the room and their chance would be gone. Realizing her indecision was wasting precious seconds she dashed through the door and across the roof to the building's ancient fire escape. She had to descend slowly as the rusted rungs were icy and treacherous.

As her feet touched the platform outside Duman's apartment, she knew she was too late. She heard the wooden door burst inward and looked through the window in time to see a bright flash. She heard four gunshots and saw Alex falling backward into the outer hallway.

Momentarily stunned, she did not see Duman turn to fire at the shadow beyond the window. The bullet went wide by inches. Katrina dove over the railing, only her past gymnastics training saving her as she landed on the snowy tarmac and rolled against the building.

A car sped past her as she ran around the front. Duman was behind the steering wheel, his eyes glittering brightly as he smiled. Katrina would never forget the look on that smug face. Too late, she thought of raising her gun.

She ignored the escaping car and hurried up the stairs. Alex lay on his back, the top of his skull disintegrated by Duman's bullet. A second shot had passed through Alex's right shoulder. Katrina looked inside the room. Three photographer's lights were pointed at the door, rigged to flash when the door opened. Alex had gone into the room blind.

As Katrina stepped back into the hall, her foot kicked two ejected shells lying on the floor. Alex had squeezed off two shots.

She gazed into the deep blue of her own gun. Even blinded and dying, her partner had shot twice. Her automatic remained unfired.

*   *   *   *   *

Katrina shuddered at the memory and quickened her pace to the Bacata Hotel. No matter what George or anyone said, she would never lose her sense of responsibility for Alex's death. And for the deaths of all the innocent people Duman had killed since *she* had allowed him to escape.

The result of his operations had always been death, she thought. She suddenly stopped to look around her. Since her arrival in Bogotá, she had felt another presence but had not seen a single suspect. Now, the feeling was stronger. More than just a sense of being watched, Katrina felt an undeniable tingle of danger.

She looked up and down the street. The entrance to the Bacata was only a block and a half ahead. The street was empty except for a few shoppers. Several people left the office building across from the hotel, but headed away from her. The scene was quiet. Nothing sinister.

You're being paranoid, she told herself. She tried to dismiss her heightened unease as an afterthought of the experience with the gun dealers and the memory of New York. She continued along the sidewalk.

Chapter 16

INTUITION

Duman twisted the small wheel between the binocular eyepieces and slowly brought the Greek woman's head into focus. The Frenchman had been right. Her hair was shorter, but stylish. She ran her hand through the fine strands, casually brushing them into place.

Her large brown eyes sparkled like rich brilliant topaz jewels, even through the binoculars. Duman pictured himself sitting across from her, watching candlelight dance in those eyes. Her clear, dark, Mediterranean skin gleamed with a light sheen of perspiration. She had accented her high cheekbones with a light touch of makeup. This Greek was a true woman, he thought. Mature, intelligent, and resourceful. Not like the oversexed fluff asleep in his hotel room. This woman approached being worthy of his attentions.

He leisurely lowered the binoculars to take in her lithe body, watching the motion beneath her loose top as she walked down the street. Tight pants hugged the slight curves of her hips. Duman could see the taut muscles flex beneath her clothing. He understood why the Mouse had fallen prey to her.

She was slim and in superior physical condition. Strength pulsated from her, but it was tempered by an uncompromising femininity. Duman wondered what she would be like between the soft sheets of the bedroom across the street. She would possess the experience Helene lacked. Youthful passion, though refreshing, could not replace years of sensual experience. After a string of young lovers, he ached for the fulfilling delights of a mature woman.

His mind snapped to attention as the woman stopped suddenly, a worried expression spreading across her face. Duman watched her search the crowds around her. He smiled. She was sensing the error of her ways. Too late. Impatiently, the terrorist willed her forward as his right hand reached for the powerful rifle beside him.

* * * * *

Early in David Morritt's career, he had accepted that he could perceive danger through some unknown sense. He didn't know whether the source was psychic, spiritual, or unconscious awareness but he did rely on it. Now, David felt his body come alive as the warning sense again passed through him.

Katrina Kontoravdis was a block ahead of him. He had seen her tense and look around. Possibly, the same danger alerted her. Where she shrugged it off, David could not be so casual. A definite reason had triggered his internal warning system.

The man tailing him was gone.

Textbook craft. All nonessential personnel cleared the area of an operation at its climax. This procedure insured the safety of any operatives during a sweep by the authorities. One less mouth to talk.

David watched the street ahead of Katrina and concentrated on the unusual and the commonplace.

The hotel was over a full block away. The crowds were thin. All traffic moved at a normal pace. No vehicles lingered along the curb. The threat did not come from the street. Working south along the sidewalk, he sought the source of his concern. Nothing out of the ordinary. Behind him, the street was even more desolate. Still, the feeling of danger persisted.

Morritt quickened his pace and closed the gap between the Greek woman and himself.

* * * * *

Katrina couldn't shake the claustrophobic feeling of danger. She could sense something closing in, choking her off. Remembering Alex's death wouldn't have produced such an intense feeling. She had never felt danger when she had thought about Alex in the past. Only remorse and guilt. This tenseness was something new. Something urgent.

She took another step toward her hotel and suddenly recognized her mistake.

She was returning to a traceable location. She had escaped Munich and traveled straight to Colombia. Her identity had changed, but little else. Any other operative would have lost themself in another country before continuing with the mission. Instead, she had left a trail leading directly to the hotel. She had supplied any stalker with an address. Now she facilitated him by returning.

* * * * *

Duman focused the binoculars on a spot behind Katrina. Several moments later, he found David. He watched him move with the rhythm of the street. Though he despised the man passionately, he respected Morritt's ability. The old man was a maestro. Over fifty and the Israeli still moved with a skill achieved by few men in their prime. Morritt could blend with the natural cover, anticipating his quarry, always ready to cover his next more. It was one of the reasons he had survived countless years in the business. "Countless years and about half a minute more," Duman muttered to himself. "You should have stayed in Israel, Jew."

The binoculars flipped back to Katrina. She approached the intersection half a block away from the hotel. She paused twice and he thought she might flee down the side street. Duman watched her and felt himself harden. He remembered the pleasure of his last night with Chanda. Momentarily, he considered abandoning his plan and taking the Greek to his bed. To experience her clinging to his body, her tensed, hard muscles pumping against his strong form...

The terrorist quickly cleared his head and turned the binoculars away from her. He panned down the street toward the Bacata. He knew the stores by heart. A women's boutique, an Italian shoe store, and a cosmetologist. The fourth shop was a small rattan importer, its window and sidewalk cluttered with baskets and furniture where shoppers had to funnel into a narrow space. Duman judged this to be the ideal shot.

Kontoravdis would die there.

He let the binoculars dangle on their strap and picked up the rifle. Holding the gun lengthwise along his body, he caressed his crotch with the smooth wood of the stock.

* * * * *

As Katrina approached the intersection, David looked left and right, desperately seeking the danger he felt. He knew his actions were becoming obvious, but he didn't care. Was the Greek at too great a risk? Should he intercept her?

His conscience bothered him. If he allowed Kontoravdis to continue, he might jeopardize her life. To use her made him no better than the man he wished to capture. But could he abandon such an excellent opportunity at Duman?

Where was the danger?

He looked at the six-story building across from the Bacata. The office tower was one floor higher than the hotel. The rooftop offered the perfect vantage point. He could hear the smooth cooing of the pigeons perched along the edge of the roof. Hundreds of the birds sat shoulder to shoulder along the length of the wall. Except in one three-foot section. Not a single pigeon roosted there.

He had found the threat. Duman had chosen well. David closed the distance between the Greek and himself.

* * * * *

Katrina paused in front of the Italian shoe store. She used the angled shop window as a mirror to study the tanned, muscular man crossing the intersection. She recognized him from the airplane the day before.

He had followed her all the way from Germany.

She walked on to the next window and paused again. The man was closer. If he was following her, he was doing a poor job of it. He must have picked up her trail near the hotel. Katrina breathed a sigh – an amateur.

She relaxed slightly now that she had identified the threat. Someone must really want her dead to have followed her from Germany. Katrina quickly prepared a counterattack, not pausing to consider who that someone might be.

She judged the man's height at five foot eleven, one inch taller than herself. She held her hands in front of her and flexed her fingers. The man moved closer.

Katrina passed in front of a cosmetologist's and shifted the satchel of money to her left hand. The cluttered sidewalk of the rattan shop next door presented the perfect defensive position. She took three more steps and stopped to gaze through the window, shifting her weight from right to left and back again. She could see her attacker's reflection in the glass.

He was only feet away.

* * * * *

David saw the rifle barrel jut over the lip of the rooftop. He propelled himself toward the Greek, intent on bringing her to the ground. But the woman dropped the bag she was carrying and pivoted to face him. Her hand shot up at his neck. Only a slight shift of his weight saved him from the disabling blow directed at his throat.

His left arm went numb as the woman dug her rigid fingers into his shoulder. He crashed into her stomach and she fell to the pavement in a tangle of baskets. David landed heavily on top of her, pinning her to the ground.

A bullet struck a tourist leaving the rattan shop. Spreading on impact, the projectile tore through the man's chest and exited through his back. The force sent him sprawling backward through the door of the shop.

Katrina saw the spray of blood erupt from the man's chest and knew the shot had been meant for her. The realization sent a wave of shock through her. She allowed the man who had pushed her down to pull her to her feet and drag her down the street after him. The front window of the corner boutique shattered as they passed.

Ducking low, they slid around the corner and ran.

Chapter 17

BREAKFAST AND RAGE

The door to the hotel suite crashed open, startling Helene who dropped her magazine onto the bed. She had risen and showered an hour ago. By the time she had dried herself, room service had arrived, delivered by the same hopeful waiter as the night before. She had voraciously eaten the large breakfast of eggs, bacon, kippers, and fresh fruit. Since then, she had spent the time lounging on the bed while she finished the excellent coffee. She was still wrapped in a towel, with no plans of getting dressed for at least another hour.

When the door slammed shut, Helene thought she felt the room shudder. She sat up and looked into the outer room of the suite. She was about to speak when the wheeled cart with her breakfast dishes sped past the bedroom door. She heard the cart crash into a wall and tip over, littering the carpet with dirty dishes. Cursing and unintelligible mutterings added to the clamor. Cautiously, she slipped off the bed and approached the door of the outer room only to duck as a sofa cushion came flying at her.

"Damn it, Richard! Watch what the hell you're doing. What's your problem, anyway?"

Duman's eyes burned with intense rage as he turned to face her. His clenched jaw made the cords of muscle in his neck stand out in high relief. He slammed his fist against the wall and an intricately framed mirror slid to the floor. Duman flexed his hands as he walked toward her. Even the sight of the slim blonde wrapped in the short towel made him angry. She had been lounging all day, the lazy, empty headed bitch. He felt an almost overwhelming desire to hit her, but brought his anger under control and shouldered his way into the bedroom.

"It was the damn Jew. He had to interfere. I had everything arranged and he..."

Duman broke off when he noticed Helene's pout turn to a puzzled frown. He lowered himself into the small boudoir chair in the corner, closed his eyes, and concentrated. He thought of the sun sinking slowly over the Mediterranean. Calmed by memories of his native land, he began to think clearly and replayed the entire afternoon. His plan was so simple. Nothing should have gone wrong. The Greek was even standing still in the street. It was perfect.

He pounded one fist into his palm as his mistake suddenly became obvious. He should have shot the Jew first. Then the Jew could not have intervened. In an effort not to underestimate the woman, he had underestimated the Jew instead. Worse, he had ignored the Hebe. A mistake Duman would not make again.

The old man was good, he thought. Good, but not indestructible. The Jew had won the first round, but he could not protect Kontoravdis forever. The Greek would die and so would the Jew. And he, Duman, would be their executioner.

✻ ✻ ✻ ✻ ✻

Helene sat on the bed and watched as Richard worked the fist of one hand into the palm of the other. The muscles of his forearms flexed repeatedly. She assumed a business deal had gone badly. For the life of her, she could not understand how anyone could get that worked up over some bit of stuffy business. Of course, he might have lost a lot of money. She could understand his anger at that. In her mind, only one thing rated with money.

In concert with that thought, she remembered last night. She thought about Richard's muscular body on top of her, under her, beside her. Never in her life had she experienced love like last night. Never in her life had she felt so alive. Sex was sex, but this *must* be true love, she thought. She needed him, needed him desperately. He brought life to her with his love. She would cease to exist without him.

They had made love for hours the night before. At times, Richard was gentle, tenderly bringing her to a climax. Other times, he was brutal. He teased and taunted until, out of desperation, she had to bring herself off. Helene rubbed her thighs together at the memory and could feel the dampness forming. In his current state, Richard would be intense, violent.

She wanted him that way. She wanted to see what he was capable of. She had to have him, now and later. For the rest of her life. She would never get enough of him. He would come with her to her grandfather's where they would secretly love through the night. Her grandfather would suspect and be furious, adding to the excitement. But, for now, she needed to have Richard's strong hands roughly grasping her body.

Richard ignored her as she walked over to his chair and knelt in front of him. Deliberately, she undid the buttons of his shirt and ran her hands down his chest. The sound of her sharp nails scratching the hairy skin aroused her further. The tingling heat between her legs increased. Still, he did not look at her.

Helene dropped the towel to the carpet as she stood. She pulled her long hair back and ran her hands over her body, pinching her hardened nipples, then pressing over her flat stomach. She let both hands slip between her legs and massaged herself until she thought she would climax. Then, she knelt again and worked impatiently on Richard's belt.

He brushed her hands away, but she persisted. Finally, she tugged his pants down to his knees and buried her face in his lap. At first, his limp condition surprised her, but it only strengthened her resolve to satisfy him. She would return some of what he had given her last night. She loved him more than she had loved anyone before. As she lowered her mouth on him, she thought about them being together forever.

※　※　※　※　※

Duman looked down at the blonde head bobbing up and down. Although her soft hair tickled the skin of his thighs as her warm mouth surrounded him, he did not respond. This stunned girl did not understand that, for one of the first times in his life, he had failed. How could this child expect sex after he had failed so miserably? She was an insignificant fool. Her greatest achievement was a multiple orgasm. She was unworthy of his attention.

He would dispose of her soon. When her usefulness ended, he could walk away from her and no longer have to listen to her whining about everlasting love.

As he watched Helene work on him, he thought of how nothing would please him more than to reach down and take her neck in his hands. He would squeeze her frail throat until the fragile bones snapped between his fingers. He could almost see her eyes pleading with him, begging him to release her as his grip tightened.

Slowly, he felt himself harden in her mouth.

Chapter 18

SWISS SWEETS

Katrina and David ran for several blocks, darting through traffic and sneaking down filthy back alleys before they dared stop. They fled both the assassin and the police, reluctant to involve themselves in any official investigation. They slowed to catch their breath and scanned the area around *Calle* 23. The wail of sirens was far behind. David turned toward the Greek woman, sensing her mistrust.

Katrina started to turn away, but stopped herself. She had no idea why she had allowed this stranger to lead her. He had given her ample opportunity to escape. And yet, she had stayed. She distrusted the man but needed to hear who and what he was. If he could not explain himself, she would leave.

She studied the man's rugged, lined face for some clue. His gray eyes had been as cold and hard as slate while he watched the street, but now she imagined she saw caring and respect in those eyes. He was attractive in a serene, mysterious way. She quickly reprimanded herself for the thought. The silence between them was becoming uncomfortable. Finally, the man spoke. Katrina was not surprised when he spoke almost flawless Greek.

"This is a rather awkward and abrupt meeting. My name is David

Morritt." Katrina looked down at the offered right hand and then back at his tanned face. When she didn't return the handshake, David let his hand drop.

"I think you already know my name," Katrina said, watching his eyes.

"Yes, I do have you at a slight disadvantage," David admitted.

"If you don't mind, Mr. Morritt, I'll reserve thanking you for saving my life until I hear more. Who, or what, are you? How did you happen to be behind me at that opportune moment?"

David smiled at the calm, even tone of her voice. "Please, call me David. What I am is an Israeli agent. Mossad, to be specific."

Katrina looked harder at him. As she connected his name with the Mossad, some of the distrust left her eyes. "David Morritt of the Mossad. I've heard of you. You helped us with airport security after the TWA hijacking. You were quite the topic with everyone discussing so many rumors of your exploits. I pictured you much older."

"Some days, I am."

Katrina smiled for the first time since the attack. David took advantage of the shift in mood and looked around at the passing crowd. "Let's get off this street," he suggested.

"Where?"

"There." He pointed to a Swiss tearoom. "A neutral location."

In spite of herself, Katrina's smile broadened.

* * * * *

An elderly Swiss couple had bought *The Chesa* after moving to Colombia in the early sixties. They brought with them generations of delicious recipes and the superior service that made their native country famous. The main restaurant was on the upper floor of the quaint, two-story building. An archway, intricately carved with scenes of Switzerland, opened onto a small tea shop on the street level.

As they entered, David and Katrina could smell the warm, moist odors of the sweet, sticky pastries, strong Colombian coffee, and flavored teas. They checked each other for dust, scuffs, and other telltale signs of the earlier attack before they passed under the arch and walked through the nearly empty room to a table near the window. David deliberately positioned himself with an unobstructed view of the street and the room. Katrina sat opposite so she could watch the street and David.

The elderly owner wheeled a tray of Swiss desserts toward the table, greeted the couple in Spanish, and invited them to choose from the array of baked goods. Katrina picked a chocolate mousse in a small cup of dark, Swiss chocolate. David chose a round, cream-filled pastry topped with sliced strawberries and chocolate shavings. Their waiter poured steaming cups of coffee and left them to settle back in their chairs. They stared at each other in wary silence. The feeling of closeness present in the street had faded and Katrina's mistrust returned. They locked eyes as though engaged in a schoolyard staring contest.

David rubbed the spot on his shoulder where Katrina had hit him, slowly working the muscles to relieve the stiffness. Now that he had met Katrina, he was uncertain what he would do with her. Complications had ruined his initial plan. Duman had seen him, so Katrina was now useless as bait. Besides, he wasn't sure if he could continue to use her as bait.

David knew he must shift his emphasis away from capturing Duman and concentrate on finding Heiden or Ulrich Kadner as he was now known. The question remained whether the lovely Greek woman sitting across from him would be an advantage or not. He had no qualms about working with a woman, but any unproven partner could be dangerous. On the other hand, any competent assistance would be welcome and potentially useful. Looking into her dark brown eyes, David knew her company would be enjoyable. He stopped that thought short. If only seeing her and reading her dossier produced this feeling, he wondered, what would happen if he spent more time in close contact with her?

This time, Katrina broke the long silence. "You still didn't answer my question. Why were you behind me? What are you doing here?"

David chose to answer the second question first.

"Our objectives are the same. Don't look so innocent," he said. "There's no sense in pretending. I know you've seen Henri Mardinaud and that you know about Heiden...uh...Kadner. I know you're after Schliemann's treasure from Troy."

When Katrina didn't answer, he continued. "Yes, well, I imagine you need more convincing. You haven't dealt with Mardinaud before, have you? Possibly, you don't know how he operates. I, unfortunately, have had many opportunities to learn what a bastard he is."

David sipped at his coffee then went on. "The Frenchman is an obsessive game player and has been for some time. His physical condition, which I'm sure you noticed, allows him to play only mental games. Over the years, he became increasingly bored with rudimentary parlor games.

Even the new computer games didn't satisfy his obsession for personal challenge so he turned to his business. Now, when he has special information to sell, it does double duty by providing a scenario he can watch and enjoy. He picks the players and uses their mutual hatred for each other to work *against* them – and *for* him. He designs every encounter for his amusement. Life and death mean nothing to him, except as added entertainment."

"And, naturally, you're after Kadner." Katrina saw something flash across the gray eyes when she mentioned the name. "That doesn't explain why you were following me," she said. "Who else knows about the treasure?"

"Only one other," David said. "Duman."

Katrina's hand tightened on her coffee cup. For a moment, David thought the fragile porcelain might crack.

"Duman shot at me?" she whispered.

David nodded.

Katrina's eyes flared and she slammed the cup down on the table. "You knew he would be after me? You just let me walk into his trap? Let me play the dupe while you trotted behind, waiting to spring into action? Did you enjoy playing the hero? Is this how you gained your reputation?"

"I know you have a right to be angry," David said as he glanced around the café.

"Angry? Angry doesn't begin to cover how I feel!" Katrina's hands gripped the edge of the table, wrinkling the lace cloth. "Duman might have killed me and you say I have a *right* to be angry? You're too generous."

David scanned the restaurant again. Nobody seemed to have overheard the outburst. When he turned back, Katrina was standing to leave. "Wait," he said.

"Forget it," Katrina snapped. "Go use someone else."

"You don't understand." David grabbed her wrist.

Katrina picked up the fork beside her plate, holding it above David's hand. He released her but continued talking. "I wanted to warn you, but I couldn't risk the contact," he explained. "A man was watching you. I couldn't rely on your reaction. You might've given yourself away. I was never far away, though. I was there when Duman made his move and I was also at the factory."

"You were at the factory?"

"Yes. You didn't really need my help, but I did take out the guy with the Cobray. The rental might be hard to explain, riddled with bullet holes."

Katrina remembered the single shot she had heard as she pulled away from the factory. Her face softened and some of the fire left her eyes. Suddenly, unbidden, the thought came to her – *he's telling the truth.* She slowly sat down. He had saved her life, even if he had been partially responsible for putting her at risk in the beginning. She wondered if she would have done any differently had the roles been reversed. She wanted to think so, but doubted it.

And it wasn't him but her own stupidity that had put her at risk. She wasn't exactly an innocent civilian but so far she had played herself as the fool. Her craft wasn't just rusty – it was all but deteriorated. But Stefandis *would not* be proven right!

Katrina reached across the table and shook David's hand. "I said I would reserve my thanks. I now offer it to you freely. Thank you for saving my life." She smiled at him as warmly as possible.

"And I ask your forgiveness for putting you in danger," David said. "I know it sounds empty now but just before Duman fired, I had given up on my plan. I'd decided it wasn't worth the risk."

Katrina was not listening. "Duman must have arranged Munich," she said.

"Munich?"

She looked up and saw the puzzled expression on David's face. Obviously, he hadn't *always* been there for her. As she briefly explained the episode in the hotel room, David's respect for her grew.

When she had finished, Katrina asked, "Where do we go from here?"

"We're on mutually beneficial missions," David replied. "Your primary interest is the treasure and I want Heiden. We're both without partners when neither of us would choose to operate that way. Together, we stand a better chance of getting the treasure and Heiden and keeping ourselves alive. Duman won't give up on you or the treasure. Working alone, we might well stumble over each other. Together, we can fight Duman and Heiden. Assuming, of course, that you would consider working with me."

Katrina watched David's warm eyes while he spoke. She felt a deepening pull of attraction toward the Israeli agent and that emotion frightened her. She remembered her last partner. She could see him slumped against the stained wall, the top of his head missing. She fought the apparition and tried to attack the problem logically.

Duman was dangerous and she was vulnerable. Even if she did avoid Duman, she had to get into Kadner's compound and escape with the treasure. She still didn't have any weapons and the supplies that had been delivered to her hotel were lost to her. With David's help, she stood a slightly better chance of getting the artifacts back to Greece. Besides, the opportunity to spend more time with this man excited her. The legend and the man.

Slowly, Katrina smiled. "I suppose you have a partner," she said.

* * * * *

They stayed for several more cups of the delicious coffee. Then Katrina accompanied David while he rented another car. They drove to a small airstrip east of Bogotá where they boarded the light aircraft David had chartered upon his arrival in Colombia. The flight to the small village in the northern jungle took an hour. While airborne, David showed Katrina the equipment he had acquired. She was impressed by the number of supplies he had gathered and unhappily compared his success against her ordeal with the drug merchants.

She watched David's face as he spoke. He had a strong profile. His smile was warm, causing his eyes to brighten and crinkle at the corners. He explained his intended assault on Kadner's compound, listening with interest to her opinion. Occasionally, he altered his plan to fit her better ideas. The equality was not only gratifying; it was something new and invigorating. The more David spoke, the closer Katrina felt to him. Her attraction deepened and, with it, her fear.

Chapter 19

SIGHTSEEING

The beige colored water of the Tequendama River erupted out of the dense green of the jungle at the foothills of the mountains. The rain fed torrent fell 475 feet to create one of Colombia's most beautiful natural wonders, the Tequendama Falls. The mist hovered over the jumbled rocks and swirled out to sprinkle the many hued tropical flowers along the banks. Small, bright birds flitted through the heavy vapor to emerge sodden on the other side. They soared upward to dry themselves in the warm sunlight and gentle breeze only to return to the mist and their game.

Duman slid down to the shore of the river and snatched up a yellow blossom touched with purple around its edges. Running like a schoolboy, he rejoined Helene and gave her the damp flower. Small droplets of water clung to her face as she buried her nose among the flower's petals. She breathed in its fragrant odors and then kissed Duman gently on the lips. Playfully, she shook the flower in his face, covering him with tiny drops, and ran down the pathway.

He allowed her to get ahead of him and then chased her along the stony path. At the base of the falls, she mounted the large steps cut into the earth, but Duman caught her at a small viewing platform halfway to the top. She collapsed in his arms in a fit of laughter. They sank to the ground, holding each other while they caught their breath. Their laughter subsided and they kissed tenderly. Duman pulled away, stood, and helped Helene to her feet. They held hands and continued to the top.

At the summit, they surveyed the surrounding countryside. The base of the waterfall disappeared into the mist where the birds still played their game of tag. Farther down, where the water ran deeper, the river lost its violence. Like a flaming border, the lush vegetation followed the twisting river until it disappeared from sight. Duman breathed in the rich odors of the jungle and the river, refreshing after the polluted cities he had visited lately. He felt a sensation of freedom flow over him. Helene ran her hand over his muscular chest and flat stomach, teasingly straying at his belt.

Behind them, a vendor sold fresh fruit from a small stand. Seeing the couple, he whistled and threw a mango over to them. He told them it was the lover's fruit. Duman took a knife from his pocket and sliced a small piece, holding it up to Helene's mouth. She bit down on it with her sharp teeth and juice ran down Duman's hand. She licked at the sweet liquid on his fingers. Smiling at each other, they continued to walk upstream along the shore.

They crunched along the gravel path for another half mile and then returned to the bottom of the falls. They walked in silence, listening to the sounds of the jungle and enjoying their closeness. In the cool shade of the huge trees, each felt the warmth of the other's body. Duman held Helene's arm until they reached the car.

They sat quietly looking at each other. Twice before, Helene had begun to speak. She touched Duman's cheek and started again.

"I don't know what to say to you, Richard. I have never felt this way."

"Don't say anything. I know how you feel because I feel the same way." Duman brushed a lock of fair hair away from her face. "I love you. Nothing like this was supposed to happen. It happened so quickly, so unexpectedly. I'm not sure I should, but I love you."

Helene threw her arms around Duman's shoulders and buried her face in his neck. Richard always said exactly the right words at exactly the right moment. She held herself against him for a time and slowly pulled away. She looked into his gentle, blue eyes.

"I have to go to Grandfather's. I don't want to leave you, but he worries. He'll send Viktor for me. Grandfather will forbid me to see you, if I make him angry. I don't care what he thinks, but he can make life ... difficult for me."

Duman avoided her eyes. He picked up the flower on the dashboard and played with its petals. "I understand. If we can't be together, at least we can remember the past hours. I only wish we could see more of each other."

Helene's eyes opened wide and she grasped the hand holding the flower. "We can! I mean, if you really want to. Do you want to?"

"Of course. But, how? You said your grandfather lived north of here and wouldn't let us see each other."

Helene almost bounced in the car seat. "Don't you see? Come to Grandfather's with me. If I introduce you, instead of him finding out about us, he will have to let us spend time together. We could be together at Grandfather's."

Duman's eyes lit up, mirroring Helene's happy expression. "You're sure?"

"Then you'll come?"

"I love you so much," Duman replied.

Helene clapped her hands together. "That settles it. I'll call Viktor and he can come and pick us up in one of the helicopters. Then we will be together."

"But not really together. Not like we have been here. You said your grandfather's home was like a fortress with guards and everything." Duman looked crestfallen.

"Well, we couldn't sleep together in the open. I could come to your room, though. I know that mausoleum and I know how the guards work. I've been sneaking around that house for years. I can get by them any time I want. Don't worry about that."

As Duman pulled out of the parking lot, Helene nestled against his chest. Exhausted from the long walk, she fell into a satisfied sleep. A smile spread across Duman's face. He looked at himself in the rearview mirror and smiled proudly. Everything was back on schedule.

*   *   *   *   *

The Hynes 5 touched down on the roof of the Hilton three hours later. Viktor Bitkowski wore the white short sleeved shirt and khaki pants that had become his uniform. He watched Helene from behind the tinted windscreen and barely glanced at the man beside her, assuming he worked for the hotel. Viktor kept the engines up to speed and began to radio the air controller at the Bogotá International Airport for clearance.

Helene and Duman ducked and ran across the roof to the helicopter. Duman easily carried Helene's and his own heavy suitcases. When Helene opened the door of the craft, he placed them in the compartment behind the seat. With a practiced eye, he gauged the amount of room available in the craft. Still calculating, he helped Helene in. Then he ran around and opened the other back door. Before Viktor understood what was happening, Duman was in the seat behind him and snapping on the lap belt.

Viktor whirled around in his seat and glared at Duman. Helene intervened and put a headset over her blonde hair. She impatiently motioned to Viktor and he turned to the control panel and flipped a switch.

"Viktor, this is Richard Wakefield. Richard, this is Viktor. He's Grandfather's right arm. Isn't that true, Viktor?" Her voice sounded strained. She feared Viktor might demand Richard leave the helicopter until he spoke with her grandfather.

Duman held out his hand, but Viktor ignored the man. "Does your grandfather know he is coming?"

"I don't have to clear everything with Grandfather. Richard is a very good friend and I want him to come and meet Grandfather. It's a surprise."

"Your grandfather does not appreciate surprises," Viktor said. He turned back to Duman who still held out his hand. Viktor grabbed it roughly and squeezed. Helene could see the muscles in Viktor's forearm bulge. She wished she could see under Richard's coat to watch the muscles on his strong arm. Viktor coolly appraised Duman as the man stared back at him.

Helene held her breath. The only other man she had seen stand up to Viktor's stare was her grandfather. Finally, Viktor released his grip and turned back to the control panel. Helene was happy to see him flex his hand before grasping the control stick between his legs. Boldly, she reached over and placed her hand on her lover's thigh.

✳   ✳   ✳   ✳   ✳

The flight to Kadner's compound took slightly over half an hour. Throughout, Viktor sat stiffly in the front seat, concentrating on flying the helicopter. Meanwhile, Helene excitedly detailed various points of interest. Below, the jungle was a single mat of green broken only by the many dirt clogged rivers and the few villages. Duman realized it would be impossible to find his way through the jungle without the detailed maps he carried in the hidden compartment of his luggage.

Duman recognized the small village that would be his destination after he stole the treasure. The otherwise primitive village had a tall radio tower and a short airstrip. The strip was perfect for the small planes used by smugglers and ideal for Duman's plan. With the treasure safely in his possession, Duman would radio a contact in M19. He would be out of Colombia in hours.

Viktor banked right and announced his intentions to land. He settled the craft beside a similar, but smaller, two seater helicopter and shut the engines down immediately. Before the blades had stopped turning, he stepped out on the cement and headed for the elderly man standing in the shade of a narrow awning.

As he walked with Helene toward the main house, Duman realized the old man was arguing with Viktor. The big German's face was a deep red, his eyes fierce with rage at being blamed for bringing the stranger. Helene grabbed Duman's arm and pulled him close. "That's Grandfather," she whispered. "Viktor must be catching hell for bringing you."

Duman smiled down at her. "You don't regret bringing me, do you?"

"You kidding? I love it. That snot Viktor deserves anything he gets. Anyway, Grandfather will like you. I know because I love you!"

As they approached, Kadner dismissed Viktor with a wave of his hand. Viktor straightened and almost saluted, then stopped himself. He stomped across the steaming landing pad to the helicopter, giving Duman a withering stare as he passed.

Helene became the young girl again and ran to the old man. "Grandfather! I've missed you so much. How are you?" She gave him a huge hug and a kiss, which he stiffly accepted. She backed up and presented Duman. "This is Richard, Richard Wakefield. Richard, this is my Grandfather, Ulrich Kadner."

Duman could feel the frail bones as he shook Kadner's hand. "*Englander?*" asked the old Nazi.

"Yes, but we can speak the language of your choice," Duman replied in perfect German.

Kadner raised his eyebrows in surprise and the suspicion deepened in his eyes. "*Nein*. English is acceptable. You are a friend of my little granddaughter and are welcome in my home, Herr Wakefield. Follow me."

The old man turned abruptly and walked through the doorway, allowing a burst of air conditioned air to escape as he entered. Duman picked up the suitcases and motioned Helene to go ahead of him. He looked back at the helicopter. Viktor stood motionless, watching him.

Chapter 20

CUPID

The way Katrina attacked the undergrowth with her machete impressed David. Out of habit, he had split the supplies almost evenly between the two packs, each weighing over seventy five pounds. Katrina had not shirked at carrying the weight nor had she complained about taking her turn to break trail. She moved with the surefooted grace and strength of a jungle cat. Unlike her, David had stumbled twice on the unfamiliar terrain. Once, she had even caught him, supporting his weight while he regained his footing. With every mile they fought through the green maze, his respect for her grew. So did the other feelings.

"You can't be that old." Slightly out of breath, Katrina's voice had a husky, appealing quality.

David's pack bobbed up as he shrugged. "Old enough."

"No, really. How old are you? I want to know when I'll be washed up."

David laughed with her and coughed when a small bug flew down his throat. Not for the first time, he wished they were in a desert instead of a jungle. "I'm fifty four. They pulled me off active duty about three years ago."

"You, too? That must have been a bad year."

"In my case, they called it 'retirement.' I squirmed my way into a couple of operations, but Assi really clamped me to a desk last year."

"But you must have been ready for a rest."

David was thoughtfully silent for a moment before he replied. "A few years after I joined the Mossad, when the initial high wore off, I thought I would be happy to see my retirement. I spent too much of my career in cheap hotel rooms and dirty back alleys. I didn't see much of the glamour or opulent life style we all expect. One time, I spent four weeks in a one-bedroom apartment without going out once. I mean that literally – I never left. I thought I would go absolutely nuts. And the killings, the death. At times, the bodies piled up until I didn't want to continue. I often questioned whether everything was worthwhile. More than once, I was ready to quit."

"So what happened?"

Before answering, David tapped Katrina on the back and moved past her. He pulled a compass from his pocket and checked their course. Like her three previous leads, she had kept them right on target. He drew his machete and began to slash at the palm fronds before him.

After a moment, he stopped and turned to face her. "I'm not sure why I don't want to quit now. I guess boredom took over. I miss the excitement and the responsibility. I miss the days in that apartment. Ridiculous, but true. Maybe I'm trying to recapture my youth. Who knows?" David turned back to the path.

Katrina watched his muscular arms as he hacked at the fronds with the heavy blade. The pair had grown closer over the three hours they had struggled through the dense jungle. Katrina feared they were becoming too close. She could sense the growing feeling and its pace frightened her. Love or even lust could only complicate matters for her. And yet, she did not fight the attraction.

David's machete suddenly broke through to a clearing beneath the canopy of trees. A small wooden shack stood in the middle. David took off his pack and motioned Katrina to the left while he headed to the right. Both stayed under the cover of the brush until they met at the far side of the building. David drew his gun and edged toward the door. Katrina counted five before following him.

David opened the door cautiously at first and then jumped through the entrance, his gun ready. Immediately, he turned back again, gulping the fresh air. Katrina looked in. The overpowering odor of rotted flesh made her back up and slam the door.

David coughed. "Looks like we've found Mardinaud's source of information," he said.

* * * * *

They had the shack cleaned in half an hour. David dragged the body of Mardinaud's operative into the jungle and buried it in a shallow grave while Katrina scraped the dried blood off the floor, straightened what furniture remained, and burned a concoction of herbs which she scrounged from the jungle. The fragrant smoke removed the worst of the smell, but nothing would completely erase the putrid odor of the corpse.

Sitting by lantern light, they discussed their plans and ate their evening meal.

"We should have no trouble reaching the compound in the early afternoon if we leave by midmorning," David said, putting the map aside. "I want to test the equipment once more before we go. I'm not happy with that one panel."

He poured a foil envelope of powder into a small pot of boiling water and stirred the dehydrated mixture. The paste turned a dark green. David consulted the package but could find no direction about the proper color. He tasted the concoction and immediately took a long drink from his canteen. He had never got used to the taste of the energy supplement. Setting the pot aside, he pulled a bag of dehydrated fruit and nuts from his pack.

From the corner of his eye, he saw Katrina pick up the pot. She sniffed at the pot, took a small sample and then devoured its contents. "Arriving by one o'clock at the latest will give us more than enough time to reconnoiter the area and plant the mortars," he said. "Mardinaud's information is usually good, but I want to see the place for myself. We'll strike at dusk."

"What are our odds?"

"Better than even," David said immediately.

"I wish I had your confidence."

Katrina finished her dinner and set the pot aside. Picking at her sweat and dirt-streaked clothing, she looked at David. "Will Duman be there?"

"If not in the compound, he'll be close by," he said.

* * * * *

Henri Mardinaud clapped his hands together and pulled his plate closer so he could mop up the gravy with a thick slice of bread. "You say Duman shot at them?" he asked after shoving the sodden bread into his mouth.

"According to initial reports," Martin Erhart said, "an unknown sniper fired two shots into the street, killing a tourist."

The fat information broker made no attempt to stifle a belch. "Do the authorities have any clues?"

Martin shook his head. "They claim it is drug related."

"The standard refrain for any unsolved crime in Colombia. But we know better. Duman must be furious. What else do you have?"

"The events were difficult to piece together," the assistant explained with some pride. "Most of the eye witnesses disagree on the details. However, one old woman claims to have seen a man tackle a woman just *before* the shot. The witness says the unknown man saved the woman."

"Morritt saved the Greek woman? Saved her and lost Duman? How like the Jew. So touching. Morritt may finally be over his late wife. Morritt and Kontoravdis are joining forces?"

"Unknown. The odds favor an alliance. Duman is already on his way to the compound in the company of Helene Kadner."

"The game progresses," Mardinaud said. He held up a glass of red wine. "To romance! Martin, I feel like Cupid."

Mardinaud drank the wine in a single gulp and put the crystal wine glass on the table beside him. "Now, tell me of this mystery interference."

Martin paused for a moment, feeling sweat break out along his spine. "The reports are sketchy at best. No solid information, just phantom data searches. I would hardly call this interference. Someone is fishing."

"But definitely directed against Kadner?"

"It would seem."

Mardinaud stared hard at Martin as he considered the reports. An unknown group had entered his little drama. Someone he did not control was trying to slip themselves past him.

"Unacceptable!"

"Oui, Monsieur."

"Find them Martin. I must know who dares defy me. They shall be made to suffer for such insolence!"

As Martin left the room, Mardinaud watched his back. It was unthinkable but Mardinaud couldn't help but wonder if he had a leak in his carefully controlled organization.

PART FOUR

KADNER'S COMPOUND

TUMULT AND COMBAT RAGED
AROUND THE WALL
WHOSE TOWER BEAMS RANG
FROM BATTERING

THE ILIAD -BOOK XII

Chapter 21

HOMARD AUX AROMATES

Duman, resplendent in a white dinner jacket and black tie, stood in the entrance to the dining room. A red coated servant showed him to a seat facing the glass doors to the garden. To his left, Kadner sat at the head of the table and Viktor sat at the other end. Both of the Germans wore black tuxedos. Duman acknowledged his host with a nod before sitting.

He slid a white linen napkin out of the wide, golden napkin ring and laid it across his lap. The table was set with fine china of ebony and ivory delicately touched with a gold trim. Golden goblets and cutlery glittered in the muted candlelight. In the center of the table, two snowy orchids floated in a Waterford crystal bowl.

The room was exquisitely decorated with several tasteful paintings and sculptures. Duman recognized several pieces that had disappeared during the late thirties and early forties. A small lamp lit each painting and overhead spotlights accented the better angles of the two statues. The collection would have been expensive – even priceless – if the Nazi had paid for the pieces, Duman thought. Knowing the spoils in this room alone could fuel the people's revolution in a small country, he began to understand and hate the men seated across from him.

Kadner seemed about to speak when Helene appeared like a spirit in the doorway. Her face was radiant. Duman could hardly believe he was looking at the same girl he had picked up at the airport. Applied with understated care, her makeup gave her the look of the mature woman he knew she was not. She had piled her long blonde hair high upon her head. Around her neck was a single diamond suspended on a delicate chain. Both sides of her floor length gown were slit from hem to mid-thigh. The nearly transparent white material was woven with threads of gold that shimmered when she moved and the daring, scooped neck revealed more of her breasts than it covered.

The three men stood as the red coated servant seated Helene. She delivered another smile to Duman, then feigned shyness by staring at her plate while the servants brought in platters of cheese and large green salads. Kadner tasted the offered wine and nodded. The servants poured and Duman sniffed deeply at the dry white burgundy. He inclined his glass to his host before taking a small sip.

Kadner picked delicately at the salad. "Helene tells me that you are a businessman, Herr Wakefield. What business are you in?"

Duman looked into Kadner's eyes. The old German didn't bother to conceal his suspicion. "People," Duman replied.

"People? Explain."

Duman stiffened at the man's tone. The ex soldier was still used to giving orders and, Duman suspected, having them obeyed without question. "I recruit talent. *Headhunter* is the term most often applied to my profession. I find candidates for particular positions."

Kadner nodded, pushing his almost untouched salad aside. The servants immediately served *Homard aux Aromates*. "Sounds as though it might be lucrative."

Duman tasted the steamed lobster before replying. "I survive."

"I have no doubt that you survive, Herr Wakefield. What are your intentions toward my granddaughter?"

Helene dropped her fork onto her plate with a clatter. "Grandfather! I will not have my guest interrogated."

"And I will not have you speak to me that way, young lady."

"Helene," Duman said soothingly, "it's all right." Blue storms swirled deep beneath the surface of his eyes as he turned his stare back to Kadner. He felt Bitkowski tense at the other end of the table. He kept his voice soft and jovial as he answered. "My intentions are honorable, I assure you. I should warn you," he added with a broad smile, "I do intend to steal her away from you."

Duman then turned his attention to a painting on the wall behind his host and inquired about the artist. Though hesitant at first, Kadner quickly warmed to the topic and the rest of the dinner progressed on a lighter tone. Yet, beneath the civilities, Duman could feel both Kadner and Viktor watching him. Neither had accepted his story.

* * * * *

Duman was stretched out on the bed when he heard the soft tap on the door. Helene came in without waiting for permission and silently turned the lock. Walking to the edge of the bed, she let her satin robe slither off her smooth shoulders to reveal a Merry Widow, silk stockings, and high heeled slippers. She bounced onto the bed, shook her long hair loose and kissed Duman full on the lips.

"Are you ready to play?"

Duman pushed her back and gently held her shoulders. He could tell she was still high from the wine. "We must talk first so I can explain things. You have to listen."

Catching the serious edge in his voice, Helene pouted. She moved back on the bed and sat propped against the headboard. "What is it?"

"Sweetheart, I don't want to hurt you. You know I love you."

Helene instantly rocked to her knees and held both his hands. "You aren't going to leave, are you? I don't want you to leave. Grandfather didn't say anything to you, did he? He didn't threaten you, or scare you?"

Duman almost smiled at the thought. He smoothed her hair and gently lowered her onto the pillows. "Of course not. How could I ever leave you? No, what I have to tell you concerns your grandfather. It may not be easy to hear."

"Oh, hell. I don't care about him." She slumped her shoulders and relaxed. "He just gives me money and sends me off to school. I hardly ever see him."

"Then, I'll just tell you straight out. I'm not in Colombia to recruit some bank executive. I am here because of your grandfather and who he really is. I'm here because of treasure."

At the mention of treasure, Helene perked up and her eyes went wide.

"Your grandfather is not who he might seem," Duman went on. "He is a…"

"I know," Helene interrupted casually. "He's really a Nazi who escaped Germany during the war."

Duman tensed, then looked over at the door to make sure she had actually turned the lock. He searched Helene's eyes, wondering if her invitation had been a trap. He only saw the same innocence, now mixed with boredom. "How do you know?" he demanded. "Did he tell you?"

"Don't be silly," Helene said. "Of course, he didn't. I'm not as stupid as you think, you know. Long ago, I recognized the paintings you were admiring tonight. I learned all about them in school. I remember the day we studied the Renoir in the library. When my teacher said it was destroyed, I told her 'no it wasn't.' I was going to say where it was when my teacher corrected herself. She said the painting might have been stolen during World War Two by the Nazis. After that, I started looking around and found more pieces that had disappeared during the war. I just put two and two together."

Duman was impressed by the little blonde perched on his bed. As she said, she wasn't as stupid as she looked. He realized she might still be useful to him.

"I figure Viktor must have served with Grandfather," she said and Duman noticed her shudder when she mentioned Bitkowski. "He almost salutes every time Grandfather tells him to do something. But I don't care about all that. That happened so long ago. After all, nobody really cares what the Nazis did any more, do they? What I want is this treasure! Do you mean the artwork? I thought about taking some, but I didn't know what to do with it even if I could get it out of here."

"No," Duman smiled. "I don't mean any of the works on display in the house. This collection is special."

Briefly, he described Schliemann's treasure. Explaining that the artifacts would require a sizable room, he asked if she had any idea where they might be. "I haven't seen any sign of them since I've been here. Your grandfather must hide them somewhere," he prodded. "Although I can't understand why. He displays everything else openly."

Helene thought for a moment, then proudly nodded her head. "That must be what he goes to look at every night."

Duman raised his eyebrows and she continued. "Every night, Grandfather disappears down into the piano room. He has done it as long as I can remember. I've followed him a few times. He plays a tune on the piano and then he moves the piano out of the way." Her eyes widened again. "Underneath is a staircase. I couldn't see down very well, but there was a big vault door. The treasure must be there."

"I think you're right." Duman kissed her on the mouth. "I don't know what I would do without you."

Helene beamed with pride and Duman smiled back at her. He was equally proud of himself; by having her reveal information Mardinaud had already provided, he solidified her involvement. Not surprisingly, she stood over him on the bed, placing her fists on her hips. "If I help you, you have to take me with you when you leave!"

Duman put a hurt look on his face. "Of course! I want you with me always. We are going to get the treasure and be out of here – together!"

Helene collapsed on top of him and smothered his face with kisses. As she worked her way lower on his body, he put his hands behind his head and smiled with double satisfaction – until he heard a shouted command in Spanish. His brow creased as he wondered who Kadner's visitor was.

※　※　※　※　※

Kadner motioned to the chair and sat down behind his desk. Frederico Santos, one of the top men of Juan David Ochoa's branch of the Medellín Cartel, sat heavily and motioned his bodyguard to leave. Kadner nodded and Bitkowski held the door for the Cartel guard. With a last look at Kadner, the German followed the Colombian into the hall.

"Who is this Wakefield?" Santos asked.

"A friend of my granddaughter's. He is unimportant."

"You are a fool if you think anyone is unimportant," Frederico said. "What do you know of him?"

"He is my concern. He has been checked out."

"My men tell me he arrived unannounced."

Kadner fought to keep his anger under control. He despised the thought of relying on these sweaty, sub human Colombians for his protection, but the thought of them spying on him was almost too much. He would have liked to throw Santos and his entire security force off the compound. However, needs outweigh desires. He forced a smile.

"Naturally, I allowed that appearance," Kadner lied. "Do you honestly think anything my granddaughter does is beyond my scrutiny? She must *think* she is free and can move without my notice."

"A cage, no matter how large, is still a cage?"

"Exactly," Kadner said. "Now, can we get down to our business?"

Frederico opened his briefcase and pulled out a sheaf of computer paper. Kadner watched him flip through the pages and thought of how much he hated the drug smuggling scum. The man's only redeeming feature was his product. The drugs killed off some of the world's population of blacks and spics. If only the Jew lawyers and money traders didn't get rich off the profits, the drug business would be perfect.

Santos handed Kadner the papers. "The top three paragraphs are the most important."

Santos watched the gray haired German scan the print and cursed his soul. To the Colombian, the Nazi was the lowest form of slime. To turn on your own, to profit from their anguish. How could a man sell out those who had been closest to him? No wonder the Germans lost the war. How could such trash defeat anyone? The man was no Colombian. He was not even a true man. He deserved the worst death imaginable.

However, Ochoa needed him so Frederico tolerated him.

Bombings, murder, terror. These were the acts of cowards who run and hide in the night. The terror worked to an extent, but the Americans controlled too much of the country with their money and influence. And dead Colombians meant nothing to Americans. The Cartel needed a different weapon to win the war against the Americans.

Direct control of the Americans was difficult, but domination of South and Central America was within the grasp of the Cartel. All they needed was access to the power of the individual countries. Unfortunately, money was not always the answer to that access.

The Cartel needed to guide those in power, those who could make life difficult for America. But controlling the leaders was not necessary. True power comes from those around the leaders. Control the advisors and the strings of the Master are yours.

And that was where the Nazi entered the strategy.

Most people foolishly expected the escaped Nazis to fade into the background and get lost in their new countries. That would have been impossible for these egotistic fanatics. After being on the verge of ruling Europe, they could not resist the allure of all encompassing power.

But they were not fools. They could not become the Hitler. They obviously could not afford to be seen by the public. Instead, they worked behind the scenes, directing the puppets while they ensured their own protection. Many still commanded great influence from their positions of absolute anonymity.

The Cartel needed to sway these men to see the advantage of helping the Cartel. Kadner identified his old friends and created dossiers on them that the Cartel could use in their gentle persuasion. In return, the Cartel protected Kadner and kept him safe from the Jews. He still had to pay for the men with his money, but he paid for the privilege of the men with his information.

And his soul, Santos thought. God, how he despised dealing with this maggot.

"You need someone who can sway opinion on this vote?" Kadner asked.

"Obviously," Frederico replied impatiently, "the vote takes place too soon for us to do anything about it. We want to prepare for the next time. I need someone close to him. You get me a name and we can work from there."

"I don't know. I'll see what I can come up with."

"Do that," Frederico said. "We wouldn't want you to become a liability."

Kadner stared back at Santos. The German knew all too well what would happen when his supply of names evaporated. Much of his life was spent plotting for that eventuality. He didn't need to be reminded of it by this sweating pile of dung. "Viktor!"

Bitkowski immediately opened the double doors and went in. The Cartel bodyguard shouldered his way through the opening with him.

"Señor Santos is leaving. Please show him the way out."

"I'll await your call, Heir Heiden," Santos said, purposely using his real name. "Please don't take too long. Señor Ochoa is an impatient man."

Chapter 22

OPERATION HARVEST FESTIVAL

Night had descended and the small sliver of moon in the starry sky did nothing to brighten the clearing. The jungle surrounding the wooden shack was silent, a deceptively lifeless calm. Nocturnal animals, insects, and birds continued to hunt, quietly springing and diving upon their unsuspecting prey. Only gentle rustlings and the anguished cries of the hapless victims exposed their positions. Intrigued by the murmur of soft voices, a single weasel risked approaching the shack with its new and strange smells. The small animal quickly lost interest and scrounged the ground, sniffing along the trail David had left while dragging the body of Mardinaud's operative to its burial place.

Inside the shack, a single lantern glowed steadily, casting long, eerie shadows on the walls. David and Katrina sat on the floor with their backs propped against the plain wooden planks. Deceptively thin blankets protected them from the hard, dirty floor. David stared straight at the lantern, almost mesmerized by the still flame. He had just finished telling her the story of his mother's death. Katrina did not know what to say. Instinctively, she reached out, covered his hand with hers, and lightly squeezed. David turned and gazed into her tender, brown eyes. She smiled at him and he returned the pressure of her hand.

"I'm sorry," she said finally. "I had no idea what Kadner, I mean Heiden, had done. I should never have pressed you into telling me."

"It's strange, but I didn't mind telling you." Seeing the honest compassion in her dark eyes, David felt a comfort he had not felt in years – not since Shana, his late wife. The sensation of Katrina's delicate hand in his warmed him. His stomach moved with a tense self consciousness. He kept his hand entwined with hers, fearing the release as much as the closeness.

"What were the camps like? I've heard things, but..."

Katrina let her voice drift into silence and tightened her hand around his. She wanted to know more about David. She understood that his time in Majdanek had begun to shape the man he was. She wanted to know that man.

Though rapidly losing himself in the memory, David was aware of Katrina's touch. In the cooling air, he could feel the warmth of her body. It seemed the most natural thing in the world to disengage his hand and slip his arm around the small of her back. But instead, she settled back against the wall, their shoulders barely touching. He began to talk, again guiding her into his past.

* * * * *

Like many of the camps throughout the German occupied territories in Poland and Austria, Majdanek was both a work camp and an extermination center. The Germans erected the camp next to a large stone quarry. Healthy men worked in the pit on starvation rations until they wasted away and became useless. They then joined those killed for being too old, too young, or too feeble to work. The ovens worked constantly, eliminating the thousands of Jews, Gypsies, and others who arrived on the trains daily.

After Heiden had killed David's mother, Dausel had pulled the boy away from the window and thrown him into one of two lines of prisoners standing by the train. Seeing the limp form of his mother tossed on the cart of bodies was too much for David. He screamed and flung himself toward the German, but a thick arm grabbed him from behind and lifted him in a vise lock while he struggled viciously. Then a soft voice spoke in his ear. Though the Polish words were harsh, the tone was soothing.

"Boy, you will only end up like her. Don't fight them here. Not yet."

David was turned around against his will. He vented his intense rage by kicking and swearing violently. "Damn you, bastard. Let go. I have to fight them. You can sit and let them walk over you, but I won't. I'll have revenge for my mother."

Even through his tears, David could see surprise and respect flicker over the stranger's face. "Strong thoughts for one so young," the man said, nodding in approval. "I did not say, *do not fight,* boy. I told you not to fight them *here.* The moment will come. Until then, we must wait. Concentrate on staying alive. There is no shame in postponing a battle that cannot be won. What is your name?"

David told him in a voice strained with self control.

"Calm down, David. Remember your namesake ruled with a sword tempered by intelligence." The man let David go and straightened his coat for him. "My name is Assi," he said. "How old are you?"

"Ten."

"Wrong. From now on, you are fifteen."

David looked puzzled. "No, I'm ten."

"Shut up and listen, David. We don't have much time. I'm trying to save your life. You are fifteen. You're almost big enough to be that old. Strong, too, from the way you handled yourself against that Goliath."

David studied the strange man whom he would later learn was an ex boxer. Assi was not much taller than David but he was huge across the chest and shoulders and his muscular arms and legs made him appear larger than he actually was. "What do you mean, save my life?" David asked.

"Don't worry about that now. Just remember what I told you." Looking around, Assi noticed a scuffle had slowed the line. Deciding he had some time left, he tried to reassure the young boy. "Who told you we have to fight the Germans?"

"My father." David straightened, his pride showing. "My father went to fight the Germans. I heard him tell my mother that he wouldn't let the Germans take his country. The Germans killed him, but I'll kill Germans for him."

"Your father was right, but we don't have time to discuss that now." The line of prisoners was moving again. Two spectacled Germans sat at a small table, dividing the Jews into three groups as they passed. One group shuffled off to the left. They were mostly women, children, and old men. The healthy men moved off to the right. The prettiest women all lined up in single file behind the table. Assi pointed at the group to the right.

"That's where we want to go," he whispered. "They're going to the work camp. Hard work, but work for the living. The others will be dead in a week, maybe less. Listen to me, David. You must do as I say. When we get up to the table, don't speak. Let me talk for you. Whatever I say, don't do anything. Just do your best to smile and nod. Do it or you won't live long enough to get your revenge. Trust me, David."

David looked into the kind eyes of the bulky man and nodded. He didn't understand, but the mention of revenge made him obey.

At the table, a German soldier asked David his age. Assi spoke quickly before the boy could answer. "Fifteen, sir."

"Why doesn't he answer for himself?"

"He is not all there," Assi said, pointing at David's head. "But he's very strong and does as he's told. He's a good worker and won't cause any trouble."

The soldier looked at David again and then impatiently waved to the right. Assi took hold of David's shoulders and led him toward the lines of men in front of the work camp barracks. As he turned away, David saw two boys from his neighborhood, but he was afraid to wave to them. They were standing in the much larger group to the left.

* * * * *

David slaved beside Assi in the stone quarry for several months. Through the bitter cold of winter and into the heat of summer, they trudged down the steep inclines into the pits. The men worked to break up the large boulders and trudge them to the waiting trains. At the end of the day, they returned their tools and dragged themselves back to the huts.

David plotted his revenge throughout the endless work.

The smoke from the ovens carried greasy ash over the camp as the fires consumed the old and unhealthy, many with children in their arms. Others died more slowly. The guards inflicted unspeakable acts of torture and cruelty on the children in full view of their mothers. Any woman leaving her place to help a child was shot. The few children, all blue eyed and blond, who escaped death were taken away to an unknown destination.

The Germans selected the most beautiful women from the daily arrivals. They were allowed to live as long as they pleased the guards. Any offense – even arriving for role call without a kerchief covering their heads

– brought instant death. A bruise or a cut meant a transfer to the ovens and death. Only perfect women were good enough for the soldiers.

The sadistic treatment was not confined to the death camp. In the labor camp, the SS troops amused themselves by subjecting the men to inhuman treatment. Each guard had his own private pastime. One specialized in dragging men to death over the sharp gravel behind his motorcycle while other guards used the speeding prisoner for target practice. Heiden and Dausel were regular participants, and often instigators, in most of the atrocities. Both were also ardent visitors to the women's compound.

Heiden's left cheek still bore a scar as a result of David's mother's final struggle. To David, it was a jagged reminder of that horrible first day. Every time he saw Heiden and Dausel, he desperately wanted to kill them. His anger built each day as the two swaggered through the compound. He would hear them talk of this woman or that. How the women had *serviced the Third Reich*. That phrase, more than anything, haunted and infuriated David.

Unable to control himself one day, David almost succeeded in getting to Heiden. Assi stepped forward to stop David, but the German mistook Assi's actions for a threat.

"You, stop!"

Assi turned to see Heiden gesturing madly. Guards brought their guns to bear on the prisoner. Assi shoved David behind him with whispered words. "Don't say or do anything."

"Guards, take that man," Heiden ordered.

The guards pulled Assi up the slope and held him in front of their commander. Heiden shoved a thick stick into Assi's stomach and he slumped to the ground. Dausel eagerly joined Heiden and looked questioningly at the Jew on the ground.

"This man has threatened me," Heiden said. "What shall we do?"

"Do you want me to take him to the other camp?"

Heiden looked at the other prisoners staring at the scene and shook his head. "He shall be my living example. He has to suffer. Death is far too easy for him and will teach the others nothing. I want him to work. But he will work with a reminder of his foolishness. He will work in pain and agony and only wish I had killed him. You there, bring me that sledge."

One of the inmates timidly brought the heavy hammer to the German. As the prisoner passed, David heard the mumbled words of a prayer.

Heiden ordered four guards to hold Assi on the ground. He raised the ten-pound hammer over his head and brought it down on Assi's foot. The German waited expectantly, but the ex boxer did not scream out in pain. By the third blow, Assi had silently passed out.

His foot was mangled, but Assi continued to work. He carried large, flat rocks because they looked heavier to the surrounding guards. Thanks to the other inmates, the ex boxer survived until his foot healed enough for him to resume his usual workload. Around that time, both Heiden and Dausel disappeared. Rumors that they had deserted the SS ranks spread throughout the camp. As time went by and the two did not return, David began to accept that he would never be able to have his revenge. He concentrated on forgetting and surviving.

✼ ✼ ✼ ✼ ✼

In late October of 1943, Berlin Command handed down an order to exterminate every man, woman, and child who had participated in the Warsaw uprising. The order included all Jews who had been in the ghetto during or previous to the battle, regardless of their age or innocence. Called *Operation Harvest Festival,* the scheduled date of execution was November second. The execution list included David and Assi, but the camp command formed a three hundred-man work detail. Good fortune and clerical error had David and Assi assigned to the detail and transported to Borki, north of the camp.

Knowing the Russians would soon arrive and fearing reprisals, some of the ranking Germans in the outlying occupied territories sought to hide their crimes. At Borki, the work crew dug up bodies from a shallow, mass grave and burned them. Working with picks and shovels, the men slaved in the half-frozen ground for months. The greasy smoke from the huge fires clung to their clothing and skin. In all, the workers unearthed and burned the remains of over 30,000 bodies.

Throughout the long days of horrifying work, Assi kept David sane by telling him stories of Palestine. Although the older man had never been there, he talked about the Promised Land and the renewed life of the Jews, safe from persecution. By 1944, when the Soviets liberated Majdanek, David felt he knew every inch of the Promised Land.

David and Assi soon discovered that the Russians did not want to take responsibility for many of the starving, sick refugees of the camps. Assi found it a relatively simple task to smuggle both David and himself away from the liberators.

After many hardships, the man and boy arrived at the northern coast of Turkey along with other refugees trying to get to Palestine. Both David and Assi wept openly when they saw the blue Mediterranean.

Their first attempt to cross to Palestine met with disaster. A British vessel forced their small ship to dock at a refugee center on Cyprus. But their hopes didn't die.

Assi learned of an underground movement within the camp. Tied to the Haganah in Palestine, they harassed the British from inside the camps. He joined the group and brought David with him.

Now thirteen, David had learned about smuggling in Majdanek and on the road to the Mediterranean. He honed his skills in the refugee camp and was soon frustrating the British, steadily working his way up in the organization until he became a respected, though young, operative. If the group wanted to be sure of safe delivery, they gave the job to David.

By the time he and Assi arrived in Palestine in 1946, David was enthralled with intelligence work.

＊　＊　＊　＊　＊

"And that was how I got my first taste of intelligence work," David said. "The intrigue and the excitement fascinated me. I loved the game of outsmarting the other man."

"And you went into the Mossad?" she asked.

"No," David said slowly. "I became a farmer."

Chapter 23

NIGHTLY VIGILS

Ulrich Kadner and Viktor Bitkowski toured the perimeter of the compound surrounding the main house. They could hear the night noises of the jungle over the quiet hum of the electrified wire. At a motion from Viktor, Kadner paused and stared past the open space on the other side of the fence. Two animal eyes sparkled from the dense vegetation, regarding the men before suddenly vanishing into the darkness.

Smiling, Kadner and Viktor walked past the guards scanning the jungle with British design night scopes, devices which magnified the available light from the stars and moon for night vision and rendered the insect attracting searchlights obsolete. The pair continued through the grounds, checking the security and discussing their guest. As always, they spoke German.

"I positioned a guard down the hall from Wakefield," Viktor said. "He and Helene have already toured much of the house. If the Englander leaves his room during the night, the guards will stop him. Otherwise, he will not be harassed. I serviced the helicopters myself and assigned a detail around them and the riverboat. Our escape is insured; his escape is impossible."

"Have you added any security downstairs?"

152 / D.A. Graystone

"Naturally." Viktor knew of Kadner's paranoia about the artifacts in the basement vault. "There are two extra men. If that is Wakefield's goal, he will not get within fifty feet of the vault."

"Very good, Viktor." Kadner grasped the muscular man's arm and steered him toward the garden. "What have you learned about him? Ochoa's lackey expressed his concern. The stupid bastard thinks I know nothing of security."

Viktor expressed his opinion of the Cartel chief by spitting on the ground. "I find nothing suspicious in his story. If his passport is a fake, it is excellent. I had trouble checking out his firm because of the time difference, but I don't think he lied about his employment. I will know more tomorrow. I still don't trust him."

"Does it occur to you that he might only be after Helene?" asked Kadner.

"He already has Helene. He is after more. Did you see him admire the paintings? He played the fool, but he knew exactly what each piece was. I'm sure he knows when they all disappeared. Could he be after us?" An unusual hint of fear sharpened Viktor's tone.

Kadner stopped and stared at Viktor's massive outline blocking the light from the house. Even at almost 65, Bitkowski was still in superior condition. He had killed men half his age with his bare hands. Kadner could not ask for a safer, more loyal companion.

"He might be, but I doubt it." Kadner said as the two continued through the garden. "Not an Israeli. Not like this. They would have just moved in and kidnapped us. Still, he might be an advance agent. Who knows? I feel his main interest is Helene. My granddaughter has turned into quite a little slut. However," he added quietly, "if this Wakefield deceives us, you may have to show the girl what can happen to her friends. If she is old enough to fuck them, she is old enough to understand the consequences."

Viktor smiled. He had often considered what being with Helene would be like. While with his whores, he fantasized about her warm, supple body.

As he watched Kadner disappear into the house, Viktor found himself hoping Wakefield would try something. Possibly, his old commander would not be so forgiving of the girl. Flexing his fists, he turned to travel the grounds again, his steps lighter this time.

✳ ✳ ✳ ✳ ✳

With weary steps, Ulrich Kadner clumped down the basement staircase. He nodded to a guard at the other end of the hallway, unlocked the door to a small room, entered, and closed the door behind him. He sat down in front of a console of five televisions and flipped a switch. The screens slowly glowed to life, displaying various scenes around the house.

Kadner twisted a knob and all the screens changed to a view of Wakefield's bedroom. Kadner focused the camera on the bed. Helene and Wakefield lay naked on top of the sheets. White stockings were draped carelessly over the headboard. The mottled red skin of Helene's neck and chest betrayed her recent exertion. Looking at the video recorder below the screens, Kadner considered rewinding the tape and watching the recorded action.

He shook his head as he removed the tape from the machine, wrote on the label, and set the cassette on the shelf. He might watch the tape tomorrow or later in the week. To delay would build excitement and anticipation. On Saturday night, if he could wait that long, he would view the entire scene from Helene's arrival in Wakefield's room to their final climax.

Thumbing the wheel again, he tightened the picture to scan over Helene's body. Regretfully, he looked at his watch and flipped the switch on the console. The picture winked out as he left the room.

He passed the hallway guard without a word and walked into a large, gaudily furnished room, again locking the door behind him. A highly polished grand piano surrounded by eighteen embroidered chairs dominated the center of the room. Kadner wove his way through the chairs, placed his fingers on the keys, and played a discordant series of notes. He heard a hiss as the Steinway rose up slightly. Standing, he shoved hard and slid the piano to one side, revealing a cement staircase below the opening.

Kadner carefully descended the steps until he faced a small keypad resembling a pocket calculator. He quickly punched a series of numbers. With a breath of hydraulics, the door moved out and Kadner backed up the steps, allowing it to swing past him. Lights came on inside the vault. He checked his watch to confirm he was on schedule and stepped through the entrance.

Kadner stood beside a clothing dummy dressed in the uniform of an SS officer. He gently ran his fingers over the material of the sleeve then turned toward the collection laid out in front of him.

A large copper shield hung on the wall. The heavily dented metal reflected rays of light around the room. Flanking the shield were thirteen copper pikes set on wooden shafts. The sharp spears angled out from the wall as though awaiting the banner of some ancient king. More pieces of copper surrounded the shield. On one side lay the silver items. Goblets, vases, and knife blades shone as they had when King Priam ruled the great city of Troy. On the other side of the copper pieces, the most valued artifacts burned in the bright lights.

The objects glowed with a brilliance that only gold possesses. A two-handled cup, goblets, and a globular bottle stood above the thousands of small rings, earrings, bracelets, buttons, dice, and two exquisite diadems. All were worked from the same glistening gold. Between the pieces, jewels sparkled like dazzling points of light.

For decades, Kadner knew, men had prayed for the opportunity to see these lost treasures again. All archaeologists would recognize these artifacts as part of the early lore of their science. However, here they rested, where only one man ever saw them. Only he possessed them. But at what price?

Kadner could feel the rage smother him. Like a lightning fast boxer, the anger jabbed repeatedly at his stomach. Sweat covered his face and drenched his shirt. His legs went weak and he grabbed the clothing dummy to support himself. His heart beat rapidly and his hands shook as his past vividly assaulted him.

The old man's nightly vigil had begun.

Chapter 24

BROTHERLY LOVE

Friedrich Heiden looked out across the deep rock quarry at Majdanek. 1943. The Jewish prisoners had just arrived at the pit and the guards were distributing tools to the line of workers. Horst Dausel whipped an inch thick length of rope across the back of one of the Jews who had staggered out of place. Heiden watched as the giant guard threw the man back into line and a guard on the other side stopped the reeling prisoner with a rifle butt in the lower back. The Jew flailed back through the line into Dausel again. This game would continue until the men tired or the Jew collapsed. Or died.

Heiden decided to let them have their fun. This particular Jew probably had months of usefulness left, but Jews were plentiful. His men needed the release. Rumors were circulating throughout the occupied territories and the labor camp was no exception. Through his contacts, Heiden heard whispers of Hitler's madness and knew the situation was out of control. Germany would inevitably fall to the enemy. Then the retribution would begin.

He held no illusions about how the world would view Hitler's Master Plan. Those responsible for the extermination of the Jews would face extermination themselves. Though not as fanatical about the Plan as many of his colleagues, Heiden naturally agreed with ridding the world of the inferior Jews. However, he had no intention of dying for his belief. He would leave Germany long before that happened.

During the past year, he had used his leave time to arrange an escape and prepare the items necessary for survival outside Germany. Heiden knew he would be hiding for years, perhaps for the rest of his life. It would require a great deal of money and a safe place to live.

Given his low status in a relatively insignificant camp, Heiden should not have enjoyed such open access to the spoils of the war. The higher ranking officials in Berlin and Paris reserved the expensive items, such as art treasures and gold, for themselves. Camp workers like Heiden usually stole only the less significant belongings of the Jews. Unless, they had his daring and intelligence.

The SS knew the value of the labor camps went beyond the obvious. Like the prisoner of war camps, the enemy knew never to bomb the civilians in the camp or the trains that transported them. It became standard practice to use the trains for shipments of plundered goods while the camps themselves became shipping depots. Heiden took advantage of this practice. With the assistance of the giant Dausel, he had brazenly intercepted and rerouted shipments destined for high-ranking members of the Nazi party while supplementing his postwar fund by supplying bogus escape routes to Jews. He shipped the jewels, gold, and artwork through Portugal to Brazil, using the names of several fictitious generals to insure the privacy and speed of the shipments. As no one dared insult one of Hitler's generals, especially in the current climate, Heiden knew the goods would be waiting for him when he arrived.

Now, the time to leave was near.

Heiden watched as Horst Dausel climbed the wooden ladder to join him at the edge of the pit. He had decided to take the sadistic giant with him. Horst had been loyal since Heiden had saved his life three years ago. His strength had been useful protection in the past and would be again during the long escape. Heiden also genuinely liked the man – their tastes in entertainment being similar.

The next day, the two would begin their official leave. Heiden had worked long hours to insure they would vacation together. After a trip to Berlin, they would be gone from Germany forever.

* * * * *

Horst Dausel waited at the top of the narrow stairs as his commander descended to the lower level. The Berlin Ethnological Museum and its collection of rare archaeological artifacts and treasures had been moved to this underground bunker when the bombings began in Berlin. Heiden used the toe of his boot to knock on the thick wooden door. Seconds later, he kicked it again and a muffled voice called out.

"I'm coming. Don't knock the door down."

The heavy door swung backward into the room and a man stepped out to meet Heiden eye to eye. The overhead light shone brightly on the two men's faces. As usual, Heiden felt uncomfortable looking at his twin brother, Anton, with his perfect unscarred face.

"Friedrich? To what do I owe this unexpected visit?"

Heiden glanced up the stairs and then looked back at his brother. "Anton, aren't you going to invite me in?"

Anton stood back and motioned him through the door, looking back up the stairs suspiciously before following his brother into the large room. Friedrich had already pulled out a bottle of Schnapps and two glasses from the desk drawer. He carefully poured the liquor into the glasses, leaving the bottle uncapped. Anton ignored the offered glass and returned to his worktable. He sensed his twin watching him as he picked up a small brush and carefully dusted a piece of crockery.

"Anton, still playing with his toys."

Anton tried to control his anger. "As curator of this Museum, I do not play..."

"Yes, yes. You have told me before. But are these treasures honestly worth that much?" Heiden taunted.

Anton shook his head and continued to clean the small shards before aligning them on the bench. "Friedrich, you are such a fool. Has the military so dulled your sense of reality? Are you incapable of seeing what is before you? Some of these objects have survived thousands of years. Are you incapable of understanding what that means?" He swept his arm around the room. "These artifacts are the evidence of great civilizations. Not like the barbaric tribes that try to de-populate the world now. These people were advanced in the Arts and Sciences."

Anton sighed. His brother would never understand the importance of his work, he thought. Though twins, they shared no common ground in their interests or personality. He pointed out two large displays centered in the room. "Those are my pride and joy," he said. His brother stared at him as though he had spoken a foreign language. "Don't you know what they are, Friedrich? How often have you been coming here? In those cases rest the treasures discovered by the great German, Heinrich Schliemann. They are priceless."

Friedrich held up his hands in mock surrender. "I have not come here for a lecture. I've no time to waste. I came to ask you a question. Are we alone?"

Anton dropped his brush on the table and glanced sharply at his brother. He stared at the SS insignia on the dark uniform for several seconds before slowly nodding his head. "We are alone, yes. Your Fuehrer has little energy left for this department. Instead, he sends my colleagues on fool's errands around the globe. I don't understand. What is this about?"

"Listen to your barbaric brother and I will explain."

Friedrich motioned for his brother to sit. Anton complied and, this time, accepted the small glass of Schnapps. Friedrich sat across from him before continuing. "Anton, the war is lost. Germany will not last much longer. Even as we speak, the enemy approaches. The end is inevitable."

Anton shrugged. "A fate predestined from the time we allowed that fanatic to lead us."

Heiden waved the remark away. "That does not matter, now. The fact remains that we must leave Germany. I have arranged..."

"I have no intention of leaving Germany," Anton interrupted. He stood and walked back to his worktable. "Germany is my home. Once Hitler is defeated and we can return to a normal existence, I will return to my studies in full force."

"You know history," Heiden said. "You know the price the losing side pays. There will be trials. Convictions. Executions."

Anton laughed and turned his back on his twin. "My poor Nazi brother. Time to pay for your sins, is that it? I have no fear, brother. You run and hide yourself away from the world with the rest of your 'elite.' I welcome the arrival of *your* enemy."

Friedrich snapped to his feet and grabbed his brother's shoulder. "We just follow orders," he shouted in his face.

"Of course, you do," Anton said, his voice low and mocking. "If you were even remotely human, you would have refused. Did your orders include torture and rape? You will face trials, but I have no worry. I didn't perform any of the monstrosities I have heard whispered about you. I have been the caretaker of these great treasures and works of art. While you were torturing people, I was unlocking the secrets of these artifacts. Not a single person knows more about this collection. The *civilized* world will hold me in high esteem for keeping this collection intact and for what I alone can tell them after years of study. You are an abomination, brother. Our mother would die if she knew what you've done."

He traced his finger down the scar on Friedrich's cheek. "Is that how you received this – during one of your tortures? Or was it during one of the rapes?"

In his mind, Friedrich could see the face of the Jew bitch that had cut him. She had marred his perfect face for life. In his renewed anger at her and his frustration with his brother, he lashed out at Anton. The blow spun the weaker man backwards and into the worktable. Friedrich watched his brother slump to the floor. Blood leaked onto the cement from a gash on Anton's temple.

"Anton?"

There was no reply. Friedrich clutched his brother close to him and started to cry. Memories of a youth spent in the company of his twin flooded his mind. Anton the meek, Friedrich the protector. He remembered the battles he had fought for Anton and the long nights of talking to help the frightened boy fall asleep. For five minutes, he rocked the limp body in his arms. Finally, Friedrich took a deep breath and eased him back to the floor.

He wiped his eyes and ran out the door, calling loudly for Dausel. The giant man immediately ran down the stairs and into the room. He absorbed the scene in one glance. Friedrich stripped off his uniform and motioned for Dausel to remove Anton's suit.

In twenty minutes, the job was complete. Friedrich Heiden, the SS soldier, lay dead on the floor and the man standing in the rumpled suit had become Ulrich Kadner. Dausel re christened himself as Viktor Bitkowski.

The plan was simple, but effective. The investigators would see a body in an SS uniform, the body of a man with Friedrich Heiden's face and papers. They would assume Anton had killed his brother and fled. The ploy would last long enough to give Ulrich Kadner and Viktor Bitkowski time to escape. However, once they discovered the absence of the blood type tattoo under Anton's left armpit, they would know the corpse was not an SS guard. Then the manhunt for the deserters would begin.

Kadner surveyed the displays set about the underground bunker and wished he could take all of them. He focused on the cases in the center of the room. His brother had said these artifacts had been his favorites – his existence. Kadner knelt next to the body of his brother and took hold of Anton's limp hand. "I will keep these safe for you, my brother. This is my last promise to you. Your treasures will live on, even without you."

He ordered Bitkowski to help him pack Schliemann's treasure into shipping cartons. While looking for a crate, Viktor returned to the main room carrying a bassinet. Without a word, he held it out and pulled back the blanket.

"My nephew," Kadner said. He suddenly remembered the death of Anton's wife in a bombing. "He must have brought him here to keep him safe."

"I'll leave him here on the table," Viktor said.

"No," Kadner said, taking the baby from Viktor.

"We can't take a baby with us, sir," Viktor said, trying to keep respect in his voice. "How can we hope to escape with a baby in our arms?"

"Anton would not leave his son," Ulrich explained. "Anyone who knows him would realize that. We must maintain the fiction of the uniform as long as possible. Even minutes may mean the difference of success or failure. We will take the child."

They put the baby in the waiting truck, along with the treasure. They stopped long enough to pick up supplies for the child and ship the crates to Brazil before travelling on through Austria and into Italy. Hiding with the child was easier than they had imagined. The young boy created the perfect cover. Who would expect two fleeing SS soldiers to escape with an infant in their arms?

After three weeks, a representative from Vatican City approached them. A faction within the Pope's organization, sympathizing with the Nazis and their crusade to rid the world of Jews, had created an underground escape route. Whether Pope Pius XII had knowledge of the secret group, Kadner never discovered nor cared. Regardless, the organization continued to smuggle wanted Nazis to safety long after the war was over.

Kadner, Viktor, and the baby sailed to North Africa aboard the yacht *Djeilan*, a ship belonging to the Countess Marga D'Andurain. In the months to come, the exact route and transportation would also see Eichmann to safety.

The fugitives hid in various countries over the next several months. In the fall of 1943, they arrived in Brazil where they remained in hiding for eight years. During that time, Kadner took the child as his son. Later, fearing the scrutiny of the Israelis, Kadner and Viktor moved on to Colombia.

In the following years, they changed locations several times. Kadner's "son" married and had a baby daughter, Helene. Shortly after the birth, the young man and his wife drowned in a boating accident. The publicity surrounding the deaths attracted too much attention. Again carrying a young child, Kadner and Viktor sought a haven.

Kadner found his protection thanks to the Medellín Cartel.

* * * * *

The old man sat alone in the vault at his jungle compound, gently running his fingers over the coarse material of the black uniform. He had bought it several years ago when he realized that his best years had been spent in the SS. He needed the uniform to remind him of his youth and his great work.

Unfortunately, he could also see his brother similarly clothed, lying on the cold cement floor, blood leaking from his head. Every night, Kadner had kept a vigil, remembering his brother. A part of him had died with Anton. He had refused plastic surgery because he felt it would deny his brother; he could not erase Anton's face from existence.

The old man ran his finger along the scar on his face.

These nightly vigils soothed the rage – almost.

His hatred of the Jew bitch was always present. He wished all Jews dead so he would never be reminded of the slut who caused Anton's death. Someday, he hoped to have revenge for his brother's death.

Then the dreams might leave him, for good.

Chapter 25

CHOICES

"You don't understand." Katrina sat up and knelt in front of David. Behind her, the lantern created a halo around her head. "I really want to hear more. We Greeks are a curious lot. Unlike most other nations, we aren't afraid to think we might learn something from others. We don't always adopt what we discover, but we sure as hell want to hear about it. A nosy nation, I guess."

"But all I've done is talk about myself. I want to hear about you," David said.

"You read my file. You already know about me." She took his hands in hers. "Besides, you can't leave me with *I became a farmer*."

David sighed and continued.

"When Assi and I finally arrived, I couldn't believe we were actually in Palestine. To my eyes, it was even more beautiful than Assi described. Of course, I was one of the lucky ones. I didn't spend much time in the relocation camps. As soon as the boat ran ashore, we scattered to avoid the British troops who by then had orders to shoot any Jews on sight. Assi and I had to sneak past three patrols on the first night. The British were diligent, but nobody was going to send us back. Even in Majdanek, I had never been as frightened as I was on that first night."

✻ ✻ ✻ ✻ ✻

David had heard horror stories of how the British treated illegal Jews and Assi had explained the convoluted politics of Palestine. Within Britain, vocal factions wanted Jews admitted to Palestine while Arabs applied pressure to keep them out. Trapped in a political vise, the British dealt swiftly with the Jews, treating them like invaders. David was young, but he understood the politics. Nevertheless, after failing once, he could not face the frustration of returning to Cyprus. He and Assi traveled inland and eventually discovered a small settlement.

"Wait here," Assi said as they peered through the darkness. He left David and scouted the outer edge of the village. He returned in minutes.

"It's Arab," he told David.

"Are you sure?"

Assi nodded, pulling the boy back over the low ridge. "You can tell from the layout. The Arabs haven't changed in centuries. Take a good look, David. That is why the Jews will settle this land; we embrace change."

Staring back at the village, David thought about Assi's words. He looked forward to and feared seeing his first Arab. From the talk at the camps in Cyprus, these people intended to rid the world of Jews, as the Nazis had. Shuddering, David followed Assi through the night.

The next morning, they came to a refugee center where they merged with the crowds. The shanties and tents reminded David so much of the camps in Cyprus that he almost ran away. Again, only Assi's insistence kept him there. Finally, Assi made contact with Albert Morritt, a man he had corresponded with before the war.

With forged papers, Assi and David joined the man and his wife. The papers listed David as their son and he promptly changed his last name to Morritt. The legal adoption would be years in the future, after the formation of the state of Israel. David regretted abandoning his natural father's name but retained Morritt out of respect and love for his new family.

A farmer from America with Polish ancestry, Morritt had immigrated to Palestine to join a small kibbutz at the edge of the Negev desert. Using methods learned from farming one of the driest sections of the Midwest, he led his small group in the unexplored techniques of desert farming. David worked beside his new parents, watching as the kibbutz used unheard of techniques to claim more and more of the arid ground.

Desperation and necessity spawned brilliance among the inexperienced. Though far from self sufficient, the group was beginning to make inroads when the British deserted Palestine. The new country of Israel proclaimed independence.

The next day, the War of Independence began.

* * * * *

Even more than he did the farmers, David idolized the fighters of the kibbutz. Assi and the boy joined the ranks of the Haganah, the illegal bands of Jewish warriors who had defended the kibbutzim when the British ruled. Now, as part of the official Army of Israel, the Haganah fought the invading armies.

The Jews scored their first decisive victory in centuries. Rather than being pushed into the Mediterranean, the Jews expanded the territory that was Israel.

After the war ended, Assi prepared to leave the kibbutz and David longed to follow his older friend. Though he enjoyed the work at the kibbutz, he was not a farmer. The work in the Haganah had left a deep impression on the young man. David had seen too many walk complacently onto the cattle cars and into the gas chambers. He vowed never to give up without a fight. He could not disgrace the memories of his natural parents by becoming a farmer while there remained so much fighting to be done.

David happily obeyed the conscription laws of the new country and enlisted on his eighteenth birthday. He excelled during his three years in the service and planned on a career in the military. Assi, rumpled and unshaven, appeared the day David signed his re enlistment papers.

* * * * *

The two men hugged each other.

"Assi! I never expected to see you here. I have news for you."

Assi looked concerned as he pushed David away. "David, you re enlisted?"

David grinned. Assi swore.

"I can't return to the kibbutz, Assi. I've done well the last three years. More than anyone else, you should understand."

Assi watched the look in David's eyes as the young man pleaded for acceptance. He could see more in those gray eyes than before. The intelligence and determination still burned steadily, but the military had added a discipline, a defined purpose, that had been absent until now. Assi could see little of the innocent ten year old from the rail yards of Majdanek. Of course, after the past years, his own eyes saw life differently, he thought. He smiled and patted David's shoulder.

"I can understand. I only wish I had returned sooner. I came to make you an offer."

The relief on David's face was mingled with curiosity. "Where have you been? What offer?"

Assi took his arm and led him away from the surrounding buildings. "I've been everywhere, David. I'm working with the Mossad. We are the most important service in the country."

David's natural pride in his own branch of the military bristled, but he held it in check as he listened. For the next hour, Assi spoke of the important contributions the Mossad had made, and would make, for Israel. David, remembering past life in the Haganah, soon caught Assi's excitement and was enthralled with the idea of the Intelligence Service.

"*And Moses sent them to spy out the land of Canaan...* Numbers 13:17," Assi quoted as his final argument. "Even Moses knew the importance of intelligence. We will do great work."

"But what is the offer?"

"Oh, that. I thought you might want to join us. I have the authorization to offer you a position. I should say, I had the authorization – until you signed your re enlistment papers."

David's shoulders slumped. In his mind, he saw himself working beside Assi on a mission vital to the safety of Israel. Assi clapped the younger man on the shoulder. "Come, little brother. We will go and see your commander."

Assi went to David's commanding officer and, with his mysterious new power, had the papers withdrawn. David left the camp the next day and accompanied Assi to the Mossad's new training facilities outside Haifa.

Since many old Haganah members staffed the new Mossad, David saw many familiar faces. As with the military, he excelled in his training and pushed himself to the limit of his mental and physical ability. In three years, David spoke seven languages and began his travels throughout the world.

* * * * *

David shifted positions, sliding down to lie on the blanket. "The desire to fight for my new country was part of the reason I joined the Mossad, but I could have done that in the army. There was more to it. The constant threat of war does something to a person. Knowing your enemies surround your country can make you either bitter or dedicated. On the battlefield, you are fighting a faceless foe, especially with today's technology. However, in the Mossad, I could face the enemy on his own ground. The battle is with the brain, not the rocket launcher.

"Then, there are the children in the kibbutz. You have no idea how satisfying it is to see them grow strong and healthy. They come from such varied cultures. Just overcoming the language problem is difficult, but they do it. They work so hard. I would hate to see them destroyed in sight of their goals. If, through my work with the Mossad, I could sway a battle or prevent a terrorist strike, I'd know I was doing something truly important."

David's love of Israel overwhelmed Katrina. In her mind, the pictures she had seen of the countryside took on a new glow. She could see David's Israel. She closed her eyes and listened to his faraway voice.

"Israel is a study in contrasts. The Negev is my favorite area. The desert teems with life, if you know how to find it. Though I could never become a farmer, my father instilled in me the love and respect of the desolate countryside. The heat is deadly at times, but I learned to survive in the desert. How to hide and how to be found.

"Some of the mountains in the north have snow on them for most of the year. Or there is Mount Carmel, outside Haifa. The view of the bay is incredible. You look down over the Bahai temple set against the blue water of the Mediterranean. The huge golden dome shines like a glittering jewel amid the gardens and green trees. The sight can leave you speechless."

Katrina looked up at David's peaceful face and thought she could see tears reflected in his gray eyes. She found herself tempted to kiss him. She quickly dismissed the notion and turned the wick of the lamp down.

In the darkness, Katrina drifted off to sleep wondering what it would be like to follow David to Israel, to leave Greece forever and spend the rest of her life with this strangely sensitive man.

Chapter 26

THEFT

Kadner's compound was a large square bordered on three sides by jungle with the river edge forming the fourth side. An electrified fence surrounded the perimeter. The jungle was cut back from the fence to create an open space for twenty feet. Men equipped with G3 rifles and British Model 1500 Night Sight scopes occupied the guard towers at each corner of the compound. David, crouching behind a stand of ferns, recognized the layout from his time in the concentration camps.

The estate house, a two story, pillared mansion, sat in the center of the compound facing the river. Behind the house, the wild beauty of the jungle was incorporated into an exquisite tropical garden. A large pool area bordered one side and a helicopter pad on the other.

David was nearly invisible in green and brown camouflage gear, his face covered by the same mottled colors. Katrina, dressed likewise, appeared beside him like a spirit. Her carefully chosen footfalls produced no sound. Breathing silently through her mouth, she knelt beside David, grabbed his arm, and tugged lightly.

They moved deeper into the jungle. Away from the compound, David dropped on the shade dappled ground. Sweat ran down the sides of his face and dripped into his hair. Next to him, Katrina stretched her cramped muscles.

They had arrived at the camp just past noon and had made several circuits of the grounds to confirm Mardinaud's information. Finding no significant deviation, they proceeded with their original plan, setting the mortars and special light show necessary for the assault. They would attack in the half dusk when the guards' own vision and night scopes were the most ineffective.

The household staff had left shortly after dinner, the locals returning to their village down river. According to Mardinaud's information, sixteen men and two dogs remained as a guard detail inside the compound. Eight men patrolled the estate – four in the towers, two around the grounds, and two in the house. The rest would spend the evening in the small building edged near the helicopter pad. The mortars would take care of that half of the security force.

"What do you think?" Katrina asked.

David rose on his elbows. "We have a chance," he said. "These guys aren't trained military. They're just a bunch of thugs. What about the helicopters?"

"We could use one of them, but they also offer a perfect means of escape for someone else. We could lose Kadner. Might be wise to take them out."

David nodded. He had considered the possibility himself. They would attack through the garden behind the house. They would be at the house, and opposite the landing pad, in one minute. Two well thrown grenades would take care of the helicopters before anyone had a chance to take off. "We'll take out the helicopters and leave by the river or the way we came," he said.

Katrina busied herself checking the ammunition of her Uzi and used a spring-loaded device to repack loose rounds into several spare clips. David watched the last vestiges of the sun sink lower into the sky and replayed the plan in his mind. Untrained as they might be, Kadner's men outnumbered them; their timing must be precise.

One mistake and they would be dead.

❊ ❊ ❊ ❊ ❊

Duman watched Kadner and Bitkowski through the bedroom window as he had for most of the day. Kadner had not appeared until late afternoon, but Viktor had spent the morning checking the helicopters, again. Then he had practiced hand-to-hand combat with the Cartel guards. The old German was surprisingly good, but Duman noticed he was at least a full head taller than all his handpicked Latino opponents.

Now, the two men sat on a small bench in the garden, talking with their heads close together. Duman suspected he was the topic of conversation and instinctively stepped back when they looked up at his darkened window. Hearing his bedroom door open, he dropped the heavy curtain and turned to find Helene standing in the spill of light from the hallway. The outline of her body was visible beneath her thin robe.

She closed the door behind her and snapped on the overhead light. "He's still at the end of the hall. I made sure he watched me the whole way here."

"Good." Duman tossed her a towel as she slipped out of the robe. "Put this on. Make sure he's not looking this way when I come out."

"Don't worry. He'll have better things to do than watch for you." She wrapped the short towel around her. "At least, he's one of the cute ones," she said as she waved to him and left the room.

Through the crack in the partially open door, Duman watched her walk toward the guard posted ten feet down the hall. Helene walked past the man, giving him a glimpse of the slight swell of her buttocks beneath the edge of the towel before she turned to face him.

"He doesn't want me," she said.

The guard regarded her silently. She let the towel drop to the floor. "Can you imagine him not wanting this?"

She knelt and unzipped the stunned man's pants. The surprised guard looked left and right before taking her head in his hands and guiding her mouth forward.

He did not hear Duman approaching from behind. Duman pulled a stiletto from a wrist sheath and slid the blade through the nape of the man's neck. The guard straightened as the knife entered his brain. Then, his body fell limply into Duman's arms. When Duman propped him against the wall, a small amount of blood welled from the wound.

Helene stood up and spat on the carpet. "I've never seen a dead body before," she whispered, staring down at the guard. She spat again.

They returned to Helene's room where she changed into a dark blue zippered jumpsuit before they slipped quietly down the back stairway. At the top of the basement steps, Duman gave a signal and Helene began speaking loudly.

"Come on, I want to show you the music room. I play quite well."

She took hold of Duman's hand and pulled him down the steps. A guard posted at the wide, double doors leading to the concert room snapped to attention and held up his hand. "I'm sorry, Señorita Kadner," he said as they approached. "My orders are that nobody goes into this room."

Helene pouted and clenched her fists at her sides. She stomped her foot like a spoiled child and her voice rose to an angry whine. "Look," she said, shaking a finger at the guard, "I live here, too. I want to play for my friend."

"You will have to consult your grandfather, Señorita. I have my orders."

Looking embarrassed, Duman came up behind Helene and gently pulled her back. "Don't worry, Helene," he said. "We can do it later. I'll talk to your grandfather. We don't want to get this man in trouble."

He smiled at the guard and the man relaxed, happy to avoid a scene. Duman placed a friendly hand on the unsuspecting guard's shoulder. The stiletto blade slipped between the man's ribs, stopping his heart in mid-beat. The guard slumped to the ground.

Duman kicked the corpse aside, pulled out a set of lock picks, and worked on the handle set in the double doors. Helene stared at the dead man. Duman had the door open in seconds and dragged the guard's body inside.

Helene walked to the piano and played the notes Kadner had played the night before. She took perverse pleasure in the thought that the same music lessons she despised and her Grandfather insisted on, had facilitated her betrayal of the old man. When she heard the soft hiss, she stepped back and tried to push the piano. Duman brushed her away and easily shoved the piano off the subterranean entrance. He sped down the steps to the vault door, recognizing the digital lock from Mardinaud's description. He snapped a mechanical device beside the keypad in the door and flipped a small switch. Lights flickered on the device until the space age safecracker signaled with a single tone. The door slid open and the light came on inside.

Duman had planned to quickly pack the artifacts but was unprepared for their beauty. A long appreciative sigh escaped his lips as he hefted the large shield in front of him and held it against his chest. He thought about the warrior who had held it last. Setting the shield aside, he ran his hand over the other pieces. For several moments, he was lost in images of ancient times, so lost he hardly noticed when Helene placed the delicate diadem around her head. Then, she toasted herself by banging two golden goblets together.

Duman heard the dull clunk and wheeled to face her. He snatched the two goblets out of her hands. "Be careful," he said. "These aren't toys."

He turned away in disgust and saw three packing crates stacked against the wall. A precaution against an emergency evacuation, he presumed.

Duman started pulling the treasure out of the cases while Helene gently set them into the Styrofoam packing. He ignored the pikes lining the walls – the shafts were too difficult to dismantle. They organized the treasure by metal. The golden items fit easily in one crate and he made a large 'X' on the top with the tip of his stiletto. If, for some reason, he could only have one box, he would take this one, he decided. He slipped his hands through the rope handles and picked up two of the crates himself, leaving the third for Helene.

They wound their way up the stairs and arrived unseen at the back entrance near the helicopter pad. They waited impatiently for more darkness. Duman had not missed the irony of the theft; a Turk was now stealing the treasure from a German. He chuckled to himself. Heinrich Schliemann would be rolling over in his grave. Helene was flexing her hands from the strain of carrying the crate. He hoped she would make it to the helicopter.

Duman glanced at his watch. "It's time," he whispered. "I'm going to set the fuse. You wait here. As soon as the explosive goes off, we'll make a run for the helicopters. The guards shouldn't see us in all the confusion. You ready?"

Helene smiled and he kissed her gently on the cheek. As he turned to run upstairs, he heard the whistle of the first incoming mortar.

Chapter 27

CONVERGING PLANS

The first mortar hit directly on target. The guard tower closest to the helicopters exploded, hurling lumber across the cement pad. David cupped his hand over the luminous display of his watch and counted off the seconds. He thumbed a second switch on the detonation panel to send a radio signal to a second mortar. A short whistle preceded the resounding thump as the mortar landed, making a two foot crater at the base of the tower to his left. Two wooden supports leaned dangerously. The guard slid off the slanted platform and tumbled to the ground. The back section of the fence was now unprotected.

As soon as she heard the first explosion, Katrina flicked one bank of switches and three more mortars whistled through the air. She could not see the impact points, but the sudden glow on the other side of the house confirmed they'd found their target. The long structure housing the off duty guards was in flames. A separate explosion blew apart the arms storage.

She flipped the remaining switches and waited. Nothing happened. She thumbed them back and forth and swore under her breath. As a last resort, she pressed a button and bright magnesium flares exploded along the south and north sides of the compound. A guard screamed as the magnified light seared his retina. She knew the man's night vision would not return for several minutes.

Powerful searchlights suddenly illuminated the compound as David crept beside her.

"The two towers by the river?" he asked.

"The mortars didn't fire."

"Don't worry about it."

"But..."

"Slight revision is all," David said. "We can take out the guards if need be."

They could hear the hum of the electrified fence over the sound of the blasting siren. David pressed a green button on his panel, producing an explosion along the south side of the house. Sparks from the exploded transformer flew high into the air and showered the grass next to the house. The hum of the fence died.

Katrina picked up a large set of wire cutters and began to rise, but David pulled her back down and pointed toward the garden. Two armed men knelt among the flowers and rapidly scanned the area around the garden. David sighted their silhouettes through his riflescope, his finger resting on the trigger. He watched the taller man point toward the helicopter pad. One of the engines revved. The two men opened fire on the helicopter and sprinted for the landing pad.

David froze, his finger still on the trigger.

* * * * *

Duman watched the flaming splinters scatter over the helicopter pad as the guard tower exploded. A guard lay near the fence, his inert body burning with a low, steady flame. Duman could smell smoke through the open door and heard several other explosions.

He made sure Helene was ready before hefting the two heavy crates. As they ran for the largest chopper, another explosion blew out the guard's quarters.

Helene dropped her crate and opened the door of the Hynes 5. While Helene primed the engine as Duman had taught her, Duman muscled the cartons into the back. He slipped into the pilot's seat and pressed the starter. The blades rotated slowly.

Duman glanced back at the garden and saw Kadner and Viktor

running toward the helicopter. At this range, their small handguns were harmless. However, the rifle in the guard tower was not. Duman knew he could wait no longer. He gave the machine maximum power, lifted straight up, and banked right over the destroyed tower.

A bullet burst through the back window and buried itself in the metal above Helene's head. The chopper lurched and lost altitude as several more rounds hit. Then they were out of the range. Duman breathed deeply and cursed as he wrestled with the controls.

Though he had not seen either of them, he knew the Jew and the Greek were responsible for the attack on the compound. They'd destroyed his carefully laid plan. Vowing to deal with the two interfering bastards, Duman pushed the stick forward and urged the unresponsive machine on. Because of their interference, he had not had time to disable the other helicopter. Worse, his own craft had sustained damage. He knew it was only a matter of time before Viktor gave chase. Beside him, Helene stared at the bullet hole inches from her head and shook violently.

✻ ✻ ✻ ✻ ✻

Viktor sped through the garden and emptied his gun at the fleeing helicopter. When it disappeared over the trees, he ran to the other machine.

"They're gone," he said, when Kadner came up beside him. Viktor opened the door of the Hynes 2. "It was Helene and Wakefield."

Kadner nodded, looking up at the dark sky. Betrayal had struck again, he thought. Betrayal surrounded him and sought to destroy him. He had dedicated his life to raising Helene. Now, she treated him no better than the rest of the world had. She was no better than the Jews. And all Jew whores had to die.

"Sir?" Viktor looked down from the cockpit.

The huge man reminded Kadner of a hopeful puppy. He remembered the young girl he had found with Viktor several months ago. More precisely, he remembered what had been left of her. Even Kadner had shied from the sight of that mutilated body. Did Helene deserve that, he wondered? "Go after them," he said absently.

"And?"

Kadner saw the expression on his companion's face. "Do what you want with Wakefield, but bring Helene back to me."

Viktor hid his disappointment. "You'll be all right?"

Kadner surveyed the compound. A single guard had survived the direct hit on the barracks. Only two towers remained standing. Still, there had not been an explosion in several minutes.

"Yes, this destruction was obviously a diversion. Go ahead. Bring back what belongs to me."

Viktor saluted smartly before slamming the door and starting the engine.

Kadner stood back and watched the blades turn ever faster.

* * * * *

Katrina ran to the fence as soon as the two men in the garden had started toward the helicopters. David waited. He immediately recognized the larger man when the German straightened to full height. Horst Dausel, alias Viktor Bitkowski. He knew the other man must be Heiden.

A part of David, long hidden, came awake. Only the desire to see Heiden's face stayed his finger on the trigger. Finally, his legs responded and he followed Katrina.

They quickly cut through the fence. "What about the helicopter?" Katrina hissed.

David looked at her face. The camouflage paint was dark and streaked with sweat, but her eyes still shone brightly through the mask. He knew what she was thinking. Somehow, Duman had infiltrated the compound. Under the cover of their attack, the Turk had made his escape. "We may be too late for the treasure," he said.

They watched as Viktor Bitkowski climbed into the remaining helicopter and lifted off, following the route of the first chopper. The other German stood and watched as Viktor disappeared over the tops of the trees. Suddenly, the old man slapped his thigh with a flat hand and strode toward the house.

David knew that gesture, remembered that walk. He had seen those actions countless times across a rock quarry.

He had found Friedrich Heiden, rapist and murderer of his mother.

"What's going on?" Katrina asked.

Unable to speak, David concentrated on pulling the wire out of the way. They squeezed through the fence and slipped between the plants and low shrubs, reaching the back of the house in seconds. David slid open the French doors leading to the dining area, stopping when he heard the sound of hollow metal scraping on cement.

"Duck," David warned.

They threw themselves to the ground behind a small planter as a guard came running around the house from the pool area. He sprinted past them and disappeared around the corner nearest the helicopter pad. They heard his footsteps slap across the cement and stop. A door opened and slammed shut. Now, at least one guard was inside the house.

When they were sure no one else was in the area, they edged around the planter. David opened the door another two feet and moved the curtains aside.

He and Katrina entered and listened to the rhythm of the house.

Chapter 28

EMPTY

Ulrich Kadner ran straight through the house and bounded down the stairs to the piano room, tripping over the guard's body by the door. The shiny black piano was still swung aside. The exposed stairway confused and frightened him. He could see the light streaming through the open door at the bottom. His rage grew. He kicked at the corpse until his heart raced from the exertion.

He yelled for Juan, the head of the security detail. Unaware that the man lay under the charred rubble of the guard barracks, the old German screamed Juan's name until his voice cracked.

Finally, another guard appeared at the top of the stairs. Pietro, the youngest and most inexperienced of the men on loan from the Cartel, was in mild shock after seeing so many of his friends killed. He'd worked with smugglers all his life and had seen much killing, but never so many of his own. Staring down at the body of his comrade, he could barely navigate the stairs to stand in front of the old German. Kadner stalked up to him until their noses almost touched.

"Where the hell is Juan?" Kadner asked in German. When he saw the guard's puzzled look, he repeated himself in Spanish.

"Dead, I think, sir," Pietro stammered. "Juan was in the barracks."

Kadner stared at the young man, then nodded slowly. " What is our strength?"

"There are five of us left, sir. The mortars destroyed two towers, the barracks, and the kennels. The power for the fence is out, but Paulo is repairing it now. One man is in each remaining tower. One man patrols the fence. That only leaves me."

"Only five men left?" Kadner said. "I had no idea." He regretted having sent Viktor off so quickly. If there were more attackers outside the fence, more killers waiting for him... "Stand guard at the top of those stairs," he ordered. "No one is to come down to this level. Kill anyone you see. Is that clear?"

The young man nodded and ran up the stairs, relieved to be away from the corpse – and the German.

Kadner descended to the vault room with sure, determined steps. He knew what to expect – and knew he would have his revenge.

The Jews, he thought to himself. Always, the Jews.

The treasure was gone.

Kadner stared at the pikes lining the wall. The spears looked naked without the rest of the treasure. He reached out and caressed the sharp points. "I should have hung banners on these," Kadner said aloud. His voice echoed in the empty room.

A small golden ring sparkled on the floor. The old man picked it up and clasped it in his palm.

"What would Anton have said?" he asked. "His own granddaughter was a betraying Jew. What shame. What disgrace on the family. A blight which must be removed."

The old man turned to the clothing dummy. In his mind, he stood in front of a mirror. He could see his own young face above the uniform.

"I will avenge this crime, my brother!" he screamed, his voice already hoarse. "I have failed you. You entrusted the artifacts to me and I allowed them to be stolen. I will have the treasure back and the thieving Jew whore will die."

The treasure was gone.

He had allowed the Jews – the *Jews* of all people – to steal it. The old man knew the Jews were responsible for the destruction of his compound. It could be no others. Somehow, they had discovered him. With that realization, Kadner knew what he must do.

The old Nazi removed the uniform from the figure and tore off his own suit. He slid his legs into the uniform pants and buttoned the fly. His arthritic hands pained while he buttoned the coat, but he barely noticed. His determination to rid the world of Jews helped erase the pain.

The jacket hung on his frame like an ill fitting rag. Loose skin from his jowls covered the neckline, almost hiding the gleaming double SS insignia. Suspenders held the pants at his waist. Kadner grabbed a handful of material and pulled the coat around his stooped torso.

He removed the small automatic from the pocket of the coat. The .22 caliber rounds were small, but deadly at close range. Brandishing the gun, he goose stepped across the room.

When he saw himself in the actual mirror, his delusion became complete. This was no old, defeated man in the reflection. Instead, a tight uniform stretched over the strong, young body of the proud, superior soldier who guided Hitler's extermination of the Jews. Coming to attention, he saluted himself.

After too many years of hiding, Friedrich Heiden was reborn.

*   *   *   *   *

Katrina followed Mardinaud's blueprint of the house to the servant's kitchen. She and David had separated, agreeing to meet at the staircase leading down to the music room. She paused and listened. Certain noise belonged to the natural environment of every home – a dripping tap, the whisper of air conditioning, the crack of a settling foundation. But other sounds belonged to the enemy – a click of a shoe, controlled breathing, the cocking of a gun. These sounds would betray a waiting attack. The difficulty, as every frightened child knows, lay in distinguishing between the two types of noises.

Katrina edged around a corner and looked out onto the empty helicopter pad. Small pieces of the destroyed tower charred the pavement. The ignored body of the dead guard smoldered against the fence. As she looked up in the direction the helicopter had taken, she wondered if Duman had the treasure. Or had he feared for his life and escaped without the artifacts. Possibly, they had disrupted his plans. She knew the answer lay down the stairway to her left.

As she crept down the hall toward the stairs, she heard a sound coming from a small alcove opposite. The wrong kind of sound. She froze and listened closely to the quiet nervous tap. Someone was drumming their fingers on a gun.

Then came a loud crash. The living room – David.

The tapping stopped and Katrina heard a quick intake of breath. Whoever was in the alcove also knew David was in the living room. But David wouldn't know about the guard. She'd have to reach whoever was in the alcove before David appeared in the hallway.

Catlike, she hurried down the hallway. When she was three feet from the alcove, David stepped through the living room doorway. The guard sprang out in front of him, his gun at the ready. David let his hands go slack at his sides.

Seeing David surrender, Pietro ignored his orders and did not fire. He wanted this man to pay for his fallen friends. He raised the barrel of the gun to use it as a club.

Katrina stepped forward and brought her own gun down on the back of Pietro's neck while David grabbed the barrel of the Colombian's gun with his left hand and punched with his right. The blow caught the guard's exposed throat and crushed his windpipe.

"I owe you," David whispered to Katrina as he pulled the young Colombian's body back into the alcove.

She motioned down the stairs. David nodded and the two crept down the cement steps. When they reached the dead guard, David pointed to the small chest wound. Katrina recognized it as the work of a stiletto. Duman's weapon of choice for quiet kills.

She could tell by David's grim face that he also recognized the terrorist's work. The piano and the stairway were directly ahead.

* * * * *

Katrina and David burst into the vault room together, their Uzis drawn. David's gun did not waver as the man in the black uniform slowly looked up at them. With immense effort, David eased the pressure off the trigger.

Heiden clasped his hands behind his back and stood rigidly, but at military ease. He would not honor the pair by standing at attention.

David looked closely at the man he knew to be his mother's murderer. The jagged scar seemed even more pronounced in the wrinkled flesh. But where there was once strength and death, there was now insanity in the Nazi's eyes. As he stared at the German, David felt an unexpected wave of pity pass over him.

In the ill fitting uniform, Heiden looked like a child in his father's clothes, a small boy trying to create an illusion of future greatness. Or, David thought, an old man trying to recreate an illusion of *past* greatness. He suddenly lost all desire to kill this man. Assi Levy would not kill this man. The years of boiling anger and desire for revenge seemed wasted on such a worthless figure.

Suddenly, Heiden began to screech at them. "Bastards. Jew bastards. You have stolen the treasure."

Katrina had seen the hatred and anger drain from David's eyes and laid her hand on his arm. "Friedrich Heiden?" she whispered.

The German held his chin high and answered in a clear, strong voice. "Yes, I am Friedrich Heiden."

"You admit you are Friedrich Heiden, formerly in charge of security at Majdanek?" Katrina said.

"And why should I not? I proudly wear the uniform of *mein Fuehrer.*" Heiden threw his hand in the air, arm straight in salute. "I serve well. My contribution to the war effort is without equal. I will not deny myself just because the world does not understand our higher purpose. I am proud that I work to rid the world of Jews, the scum of creation. My only criminal act is not having killed more. I serve Hitler and I serve humanity for the greater good. We were unsuccessful before but the purifications must continue."

"Humanity?" David said, unable to help himself. "You are a murderer. Pure evil!"

"What do you know of anything?"

"I was there," David whispered. "I was at Majdanek! My mother gave you that." David pointed at the scar on the old man's left cheek.

Heiden slowly ran the tip of his finger down the side of his face. He flushed as the rage within him built and the scar stood out in white relief. With extreme effort, he regained control. The spawn of that Jew bitch – fate smiled. He kept his left hand behind his back, waiting for his opportunity.

"You know nothing of my mission," he sneered. "How could a Jew understand the thinking of a great mind like Hitler's? It's no wonder we rid the world of your inferior stock. We will build, we will create, but first we must cleanse. Hitler leads the world into the greatness that it can become. Who are you thieves to sit in judgment?"

David heard the rhetoric spouted in the present tense and realized the old man had retreated into the past. A pitiful lunatic playacting at being a soldier again. God forgive me my thoughts of revenge, David thought. Disgusted with his anger, he lowered his Uzi.

Heiden lunged suddenly, swinging the automatic toward David's head. David saw the flash of metal and swung at Heiden with his free arm. The blow hit the Nazi below his right eye, sending the frail man backwards. The gun clattered to the floor. Heiden twisted and tripped over the cuffs of his pants. Unable to stop his awkward dance, the old man staggered into one of the pikes. The point pierced his chest, driven deep by the German's own weight.

David watched in disbelief as Heiden's body fell to the cement floor. Katrina stooped to check for a pulse but she knew instantly that Heiden was gone. A flash on the floor caught her eye and she picked up the ring that had fallen from Heiden's hand. She slipped it into her pocket as she stood.

David stared down at the old Nazi. He wished he could summon the earlier rage and enjoy the satisfaction of seeing Heiden dead. Instead, he felt a burning guilt. He remembered the words from the Nuremberg trials. "The heinous crimes scream for punishment, but we must have justice. Justice under the law. Without law, we become our enemy." With a final look at Heiden's corpse, he walked out of the room.

Chapter 29

THE BATTLE

Helene huddled in the copilot's seat. This had begun as a game, she thought. Now she realized the seriousness of her actions. She had seen Viktor running through the garden firing his gun – with her grandfather close behind. Her grandfather had shot at her! She looked into the darkened back seats. Could those crates mean more to her grandfather than her own life?

She knew the objects had been missing for over forty years, but they hardly seemed that important. The bits of metal were not as beautiful as the King Tut treasures. However, if they were worth that much to her grandfather, they might be worth as much to others. That meant mounds of money. Brightening, she turned to Richard.

"Are we going to Bogotá?"

He nodded but didn't look over at her. He held the control stick with both hands. For the first time, Helene noticed the sweat standing out on his forehead and the difficulty he was having. She looked down at the blackness of the jungle below and then ahead at the distant lights of the city.

"Won't they know where to find us if we go there?"

"They don't have to."

Helene looked back at him and then through the side window. Another helicopter came into view.

Viktor.

If her grandfather would allow Viktor to shoot at her, what else would he let the huge German do? She had heard whispers of Viktor's sadism. One night, she had even heard the screams of one of his whores.

"Lose him!" she yelled at Richard. "I thought this was the faster helicopter. You promised me that we would get away. You said 'no problem.' You said they wouldn't catch us. You promised!"

Richard released one hand from the stick and, for a moment, Helene thought he was going to strike her. Then the chopper lurched and he had to grasp the control stick again.

"We were hit," he said. "We lost the hydraulics. I can't outrun him. I can't even keep us in the air. I have to set down. Then I am going to get rid of the bastard, for good."

Helene looked over at the helicopter beside them and chewed nervously on a strand of her hair.

✳ ✳ ✳ ✳ ✳

Duman spotted a field outside Bogotá. Unfortunately, it was big enough for both helicopters. But he had no choice. He descended.

The landing was hard, almost jarring his hands from the controls. Helene was thrown sideways and her head struck the doorframe. She slumped to the side and Duman could see the large bump already forming below her left eye. Ignoring the girl, he shut down the engine immediately and grabbed the MAC 10 beside him. As he opened the door of the chopper, a brilliant spotlight blinded him.

Viktor landed his craft twenty feet from the Hynes 5. Duman let loose a short burst of automatic fire and the spotlight exploded.

The German dove to the ground as the light went out and crawled to the right. He glimpsed a fleeting silhouette but didn't fire. He couldn't risk killing Helene.

Duman worked feverishly on the MAC 10. The gun had jammed. He tossed the useless metal on the ground and reached into the helicopter for his revolver. Suddenly, a powerful arm reached around Duman and dragged him backwards. An instant later, he was lying on the ground, Bitkowski towering above him and pointing a .45 caliber at his groin.

"Where is the satisfaction if you just shoot me?" Duman taunted in German. "Wouldn't you rather kill me with your bare hands? Aren't you the Master Race? I saw you with those putrid Cartel boys. Are you afraid of a real man? Come on, you German pussy. Be a man for once."

Viktor tossed the gun aside, flexed his massive hands and swung his arms to loosen his strong shoulder muscles. Without speaking a word, he backed off three steps and motioned Duman forward.

Viktor dwarfed the terrorist. Duman knew that at six foot seven, the German had a serious advantage in reach and weight. But the German was at least sixty years old. Duman had KGB training in unarmed combat but he never really practiced. Bombs and guns were Duman's solution. Moving with feigned awkwardness and pain, Duman took one step and launched himself into the air. Both feet connected with Viktor's face.

Viktor landed on the ground in a sitting position, blood gushed from his broken nose. Duman recovered from the kick and turned to the helicopter, trying for the revolver.

Viktor jumped to his feet and grabbed Duman's collar, yanking him around. The terrorist thrust his knee into the German's groin. Viktor grunted and doubled over. Duman dug his fingers into Viktor's thick neck, trying to tear the carotid. But Bitkowski flexed muscles were rock hard. He pried Duman's hands apart and tossed him into the side of the helicopter. Duman hit hard, his head snapping into the metal fuselage.

Dazed, Duman tried to prop himself up as the giant stepped toward him. From the small of his back, Viktor drew a knife with a long, thick, double-edged blade. Steadily, he approached Duman – the knife ready to slash at the terrorist. Duman fought to make his body respond. Then Duman saw an arm and the barrel of a gun poke through the door of the helicopter. Helene leaned out and pulled the trigger.

Viktor's huge chest exploded into a mushy pulp. He took another step and the gun exploded twice more. The giant fell.

Duman stared at the smoking revolver, then raised his gaze to meet Helene's. Her eyes were bright with confidence and, for a moment, he almost respected her.

"Well?" she asked. "Does the other helicopter work any better than this one?"

* * * * *

"We're here, Sweetheart."

Duman turned off the Jeep's ignition and looked at the tousled blonde in the seat beside him. Asleep, Helene looked small and helpless – an innocent child except for the huge bruise under her left eye. He had trouble reconciling this girl with the woman holding the revolver. He wondered who had taught her to use a handgun. Whoever it was, he silently blessed them. Duman nudged her, then got out of the Jeep and walked around to her side.

Helene stretched and yawned, rubbing the sleep from her eyes with her fists before she remembered the bruise. She cursed and then asked, "What time is it?"

"After midnight," he said, taking her hand.

"Where are we?"

Duman ignored the question. Helene looked disoriented as he pulled her across the sodden grass toward a small shack. A crack of light barely showed beneath the wooden door. "Richard, what are we doing here?" she asked.

"Getting the hell out of this country," he said. "We still have the Cartel to worry about. They won't be happy that we broke up their little spot in the jungle. Those boys have some major egos and we just gave them quite a kick to their egos tonight. You have to be prepared for them because they will make Viktor seem like a really nice guy."

Duman was happy to see the fear creep into Helene's eyes. He was sure the Cartel would be looking and the last thing he needed was those greasy thugs sneaking up on him.

Duman knocked once and opened the door.

A man wearing a leather bomber jacket was sitting at a table. He looked at his watch and snarled as they entered. "About time you got here. Thought you weren't going to make it before dawn. Or before I got so pissed I couldn't fly." He set a half-empty bottle of Scotch on the table beside a blue pilot's cap and stood up to shake Duman's hand.

"Helene, this is Captain Michael Smithers. Captain, this is Helene."

Helene stepped out from behind Duman and the man whistled softly. He all but ignored the black eye, instead concentrating on the front of the zippered jumpsuit as he took her hand. Then he remembered Duman was standing behind her and forced his eyes to meet hers. "A lovely flower you have brought with you today. Pleased to meet you, Helene."

"Likewise, I'm sure." Helene swelled her chest until the pilot's eyes dropped again.

Smithers took a last pull from the bottle and picked up his cap. "Shall we go?"

Duman told him about the three crates in the Jeep and led Smithers outside. In minutes, they had the crates loaded in a waiting DC 3. Smithers took his place at the controls and revved the plane's engines. Helene sat next to him in the copilot's position and Duman sat in the navigator's chair. Smithers taxied to one end of the dark field before pressing a small button. The remote unit emitted a tight radio signal to a gas powered generator inside the shack. Lights flared along the runway.

The overhead speakers crackled as Smithers picked up a microphone and threw a switch on the control panel. "Ladies and Gentlemen, this is Captain Smithers speaking. The tower has given us a green light and we are beginning our takeoff. Please fasten your seat belts and extinguish all smoking materials. The crew and I hope you enjoy your flight and thank you for flying Outlaw Airlines." Beside him, Helene giggled, then gasped as the wheels barely cleared the trees at the end of the runway.

"Don't worry, little lady," Smithers reassured her. "I haven't hit them yet."

Duman came up behind her and knelt between the seats. "Relax," he said, placing his hand on her arm. "We're with one of the best pilots in South America."

"What do you mean *one* of the best?" Smithers said. He grinned at Helene. "Besides, look at the copilot I have."

Helene snatched his blue pilot's cap and examined the insignia before placing it on her head. "What does RCAF mean?" she asked.

Smithers glanced at the cap. "Royal Canadian Air Force."

"You were in the Air Force?"

Smithers nodded. "A Captain, no less."

"What the hell are you doing in Colombia?"

"Nosy little thing, isn't she?" Smithers said to Duman.

"I should have warned you." Seeing Helene's hurt look, Duman smiled. "Don't worry, Sweetheart. He loves to tell the story. Go ahead, Mike."

"If you insist," Smithers sighed. "You have to understand that I spent most of my life serving my country. I learned to fly during World War II – the Big One. The military was my life. Worked my damn tail off, no pun intended. Put in extra hours, flew extra missions. Hell, I flew everything the damn bastards gave me. Then, they came to me one day."

In the eerie light of the cockpit, the pilot's eyes glittered dangerously. "This big brass tells me I'm old. Too old for the new high tech shit. Going to replace me with a bunch of kids that still need their arses wiped for them. I had more experience than any of them ever would. Anyway, the deal boiled down to early retirement or stay a Captain, forever tied to a desk. Closest I'd get to a plane would be flying to Disneyland on my holidays. I told 'em to take a flying one."

Smithers lovingly patted the wall of the cockpit. "So, I took all the cash I had and bought Brenda. Named her after the whore that stole my cherry. Uh, sorry, Miss," he said with a sheepish grin. "Anyway, there's only one place to make big money and have the most fun flying. I came down here ten years ago and I've been here since. I've flown loads of Colombia's finest into Florida from the Keys to Miami. I've run guns into Nicaragua. Hell, if it grows in South America and there is somebody willing to buy it under the table, it has been in this plane. If there's money in it and it takes a plane, I'm your man."

Helene tried to hide a yawn with her hand.

"Why don't you crawl in one of the bunks in back?" Smithers suggested. "Pretty young girl like you needs her sleep."

Helene headed toward the back of the plane and Duman slipped into her vacated seat. He pulled out a chart of Jamaica, but watched Smithers out of the corner of his eye. The mention of cocaine reminded him of the pilot's ties to the Cartel and made him wonder who would hear of this flight.

* * * * *

"Disgusting. Absolutely disgusting. I am shocked." Henri Mardinaud pushed his half-finished meal aside and flopped back on the chesterfield. "How could David Morritt allow this to happen? I was so happy to see him emerge from retirement. He has disappointed me."

"You knew the game would end," Martin Erhart said. "Now, we move on."

"The game ends when I declare a winner," Henri said. "I have not seen a winner. You are certain Duman is on his way to Jamaica?"

"They should be on the island, shortly," Martin assured him.

Mardinaud shook his head. "I don't want it to end this way," he sighed. "I pictured a much stronger ending. How could Morritt have allowed Duman and the treasure to get away?"

"I doubt either held much fascination for him compared to Heiden. I don't see what can be done about it. We must accept certain disappointments." Martin was completely satisfied; he knew that the play was not over for Duman.

Henri threw himself forward on the couch. "Nothing to be done?" he exclaimed. "There is always something to be done. Sit your little defeatist derrière down in front of that computer screen and I'll show you what can be done."

Martin did as he was told, calling on the immense database in anticipation of his employer's request. "What am I looking for?" he asked.

Mardinaud put his plump fingertips together and answered slowly. "A Jew. I need a Jew in Bogotá. Someone who knows either David Morritt or Assi Levy. Someone they would trust. We will send our Israeli a message. If Morritt cannot find Duman on his own, we will supply him with a map."

Martin worked on the computer for exactly 63 seconds, then turned to Mardinaud. "Max Bokman. He and Assi Levy have a long history. Assi would trust him with his life."

"And, therefore, so will Morritt. Contact Bokman and have him pass on a message to the Jew. Give him all the information he needs to find Duman."

Martin made several notes on his pad. "A dangerous game," he said. "Duman will not like this."

"I told you before, don't let Duman concern you. I can handle him."

Martin was surprised at Mardinaud's tone. For one of the first times, he suspected his boss was unsure of himself. He knew Mardinaud was thinking of the unknown player in the game. The fat information broker had worked for hours to discover the mysterious force intruding on his little game. But he had discovered nothing because there was nothing to discover – at least where Mardinaud was looking. He sought a connection with Heiden while the link was elsewhere. And the frustration was beginning to show. He would never admit the frustration he was feeling at not knowing but the unknown was the only thing Mardinaud truly feared. And how fearful should Martin be if Mardinaud discovered the truth? Martin tried to shake off his own fear and focused on Mardinaud again.

"Tell me what is wrong with this plan?"

"I beg your pardon, Monsieur?"

"What is wrong with this plan?" Mardinaud repeated. "Why is it destined to fail?"

Martin shrugged and the fat man made a sound of disgust. "Because Morritt is not as stupid as you," he explained. "Morritt will suspect a trap as soon as Bokman contacts him."

"Bokman would never betray him."

"No," Henri said patiently. "Try your best to keep up with me. Morritt will suspect the *information*. He will not go to Jamaica just because Bokman delivers the message. Morritt is too smart to walk into a trap. He needs motivation."

"Motivation?"

Henri motioned him back to the keyboard. "Who do we know in the opposition in Israel? Someone who would like to see the end of Assi Levy."

"The list is quite long," Martin said after a few seconds. "Oslin is at the top."

"Yes," Mardinaud replied, considering the name. "Yes, he will do."

"I will see to the calls and insure all is in place," said Martin. *Including my own surprise*, Martin thought. *This close, I must start considering how I will hide the money.*

Chapter 30

THE MESSAGE

"We may have a problem," David said, stepping into the car.

"What does that mean?" Katrina asked from behind the wheel. The small dome light revealed dark circles under her eyes and dirt smudges on her cheeks. It was already past six o'clock in the morning and her face was worn with fatigue.

After leaving Heiden's compound, they had worked their way through the dark jungle. It had taken nearly seven hours to retrace their steps back to the village and their waiting plane. Neither had slept during the short flight to Bogotá although both were exhausted. David fought the memories of the camp and Katrina brooded over the loss of the treasure.

So much had happened in the last twelve hours. Now David wondered if it was all beginning again.

"What did they say?" Katrina asked when he hesitated. "Did you get through to Assi? Are they going after the rest of Heiden's collection?"

David pulled the car door shut. "I'm not sure. Something isn't right. I can't reach Assi. An old friend of his will meet us at a café near here. We can trust him. Besides, I could use a strong cup of coffee."

"I'm all for that," Katrina sighed.

She followed David's directions and soon pulled the car to the curb behind a long, gray limousine. A uniformed driver lounged against the front fender. He barely seemed to notice them, but David knew better. The expert eyes of the ex commando had identified and cleared them.

The owner of the café glowered at them as they entered. David ignored him and led Katrina to a booth in the back where a plump man dressed in a light coat and open necked shirt smiled and stood. A look of concern replaced his smile as he silently grasped David's hand and pulled him close. David returned the embrace before following Katrina into the booth.

The man motioned to the café owner for two more coffees and sat down.

"David, it's good to see you," he said. "Are you all right?"

"Fine, Max. This is Katrina Kontoravdis. Katrina, this is Max Bokman."

"Very pleased to meet you, Miss Kontoravdis." Bokman briefly shook Katrina's hand and turned back to David before she could reply. "You've had a bad time?"

"We survived," David said. "What's happening? Why can't I reach Assi?"

"You might be in a better position to tell me. I had a call at three this morning. The caller told me you were in Colombia and stirring up hell."

"Who called?"

Bokman shook his head. "I have no idea. They just told me that you had started an international incident and said I should contact Assi."

"International incident?" David said slowly. Whoever he was, the caller knew about Bokman's past association with Levy. Access to that type of information pointed to one man.

"Mardinaud," David muttered. He looked up at Bokman. "I couldn't reach Assi," he said.

"So you said. My conversation with him was very short. He's in trouble, David. Political trouble."

"Because of me?"

"Precisely. What did you do?"

David recognized a tone of disapproval in Bokman's voice and briefly recounted the events of the past few days. Max was silent, but nodded occasionally. At the end of the tale, he cursed.

"Everything is happening too fast," he said. "The machinery doesn't operate that quickly in this country. An official protest lodged overnight? From what Assi told me, word reached Oslin just after the attack. You know Assi's position was tenuous. Too many are out to get him."

David remembered his own conversation with Assi. The Mossad director's enemies would pounce on this new scandal. "He didn't resign, did he?"

"They didn't give him the option. He had to step down while they investigate the Colombian government's claims. I was talking to him when Shamir called for him. Assi's personal network is still in place and they got my message to you. They're protecting him, for now. God knows how long that will last."

David stared at Bokman. "This could finish Assi. When they connect him to Heiden, they'll crucify him."

"You're in danger as well. You'll be arrested on sight if you stay in Colombia."

"Mardinaud," David repeated.

"If the Frenchman is involved, it might explain the rest of the message," Bokman said. "According to the caller, I was to tell you Duman is in Montego Bay."

"That fat bastard," David swore. "Max, I appreciate the information, but I think you'd better leave. Do what you can for Assi and forget about this meeting. The Medellín Cartel was guarding Heiden."

"They don't concern me."

"They concern me. I don't want your association with me to make you a target."

"Don't worry about that," Max assured him. "I will leave, though. As you say, I might be able to do Assi more good than I can you, David. My plane is at your disposal. It's fuelled and waiting for you. Let me have your keys."

Katrina handed him the car keys as he continued his instructions. "I'll leave you the limo. Whatever you decide to do, the driver has a key to a locker at the airport. My people are stocking it as we speak. You'll want to change before going through security. There's also a briefcase with everything else you'll need in the way of money. My name will get you to the plane, but security is tight. Don't take anything you wouldn't take through Tel Aviv. Good luck, David."

David shook the older man's hand and thanked him. Bokman waved off the thanks and turned to Katrina. "A pleasure to meet you, my dear. Take care of him, will you?"

Katrina stared into his small, dark eyes and noticed how the puffy flesh around them creased as he smiled. She already liked and trusted the man.

Humming to himself, Bokman walked out of the restaurant and spoke to his chauffeur before driving off in the rental car.

* * * * *

"I never understood what a bastard Mardinaud is," Katrina said. "He just expects us to walk into whatever trap Duman has laid for us? To hell with his little games. To hell with Duman and to hell with the treasure."

"I wish it was only Duman," David said. "Mardinaud is smarter than that. He's left me no choice. I have to go to Jamaica."

Katrina's hand stole over his. From David's reminisces, Katrina knew how much he loved Assi. David would never turn his back on his friend, no matter what the danger. "When do we leave?" she asked.

"*We* are not going anywhere," David said firmly.

"You're going after Duman, aren't you?"

"If I can't get Duman, Assi is finished. With Duman, I can claim that the Heiden connection was an elaborate plan to get the terrorist through the treasure. We can make Colombia out to have harbored both Heiden and Duman."

"So," Katrina asked again, "when do we leave?"

"You don't have to come with me."

"Your concern is touching, but I am coming."

"Mardinaud will have told Duman about us," David warned. "We'll be walking into a trap he's had hours to set. I have to go, but you don't." He peered into Katrina's eyes. "Do you want him enough to risk going to Jamaica?"

"Yes," she replied. But she wondered if she really meant that she wanted David enough to risk going to Jamaica.

* * * * *

David opened the locker and took out two small suitcases, one white and one blue, and handed the white one to Katrina. While she headed for the ladies room, he grabbed the other case and slammed the locker shut. A half hour later, they met outside the airport's coffee shop.

"Are we fools for going to Jamaica?" Katrina whispered.

David shrugged and reached to carry her suitcase for her. She glared at him. "If I can slug a pack through the jungle, I can carry my own suitcase."

David pulled his hand back as though the bag was on fire. "You just look so beautiful," he explained. "I couldn't help myself."

Katrina's serious mask broke into a smile. She kissed him on the cheek as she handed over the bag. "My shining knight," she teased.

Without warning, a short man shoved a fistful of pamphlets at the couple. "Rise up and battle the overlords," he cried. "Join the Communist Party of Colombia!"

Katrina slammed the heel of her hand into the man's chest, causing him to stumble backward. He regained his balance and immediately started toward her again. David stepped between the two. One glance at the menacing look in the Israeli's eyes and the campaigner backed off, muttering to himself as he turned away.

Katrina stared straight ahead and didn't speak while they boarded the plane. "I guess I should be glad we made it without being arrested for assault," he joked.

Katrina whirled on him, then looked sheepish when she saw his grin. "I'm sorry about that back there," she said.

"That's okay. After the last two days, overreaction is natural. Maybe you just don't know your own strength. That guy sure picked the wrong person to convert."

"It's just that I have never agreed with the Communist Party. It goes back to my childhood."

David waited, but Katrina was silent, staring out the window of the plane.

"Well?" he prodded. "I told you all about my childhood. You can't leave me hanging like this." He reached for her hand and Katrina settled back into her seat with a sigh.

"I never knew my mother and father," she said. "The Communists killed them."

David regarded her silently for a moment, noticing how the sparkle had disappeared from her eyes. He heard himself in her tone and recognized the protective cocoon of denied emotion.

"What happened?" he asked.

"When the Communists swept southward toward Athens in 1948, they tried to swell their ranks with volunteers from the surrounding villages. The mountain people didn't want to fight so Moscow ordered the Albanians to draft all able bodied male villagers into the new army –

forcibly, if necessary. As news spread of the conscription, the village men left their families and hid. The Communists mined the roadways as a deterrence."

"And your father? Was he one of those who fled?"

"Just before the Communists entered the village. He didn't have any choice. Nobody ever saw him again," Katrina said. "My mother was pregnant with me at the time. That made her one of the lucky ones.

"At first, the bastards were almost humane although they used the villagers as slaves. The women were forced to farm, cook, and entertain." Katrina shuddered, remembering the stories she had heard. "But the women wouldn't cooperate. The Communists resorted to brute force and terrorized the women until they performed."

"But your mother was spared all this?"

"For a time, but the tide of the war was turning. Their forces had rapidly thinned and the Albanians started drafting all women between the ages of sixteen and fifty. My mother went to fight just after I was born. I never heard how she died."

Katrina's eyes brightened slightly. "My maternal grandmother, Anna, raised me. She was an amazing woman. All her children and most of her grandchildren had been taken away from her, but she never gave up. One night, she gathered the remaining villagers and led them through the mountains to the one of the Royalist battalions. The Greek troops took us to a relocation center, but we left immediately for Athens."

Katrina turned to David and her voice became more animated. "She gave me an education far from the traditional Greek upbringing. I learned about being strong and independent. She always told me, 'woman or not, you can do anything.' She taught me to survive."

David said nothing, but raised the armrest and pulled her against his shoulder.

Katrina sighed, the strength going out of her voice. "The Communists took my father and mother from me and kidnapped over 100,000 of my people, mostly children. Over half of them are still behind the Iron Curtain. I'll never forgive them."

David gently covered her with the blanket. He listened to her breathing until it became deep and regular. Then, he too fell asleep.

✳ ✳ ✳ ✳ ✳

"How did you find me?"

Henri Mardinaud smiled at the note of surprise in the voice coming over the speaker phone. "You're joking," he replied.

"Smithers," Duman said, more to himself. "What do you want?"

Mardinaud chided him. "You're not very civil to me today. I take the time to call you and you snap at me."

"I don't have time for this."

"I quite agree," Mardinaud said.

"What does that mean?" asked Duman. "What do you know?"

Henri ignored the questions. "Congratulations on acquiring the Schliemann artifacts," he said. "I understand you left some destruction in your wake."

"Not me. That was the Jew."

"Which brings me to why I called."

"Yes?"

"Morritt knows you are in Jamaica. He's on his way."

Duman was silent and the line crackled. Mardinaud waited.

"You told him," Duman said finally.

The fat man sounded innocent. "What profit would there be in betraying you?"

"None. Believe that," Duman snapped. "How and when is the Jew arriving?"

"I'm quite sure I don't know. Besides, telling would be unfair. However, considering Morritt's resources, a private jet is not out of the question."

"And the Greek?"

"I understand they have become quite inseparable."

"Yes, insufferable."

"Oh, very good," Mardinaud chuckled. "You have retained your sense of humor."

"And my sense of revenge," Duman said. "This is not finished, Frenchman."

The line went dead.

Martin Erhart leaned forward and pressed the disconnect button, then studied his employer. The fat man looked disturbed, possibly even frightened. Duman's threat had found its mark. Perhaps, Mardinaud had gone too far.

"Monsieur, a question?" Martin asked quietly.

"Yes, Martin?"

"Who are you more afraid of, Duman or Morritt?"

Mardinaud paused for a long time. "In truth," he said finally, "whichever one survives."

PART FIVE

JAMAICA

LET US ALONE...
IN SINGLE COMBAT DUEL...
WHOEVER GETS
THE UPPER HAND IN THIS
SHALL TAKE TREASURE
AND THE WOMAN HOME.
                    THE ILIAD -BOOK III

Chapter 31

WHITE SANDS

The tall Jamaican slapped a tile on the table. The man watching the game smiled, nudging the tall man's opponent. "Michael's got you," he said. "Game be done, soon."

Michael's opponent leaned forward and examined the arrangement of dominoes, then snorted and sat back, looking at his own pieces. He played his tile, but Michael did not notice. He was watching a white couple cross the baked tarmac. They avoided the long terminal of the Montego Bay Airport and headed to the left, passing through the hangar reserved for VIPs.

Michael's opponent noticed the tall man's stare. "You best be watchin' the game instead o' the scenery."

Michael flashed a row of brilliant teeth. "Like to give that one the big bamboo."

The three Jamaicans laughed and returned to the game. Michael took off his hat and tossed it on the ground beside him before making his next play.

* * * * *

"What do we do now?" Katrina asked.

They had avoided discussing their plans during the flight, each appreciating the brief respite. But now it was time to confront the situation. "We're safe, for awhile," David said. "But Duman knows we're headed for the island. We won't be able to hide for long. We need weapons."

"Do you have any contacts here?"

"Nope. What about you?"

"I vacationed here once." Katrina did not elaborate.

The thought of Katrina enjoying the island with someone else bothered him. And his senseless jealousy bothered him even more. Frustrated, he turned to flag down one of the passing cabs. His frustration grew as Katrina whistled sharply. A cab immediately answered her shrill call.

"We can take care of the hotel after," she said, climbing into the back seat. "I know where to get what we need."

David let the driver take the bags to the trunk and settled himself beside Katrina. When the driver slid behind the steering wheel, Katrina leaned forward. "Take us to the market."

The driver stepped on the gas, throwing his passengers backward. As they struggled to right themselves, both missed the tall Jamaican watching them from inside the hangar.

The man stepped out of the shadows, tipped his hat, and motioned to another taxi. Once inside, he nodded to the driver and the vehicle sped after the white couple.

* * * * *

"This is where we get our weapons?" David surveyed the rows of tables lining the street. "Fruits and vegetables?"

"Come on," Katrina said, taking his hand as she propelled him along the booths of the open market. She understood his anxiety at the unfamiliar place, but could not resist taking advantage of his discomfort. David was out of his element in the strange locale and it was obvious he hated not being in control. She knew David Morritt did not follow, he led. "You'll love this place." She pinched his ribs to tease a smile out of him. "Relax," she said. "I'll take care of you."

"You don't have to enjoy yourself so much."

"I don't have the faintest idea what you mean." Katrina made an exaggerated show of fluttering her eyelashes, then her face grew serious. David tensed as she placed a restraining hand on his arm. "Trust me?" she asked.

"What do you want me to do?" he whispered.

Katrina spoke quickly. "Do exactly as I say. Turn when I tell you. Then, as fast as you can, pick out our dinner. Okay, now!"

David twisted around, confronting the table of fruit. His shoulders slumped as her words sank in. Behind him, he could hear Katrina laughing. He turned back and grabbed her by the shoulders. He kissed her and could taste the salt from her tears.

"I'm sorry," she said, trying to catch her breath. "You just seem so serious. I must have caught the fever of the island."

David shook his head and gave her another kiss. He knew he was being too serious, but relaxing with his new emotions was difficult for him. He had not felt this way about a woman in many years. "I promise to relax," he said, "if you promise never to do that again."

"I promise," Katrina said, putting her hand over her heart. "I do want you to buy us dinner though."

"And you will be doing?"

"Woman's work," she said. "I have to go buy our guns. I'll meet you back here in less than half an hour. Can you handle dinner, or do you want a list?"

David drew back his hand in a playful swat, but Katrina slipped away. He felt a flash of concern as he watched her fade into the milling crowd. He didn't like letting her go off alone, but she knew this island and he did not. He had to let her work as she saw fit. And he suspected her confidence needed a success.

David turned back to the table and began picking out their dinner.

* * * * *

In their third taxi of the day, Katrina and David stopped at a pair of wide, ornate gates. An engraved, bronze plaque announced the name of the establishment – *WHITE SANDS*.

After registering, they crunched along the white gravel path which wove around the resort's twenty, white stucco bungalows. Colorful flower gardens surrounded the small palms, breadfruit, and banana plants. White cement benches provided a view of the rocky shore, blue water and small craft moored at the adjoining marina. Closer inspection revealed an oily sheen covering the water, marring the picture postcard perfection. David scanned the area several times but saw nothing unusual. Except the lack of sand, white or not.

At Bungalow Eight, he pulled a key from his pocket. "I hate this," he said, more to himself than to Katrina. He took another look around. "I don't like playing Mardinaud's games."

Katrina was lost in her own thoughts. She remembered Alex dead in the New York apartment's hallway, propped up against the cheap wallpaper. "The treasure might not be worth it," she said softly.

"The treasure isn't, but Duman certainly is. He deserves to die. I want to see that happen. Besides, it's my only chance." David's voice was harsh in its half whisper. "With the reception Mardinaud has arranged, I'll be lucky if they don't put me in jail when I return home. That's assuming I can even get back in. The world press will crucify Israel. Someone will have to take the heat. I'm the logical choice, but Assi will catch it even more. There are people who have been waiting years for the chance to get Assi. I'll just be an extra piece of meat at feeding time. If I'm going to get out of this, it's now or never. And I don't like the idea of never."

The interior of the miniature bungalow was more like a hotel room. David opened a closet to the left of the entrance and peered across the hallway at the small bathroom opposite. Straight ahead, he could see the Caribbean through the sliding glass patio doors. He stepped around the corner created by the bathroom to set the suitcases and the string bag of groceries on the lone, king size bed.

"Don't put those on there," Katrina ordered. "I'm going to be in there as soon as I take a hot bath."

David snapped to attention and saluted. He moved the bags over to a stand against the wall and rummaged through the blue case for his shaving gear. Katrina pulled her newly purchased automatic out of her purse.

"Make you a deal," David said. "Give me a minute to have a quick shower. You check your guns. Then, the bathroom will be all yours while I get our meal ready."

"That's a done deal," Katrina grinned.

He motioned toward the gun. "Gonna tell me where you got those?"

"Easy," she said. "I went to this little bar I remembered. I wasn't there two minutes before a local asked if I wanted to buy some mind mellow. I said no to the drugs, but told him I wanted some guns. He introduced me to the bartender. The whole deal took ten minutes. The boys on this island are different from the sleaze in Bogotá, more laid back. All they want to do is make a deal and a double cross is just too much work in this heat."

"Such resourcefulness for an innocent little girl," David said.

Katrina only nodded and ejected the clip from the gun. In three swift movements, she disassembled the automatic. "While you're at it, check mine," David said, disappearing into the bathroom. He was happy to see her confidence, marred by the episode with the Colombians, return.

After stripping out of his clothes, David lathered his face and scraped the razor across his beard. His eyes were bloodshot and dark bags hung below them. He puckered his face, staring at the complex design of wrinkles. At that moment, more than ever before, he felt his advancing age.

How could he justify being here, he wondered? Katrina was almost fifteen years his junior and appeared even younger.

David stepped back and looked at his body in the mirror. His muscles were still firm, but gray lightly tinged the dark hair on his chest. Nevertheless, he thought, the overall effect wasn't bad. His were mature, good looks. Possibly, he did have enough years left for the beautiful woman waiting in the other room. He hoped so because, he now realized, he was falling in love with her.

The shower slightly revived David's weary body. He briskly toweled dry, then ran a deep bath for Katrina, adding the bath crystals generously left by the management. As the water foamed, he envisioned how she would look buried in the bubbles.

Katrina knocked on the door, causing David to jump guiltily. "You just about done?" she called.

He opened the door and bowed. "My Lady. Your bath awaits."

Katrina was wearing a thin, silk robe. The two of them standing together, she in her robe and he wrapped in a towel, seemed oddly comfortable to David. He felt relaxed and at ease, as though they had been together a lifetime. But the sensation of familiarity did not prevent his arousal. As though sensing his thoughts, Katrina slapped his backside, pushed him out of the bathroom, and slammed the door.

* * * * *

206 / D.A. Graystone

David could hear Katrina getting out of the bath. He placed a bowl of fruit salad, plates of bread and cheese, and chilled bottles of *Red Stripe* beer on the bed.

"A picnic! That looks magnificent."

David turned and felt his heartbeat quicken. The ankle length robe clung to Katrina's body in spots where she had not dried herself completely. Her face, freshly scrubbed of travel dirt and makeup, glowed with a warm flush. Her brown eyes sparkled in the candles he had placed around the room. "*You* look magnificent!" David said as she came over to him and gave him a light kiss on the cheek. He drank in her exotic scent. The gun had not been her only purchase.

Katrina sat on the bed and attacked the food. "How are we going to find Duman?" she asked, forking a piece of melon into her mouth.

"He may find us."

"We're going to have to show ourselves eventually." She noticed David's faraway gaze. "What's the matter?"

David shrugged and tore off a piece of bread. "Homesick. I wanted to come out on this mission so much and yet I miss home. I miss Israel. I always did – no matter what mission I was on. But I think it's worse this time." He took her hand in his. "Worse because I have someone I want to show my country to."

Katrina gently kissed his knuckles. "Tell me again what I'll see," she said.

While they ate, David talked about Israel. He thought he had told her everything before. But now, as he traveled the country in his mind, he remembered more and more. The beauty and the danger. The contrasts of the geography and the people came alive in his words. He spoke with bursting pride of the ancient times of the Bible and the modern technology of the *Sabras*, the second generation Israelis.

When he had finished, both were surprised to see it had grown dark outside. David cleared away the dishes. As she lounged against the thick pillows, Katrina realized she would follow David to Israel – if he was allowed to return.

"In my country, a man would not do that," she said, pointing to the dishes. "That's woman's work."

David moved across the room and lay down beside her. "In my country," he said, "equality has advanced. Except among the more religious sects, of course. In the early days, when the country was young, able bodied men were scarce. Even with women enlisting, the Arabs severely outnumbered us. The women still serve in the forces and we respect their abilities. Golda Meir was not an exception for Israel. You know how it is with us Jews; we hate to waste anything. Equality was a necessity, at first. We eventually learned it was an asset."

"And what about in bed?" Katrina asked with a slow smile. "Is equality an asset there as well?"

"Dominance is inconsequential. The most important goal is satisfying your partner."

Katrina parted her robe to reveal her round breasts and hard nipples. "An admirable goal," she said. "Tell me if I succeed."

They kissed deeply. David moved his mouth down her neck and between her breasts, losing himself in her warm perfume. She surrendered to his touch, allowing small shudders to shake her body. Slipping her hands under his robe, she caressed his tight muscles, scratching his back lightly with her nails. Mouths and hands tenderly explored each other's body. With infinite patience, they brought the other to the edge, only to retreat and begin rebuilding the passion. Wax pooled around the candles, yet they continued to express their love.

Neither noticed the slight noise outside their bungalow door.

* * * * *

The man crouched in front of Bungalow Number Eight, the bright moon glinting off his gray temples. He could hear the muffled sounds of lovemaking. He smiled. This would be their last opportunity, he thought. As he remembered the exciting figure he had seen through the binoculars, a spark of jealousy flared and quickly winked out. Soon, he told himself. Soon he would have his revenge for that missed shot and for the interference at the compound. He had wanted to see them die, to make them suffer, but he'd grown weary of the pair. He would swat them out of existence as he would an annoying fly.

The man opened a small case beside him. He removed a *Do Not Disturb* sign, three brass screws, a screwdriver, wire, and a small detonator. Then he went to work.

When finished, he replaced his tools in the bag and walked back down the path, turning back to admire his creation. He squinted in the half-light at the bungalow beside Number Eight and the sign on its door. He glanced back at Number Eight. Nothing could be more natural than the tiny sign, he thought and smiled again. The thin wire would be invisible, even in bright sunshine. In the morning, the two inside would open the door and the detonator would trigger.

After that, the Greek and the Jew would not be around to bother him any longer.

Chapter 32

DEADLY ILLITERACY

A sunbeam streamed into the room, bathing Katrina and David in its warmth as they lay entwined in each other's arms. Though both had been awake for half an hour, neither wanted to stir from the rumpled sheets. David toyed with Katrina's hair. Katrina looked up at him. "Don't tell me about any gray ones," she murmured.

"I thought that was why you had it highlighted, to cover up all this gray."

"Bastard, I'm only thirty-four. I'm not old yet!"

"That's what I keep telling everyone," David laughed. "The difference is, I know I'm lying."

Katrina rolled onto her stomach and propped herself up on her elbows. "Could have fooled me last night. I would have put you around eighteen."

David kissed her forehead. "I would have put you around that age, too."

"God, no. Don't you know that women reach their peak at forty and beyond? I'm just beginning to come into my own."

David rubbed his chin thoughtfully. "Hmm. That would work out about right. Give you twenty years in your prime and then I'll be dead.

Actually, you'll probably have killed me. I could go out the way every guy dreams."

Katrina made a move to hit him, but David was already up and out of bed. "I'm going to shave and shower," he said. "We'd better get going. I think we've used up too much of our lead time."

"You have your shower," Katrina said. "I'm going out to see about getting us some breakfast."

❊ ❊ ❊ ❊ ❊

After shaving, David turned on the shower and stepped under the spray. As he pulled the curtain closed, he heard the bathroom door open. He stuck his head out. "I thought you were going to get us breakfast."

Katrina dropped her robe to the floor. "I'll join you and we'll go out for breakfast together. It'll be faster in the end."

David looked at her standing naked in front of him and smiled. "I doubt it."

After a long shower, they dressed quickly and checked their guns. As enjoyable and restful as the past twelve hours had been, neither of them could forget Duman was waiting for them somewhere on the island. Now that he had accepted the need to leave the bungalow, David wanted to get on with their plans. He could almost see Israel slipping through his grasp.

Katrina sensed his impatience and kept pace with him. She, too, had her visions. All she could see was Alex bleeding on the carpet.

❊ ❊ ❊ ❊ ❊

Asabi pushed her cleaning cart along the gravel, cursing when the wheels caught in the loose stone. She waved at her friend Chi, the maid who looked after the other ten bungalows. Chi had told her about the job and talked the boss into hiring her. And Chi had taught Asabi everything she knew.

Asabi looked at the door of each bungalow as she passed, watching for the signs that told her when to make up a room. Not that she could read the words. She couldn't read a single word, not like Chi. One day, Chi had promised, Asabi would know how to read. Chi would teach her.

For now, Asabi watched the colors. Blue, like the sky, meant the people did not want to be disturbed. "Never go in the rooms with blue signs," Chi had told her.

Green was the sign she watched for. Green meant she could go into the bungalow. She made up the beds, cleaned the bathroom, and left fresh towels. Dirty work, but Asabi loved going into the rooms.

The rooms held promise for Asabi. Chi had told her about the last maid at the resort. That maid had done such excellent work, one of the guests had hired her. She had moved away from the island and now lived in luxury in the United States.

That was Asabi's dream.

Asabi stopped and squinted at the door of Bungalow Eight. The sign hanging from the doorknob was wrong. It was not blue and it was not green. It was gold.

She looked back at Bungalow Seven. A blue sign. She looked ahead at Bungalow Nine. A green sign.

Asabi leaned back and looked down the row of bungalows. Chi's cart sat outside one of the doors. Asabi could go down and bring Chi, but the boss did not like the women gabbing. If Chi came here, the boss might think that she, Asabi, couldn't do her work alone. She might get fired.

Don't bring Chi here, Asabi thought, bring the sign to Chi. She crept up to the door of Bungalow Eight, bent down, and grabbed the sign.

The explosion was deafening. Blood and debris flew through the air for forty feet. The blast flattened the miniature palm beside the walk and toppled Asabi's cart, scattering towels and cleanser. Several bungalows away, Chi began to scream.

The echo of the explosion faded.

There was no sound from within the remains of Bungalow Eight.

Chapter 33

CONTACT

David heard someone screaming as he regained consciousness. His head was pounding and his ears were ringing. He squinted to bring his blurred vision into focus. Everything looked dim, as though a shroud hung across his eyes. It must be evening, he thought. The screaming continued, sounding far away and muffled.

Suddenly, he became aware of the weight on top of him. "Katrina?"

He barely recognized his own voice. It sounded like the voice of a stranger calling out from deep within a tunnel. He gently rolled Katrina on her back and rose up to his knees. The movement made him dizzy and he grabbed the closest means of support. The room completed one more spin and settled. He realized he was on the bed and holding onto the headboard.

David felt for Katrina's pulse. It was faint, but steady. He checked her nose and ears and found no blood. He said a silent prayer of thanks.

The screams came from outside, he realized. And it wasn't really evening. Clouds of dust floated in the air, creating a thick haze. His memory returned.

He had been heading for the door of the bungalow when Katrina had stopped him. She had put her fingers to her lips and motioned to the door.

Someone was coming up the front walk, very quietly. They both had stepped around the corner formed by the bathroom. There had been a bright flash followed by total darkness.

Katrina's body must have shielded him, absorbing the worst of the explosion. The shape of the front hall had directed the force of the blast past the foot of the bed. David's eyes followed the path of destruction. The patio doors were gone. The curtains hung in shreds with bits of wood caught in the material.

He looked down at Katrina and slapped her face lightly. Her eyes flickered open. She immediately squeezed them shut and moaned. David smoothed her hair and tried to shield her from the light. "Katrina," he said softly, "can you hear me?"

"Barely." Her voice was husky and deep. "God, my head. What the hell happened?"

"An explosion." David's hearing was returning and his voice began to sound normal. "A bomb left at the front door. You have to get up. We can't stay here."

She tried to sit up, but fell back on the bed, grabbing her head. "I don't want to."

"The hell you don't," David said sharply. "Get up, you stupid bitch! Some partner you turned out to be. I knew I should have had a man for a partner. Stand up before I leave you here."

Katrina's eyes sprang open and David could see them flash with anger before she looked away. She sat up and he could almost feel the pain that shot through her body. When he tried to help her, she slapped his hand away and struggled to the side of the bed. He watched her delicately check her body for injury. Finding no serious damage, she looked at him again and grinned weakly. "Mr. Pop Psychologist," she said. "All right, it worked. I'm up. Now help me or I won't stay that way."

David took her arm and helped her to the patio, pausing to let their eyes adjust to the outside light. "I didn't expect this of Duman," he said. "I thought his ego would demand he confront us in person. My mistake almost got us killed."

"Our mistake," Katrina said, softly.

David looked back through the destroyed front door. He saw the blood sprayed on the gravel walk outside. Someone had been at the door, he thought. Not Duman. That was too much to hope for. Whoever it was, they had been blown apart. "We have to get out of here before we're seen," he told Katrina. "Maybe we can get you off the island."

"Not likely," she said.

"Bokman's plane should still be here."

"I mean, not likely that I would go. Don't you still want him?"

Katrina felt a measure of strength returning as she stared at David. His jaw was set and he was breathing rapidly. She searched his cold, gray eyes and then nodded. "I want him too," she said firmly. "I'm not leaving. You want him so you can return to Israel. I want him to return what he took from me three years ago."

David smiled, relieved she was staying. He glanced again at the front door. "It's only a matter of time before somebody comes to investigate. We'll have to disappear for awhile," he said. "We need time to regroup."

As they crunched through the broken glass of the patio doors, they could hear voices nearing the front.

But everyone was too excited about the explosion to notice one more dust covered couple. As they slipped away and walked casually along the marina, they could hear the rapid exchange of the Jamaicans surveying the damage from the bomb. Katrina stopped for a moment to view the scene. A maid had screamed herself hoarse, but otherwise suffered no apparent injuries. Someone else had not been so lucky. The remaining pieces of that other person would be blotted up and taken away in a small plastic bag.

Having seen enough, Katrina allowed David to pull her away from the resort and onto the hot street. They stepped into the first available alley and brushed plaster dust off their clothes. They started to leave the alley but Katrina put her hand on David's arm.

"Duman."

"Of course," David replied.

"No, Duman!" Katrina pointed down the street at a tall man leaning against a car. Although trying to appear casual, he was obviously watching the activity around the explosion. David thought back to the photos and descriptions he had seen of Duman. Always cautious about having his photo taken, not many clear shots of Duman existed. However, four years ago, a forger had offered pictures for sale. He claimed they were taken of Duman for passports that the terrorist had requested. The forger's rather painful and spectacular death lent some credulity to his story. David mentally compared those pictures to the man leaning against the car. Ignoring the obvious changes that scissors and hair dye can achieve, David was forced to agree.

Suddenly, Duman straightened and all pretense was gone as he stared at the bungalow. David and Katrina looked away from Duman toward the wrecked front of their room. Two policemen had just exited from inside the bungalow. They delicately stepped through the remains of the maid and her cart. Stopping in front of a third man, they saluted and fell into conversation. Though too far away to hear, David could guess the conversation from their gestures. Both were shaking their heads and pointing toward the bungalow. Obviously, they were surprised to find it empty.

David turned his attention back to the terrorist. Duman was smiling. Obviously, he had misinterpreted the gestures and the Turk assumed his bomb had been successful.

"He's going to leave," Katrina said, also having seen the smile.

"We can't take him here," David said. "We could never get close enough before he saw us."

"We need a car."

"There," David said, pointing across the street. A man had just left an early 70s model Chevrolet and was heading down the street. The couple watched as he rounded the corner. "With luck, he won't have forgotten anything."

David and Katrina exited the alley and headed down the street at a leisurely pace. Katrina looked back at Duman. "Okay, cross now, he's looking away."

Briskly but not too quickly to attract any attention, David and Katrina went directly to the Chevy. In seconds, David was behind the wheel and working on the ignition wires. Katrina kept watch on Duman. "He's getting into the car. He must think we're dead. He's pulling out and heading straight."

The engine coughed once and then started. David immediately put it in gear and pulled out into the street. He grabbed a straw hat off the seat and slipped it on his head. Staying well back, he began to follow Duman through the crowded streets.

David glanced at the gas gauge. "Not much fuel. I hope this is a short trip."

Katrina looked through the glove box and found a street map of Montego Bay. "I think he's heading toward the outskirts. There isn't much town left after about five more blocks. If he turns left just up here, he's heading out into the country. We aren't going to have much cover."

Duman made the left hand turn and David followed. He tried to let Duman get a little farther ahead but even the sparse traffic was beginning to push him closer. In five minutes, they had left the city and were driving along a narrow two-lane highway. Duman was three cars ahead but didn't seem to be paying too much attention to anyone behind him.

After passing a shantytown of small corrugated tin and wood shacks, the scenery quickly changed to sugar cane and palm trees. "Road coming up on the right," Katrina warned David.

David slowed as Duman turned off onto the dirt road. Instantly, a dust plume appeared behind Duman's car. Only one car followed him off the highway before David and Katrina made the right hand turn. Even if Duman was suspicious, he would not be able to see David and Katrina through the thick clouds of dust.

The sugar cane had disappeared and the coast was visible again when David glanced down at the gas gauge. It was already touching empty.

"He's turning off. Looks like a house."

"Duck down, don't let him see you," David said, pulling the hat over to the right side of his face. Out of the corner of his eye, David saw Duman pulling into a garage at the side of a beachfront property. David continued on until they were well past the property and were out of sight from Duman. Pulling off to the side of the road, David checked his handgun while Katrina did the same.

Katrina and David jogged back toward the house. The front of the house was open to the road with a detached garage off to one side. A single story, the house had many large, open windows and very little cover except along the sides of the property. David and Katrina avoided the open front yard and skirted the property along the brush and palms that separated it from its neighbor. Halfway to the beach, they reached a low wall. Peering over, they looked down a small steep hill that ended at the sand. A basement level under the hill exited onto a stretch of beach that ran from the back of the house to the surf about twenty yards away. There was a small boathouse and dock with a speedboat moored beside it. Although Duman had another escape route, they had little access from the back.

"As bad as it is, I think the front is still our best bet," Katrina suggested.

"At least with the windows, we will be able to see if Duman is in sight," David agreed.

"We can make it most of the way across the yard behind the garage. The front door isn't too far from there," Katrina said.

David nodded and they headed back toward the garage.

Chapter 34

RESCUE

David and Katrina carefully scanned the windows on the left side of the house for over five minutes. There was no flicker of movement so they made the dash to the front of the house. Katrina grabbed the handle of the front door but it was locked. David pointed to the large open window beside the door. He pulled a knife from his pocket and unfolded the blade. He made short work of the screen and the two of them slipped through the window. "He's making it very easy," David whispered. "Watch for motion sensors."

From the front foyer, two hallways branched off left and right. To the left was a sparsely furnished living room. To the right was a narrow hallway with at least three doors. Katrina, already knowing Duman was not in the living room, pointed to the right. David hesitated and then nodded. As silently as possible, Katrina started toward the first doorway.

David worked through the living room and adjoining dining room quickly. At the back of the house, he found himself in the kitchen. A glass patio door opened onto a deck that overhung the exits from the lower level. David checked the boat and the dock but could see nothing but the speedboat. The back half of the boat was covered with a large tarp but otherwise the boat appeared to empty. David turned and saw an enclosed stairway going to the lower level of the house.

Katrina had still not appeared at the end of her hallway. David knew that, if Duman was downstairs, he could hear them at any moment. Not waiting for Katrina, he quickly descended the stairs. At the bottom, he was faced with several closed doors. Gloomy half-light found its way from windows at the beach side of the basement. Quietly turning the knob of the closest door, David hurried through the threshold. The room was pitch black. David groped along the wall until he found a light switch.

Blinking in the sudden light, David was faced with a room full of munitions. Boxes of guns and ammunition were piled against the farthest wall. David did a quick inventory, hoping to find a better weapon than his handgun. A large open crate produced a Kalashnikov AK-47. Checking the smaller ammo crates, David found several boxes of 7.62 caliber magazines. David rammed one into the assault rifle and put two more in his belt.

Turning back to the door, David froze. Two small wires ran into the room along the top of the doorframe. David quickly scanned the door for an alarm but the wires continued along the baseboard and disappeared behind the crates. Puzzled, David flicked out the light and shut the door. As quickly as possible, he began to search the other rooms.

* * * * *

Katrina had searched the first two rooms and found no sign of Duman. A computer in the first room might be helpful uncovering some of the terrorist's cells but that would have to wait for later analysis. The second room was a small bathroom. Finally, Katrina reached the third door. From there, she could see the kitchen and the blue water through the large patio door. Her gun ready, she turned the doorknob and rushed into the room.

She briefly took in the young girl tied to the bed before turning and scanning the room. Confident that only the girl was in the room, she walked over to the bed. The blonde girl was wearing a white top that had been torn open. Her skirt and panties lay in a heap against the wall. Below her left eye was a dark, ugly bruise where she had obviously been hit.

Putting her gun on the bedside table, Katrina tried to comfort the girl. "Just relax. I'm going to untie you and get you out of here. You don't have to worry about that bastard any more."

Helene stared at Katrina for a moment and then began to whimper. "Thank you. Thank you. Thank God you are here!"

Katrina worked on the knots and soon had one hand untied. Leaning across the girl, Katrina worked to free her left hand. As soon as Katrina had the arm free, Helene brought up her legs and placed her bare feet against Katrina's chest. With all her might, the young blonde pushed with her legs. Totally unprepared for the attack, Katrina flew backwards across the room and crashed into the dresser.

Dazed, Katrina could not understand the reaction from this girl she was rescuing. She watched in disbelief as Helene snatched up the automatic from the bedside table and pointed it at her. She could see Helene struggling to pull the trigger. Her back in agony, Katrina fought to get up before the girl realized the safety was on.

"Richard," the girl began shouting as Katrina got to her feet. "Richard, hurry, they're here! The Cartel is here!"

Chapter 35

THIEVES

David had almost worked his way to the beach side of the basement when he heard the large crash from the main floor. Almost as soon as he heard a woman start calling for 'Richard', there was a scrapping of metal on concrete from the back. David pictured Duman relaxing on the patio while they wasted time searching rooms. By the time David reached the back door, he saw Duman climbing into the boat. Duman seemed almost frantic, swearing loudly in Turkish and searching beneath the tarp. In a rage, he threw the tarp over the side of the boat onto the dock. David thought he might be looking for a weapon. If the terrorist was without a weapon, now was the time to act.

Shouldering through the door, David started firing the AK-47 in short bursts. Running across the sand while firing, David's aim was off. The bullets tore up the dock and one shattered the windshield of the boat. Before David had taken five steps, Duman had picked up an AK-47 of his own from the front of the boat and was spraying the back of the house. David veered to the left and rolled behind a large brick barbecue pit. Peering around the edge, he realized that not only was he out of sight, so was Duman. The boathouse blocked Duman from view.

The speedboat roared to life. David looked again. There was a line tied to the back of the boat. Duman would have to untie that line to escape. This would be David's only shot.

* * * * *

Katrina tried to ignore the pain and slowly got to her feet. Her first step almost took the leg out from under her but she braced herself against the wall. Helene suddenly realized why the gun would not fire. She turned the gun in her hand and saw the small safety switch. As Helene flipped the safety off, Katrina launched herself across the room. She grabbed the gun in Helene's hand as the girl pointed it back at her. A round went off, grazing Katrina's right shoulder. Katrina grabbed the gun with both hands and twisted viciously. The young girl screamed and released the gun. With both hands still wrapped around the gun, Katrina viciously backhanded the girl across the face. The added weight of the handgun sent Helene sprawling across the bed as automatic weapon fire shattered the silence from the beach.

Katrina ran to the door of the balcony and looked out. She could see Duman in the boat firing toward the house. She couldn't see David but suspected he was Duman's target. Duman suddenly stopped firing and started the boat. Katrina pulled the screen door open and ran onto the balcony.

Ten feet off the ground, she had an excellent vantage point. Pointing the handgun at Duman, she called out to the terrorist as she fired. A wave tossed the boat and the bullet went wide, burying itself in the control console of the boat.

Duman turned and crouched down behind the seats of the boat. For the briefest moment, shock registered on his face when he saw Katrina. Then, he smiled.

"I should have known. You bitch! Where did you put my treasure? Thieving Greek bitch. Is that the Jew hiding behind my barbecue? Wouldn't think you'd get that close to an oven, Jew! Why don't you come out where I can see you?"

Katrina aimed the handgun again. Before she could fire, Helene ran out of the bedroom and slammed into Katrina's back. The automatic went over the balcony and landed in the bushes below. Helene's momentum pushed Katrina against the railing. The wooden rail snapped. Katrina barely held her balance before pushing Helene backwards. Pulling the young girl off her back, Katrina twisted her around. Wrapping one arm around her throat, she looked down at Duman.

"Now I have a hostage for a change," Katrina said.

"And you think I care?" Duman said, picking up something from under the console. He fired a burst of gunfire at David. "Stay there, Jew. I'll deal with you in a minute."

Though David could not see Duman, he suddenly understood the wires he had seen in the house. Ignoring the bullets hitting the bricks, he ran out from behind the cover of the barbecue and screamed up at Katrina. "The house is wired! He's going to blow the house!"

Katrina responded instantly. Putting her hands under Helene's arms, Katrina tossed her through the break in the railing. The young girl had barely cleared the deck when Katrina dove off the balcony into the brush. Hitting the ground hard, she rolled behind the wall as the house behind her exploded.

David cleared the boathouse and brought the AK-47 up just as the house exploded. The force of the blast sent him sprawling into the sand. His rifle flew out of his hands and landed five feet in front of him. Ears ringing, he struggled to get up as debris rained down around him. A large board hit him in the back but he ignored it as he stared at Duman. The terrorist had retrieved his rifle and had it pointed at David.

"And so it finally ends, Jew," Duman said, smiling broadly.

David smiled back. Duman's smile faltered briefly, not understanding David's look.

"Yes, so it finally ends," David said as he watched the red sniper scope dance across Duman's forehead. Without warning, the back of Duman's head exploded as the high-powered bullet ripped through his skull.

Not pausing to enjoy the terrorist's death, David rolled across the sand and grabbed his rifle. Coming up on one knee, he turned the barrel on the bushes bordering the property. He scanned back and forth but could see no one.

Dropping the gun again, he ran to the side of the house. Katrina was just coming to. Gently he carried her away from the burning house and then went back for the other girl. She was unconscious but breathing evenly. David dragged her into the shade of the palms beside Katrina.

"Duman?" Katrina asked.

"Quite dead. If you can move, we'll take the boat. You need a doctor."

"I'm mobile," Katrina said, standing to prove it. She winced and cradled her arm. "But I'll take that doctor. I think my arm is broken. Where is the treasure?"

"Duman said we stole it. I think it was under the tarp. Likely some Jamaican has it and doesn't even know what it is."

"What about her?" David asked, pointing at the unconscious Helene.

"I have no idea who the hell she is. One of his women, I guess. All I know is, she tried to kill me."

"Then leave her. Let the Jamaicans work it out. It will give them something to do other than look for us."

David started toward the bushes. "I want to see if our savior left anything behind."

Before he took two steps, they could already hear the sirens approaching. Looking annoyed, Katrina shook her head and headed for the boat. "No time."

Taking the boat, David steered away from the sound of the approaching sirens, staying close to the coast and it sparse covering of palm trees. Katrina dragged the tarp over what had once been Duman.

EPILOGUE

I WANT TO GO HOME,
AND CAN THINK OF NOTHING ELSE.
THE ODYSSEY-BOOK V

EPILOGUE

TWO MONTHS LATER

Katrina stared at the beauty of the incredible view. Rows of citrus trees lined the flat area below. A complicated irrigation system watered the thirsty plants that produced the Kibbutz's famous fruit. The grove, a legacy left by David's adopted father, stretched farther every year. The number of trees had quadrupled since the old man had died. According to Kibbutz members, the next two years would see the grove expand to twice its present size.

Katrina looked past the orchard at the endless desert, amazed that the reddish barren ground could be so lovely. In her mind, she could see the floor of the desert covered with the vegetation of the future. She gripped David's arm as an idea struck her.

"Can we be married right here?" she asked.

David laughed, pointing at the ring on her finger. It was the gold band she had picked up at Heiden's. She had been hesitant to use it because of what it might mean to David. He had insisted because he knew it represented her past – not his. His past could finally rest. "We already are married," he reminded her.

"I know, but I want to do it again – on this spot."

He tenderly brushed her hand with his lips. The arm had healed over the past two months, leaving her only slightly stiff. "Whatever you wish. I'm so glad you're happy here."

Katrina's dark brown eyes seemed to penetrate his soul. "Are you happy here?" she asked.

"I'm happy anywhere, as long as you are with me."

Katrina smiled.

"What?" David asked.

"The call from Assi?" Katrina asked.

"Oh, no, nothing like that. He was just giving me an update, if you could call it that. He was rather insistent that we visit this weekend. Said he had something to run by me that he thought might be of interest."

"About Duman?"

"No, likely a new training class or some such thing. Nothing about Duman, there hasn't been a peep. Nobody has taken credit for the kill. Most think that I did it and that I'm trying to cover it up for some reason. Assi couldn't care less since it has solved his problems. Bringing in Duman has given Assi some much-needed breathing room."

"And the treasure?"

"Again, nothing," David said. "Duman thought we had taken it. Where it is now is anyone's guess."

"I would have loved to have seen the treasure," Katrina said wistfully.

Katrina was about to speak again when several gleeful cries from behind made her turn. Children swarmed around Katrina and led her back to the Jeep. As he followed them, David considered her question about his happiness.

The truth was, he had never been happier. He wanted to stay with Katrina forever. After their marriage, he had been content to move to the Kibbutz. He had even enjoyed supervising the occasional training session. Katrina would join him as an instructor as soon as she received her clearance. All was well. Last night, even the visiting Major Yaacov Sigura had pronounced David "domesticated".

David was unsure whether to cringe or smile at the pronouncement but he was sure his days as an active agent of the Mossad were behind him. With Katrina in his life, he doubted there was another mission that could interest him enough.

* * * * *

Martin Erhart hurried into Mardinaud's office and slipped behind the computer console. He had been busy helping his wife settle into their new home when he received the summons from his boss. She adored the new place and he was pleased with how often she demonstrated her new joy and the inventive ways she demonstrated her gratitude. She assumed he had received a bonus and a promotion. The rest of the world thought the money was an inheritance from his wife's late "Uncle Ivan" – totally documented even if the documents were technically forgeries. Luckily, Mardinaud was too consumed with the latest tidbit of information to be overly concerned about Martin's recent wealth. For the sake of his own health, Martin hoped that would continue.

Henri Mardinaud looked up at the large screen as Martin Erhart typed in the retrieval codes. A name flashed on the computer screen. "Sammon Abdel Nasser," the information broker read aloud.

Mardinaud leaned back into the chesterfield and sighed deeply. "Sammon Abdel Nasser," he repeated. He smiled. "A Jew using an Arabic name. The man has a sense of style. I'll have to give him that."

Martin turned around in his chair. "I contacted Assi Levy, as you instructed."

"Very good." The fat man leaned farther back on the couch and rested his head. He shut his eyes and appeared to go to doze off.

"What will David Morritt do when he finds out who Sammon really is?" Martin asked.

Mardinaud pulled his head up and looked at his assistant. "He'll come after him, of course," the Frenchman replied, a wicked grin forming on his face. "Then, the game will begin."

*   *   *   *   *

April 22, 1996
Moscow, Russia
Since the end of World War II, the Soviet Government has denied accusations that its soldiers looted Germany following the surrender of the Nazis. In fact, the various governments have adamantly denied the suggestion that troops gathered treasures during the invasion. However, in a reversal of that position, the Soviet Government has admitted to possessing over 300,000 pieces of art, more than two million rare books and countless other items liberated from Germany at the end of the war.

According to a government spokesman, the looted items have been housed in basement archives for over fifty years.

A further twist to this story comes as Helene Kadner, a minor celebrity from the early 1980s, has filed suit in the International Court of Justice in The Hauge for the return of some of that looted treasure. According to documents released by the Soviets, along with impressionist paintings by Manet, Renoir and Matisse and a rare Gutenberg Bible are 260 pieces of Trojan gold, treasure discovered by the German archaeologist Heinrich Schliemann. The discovery of the Schliemann artifacts actually casts further doubt on the story of Helene Kadner.

Following her arrest by Jamaican authorities in the early 1980s, Helene Kadner claimed to have been the lover of the international Turkish terrorist, Duman. According to Ms. Kadner's story, which became a best-selling book and a hit movie despite having no real evidence, she was the granddaughter of an escaped Nazi war criminal, one Friedrich Heiden. Heiden supposedly acquired the treasure during his escape from Nazi Germany in the last months of the Second World War.

According to Ms. Kadner's account, Duman seduced her to gain entry to her grandfather's home and stole the treasure out from under the noses of the Medellín Cartel. After escaping to Jamaica, Duman disappeared with the treasure after he thwarted an assassination attempt by the Cartel by detonating the home they were living in.

Ms. Kadner's supporters point out that since the time in question Duman has not surfaced. In fact, anonymous, highly placed US Government sources have confirmed Duman's death – though not in Jamaica. The various stories have the terrorist killed by several different groups including the DST, a CIA hit squad, the Greeks and the Mossad. Meanwhile, critics argue the public should not be duped by so-called "non-fiction" and hope that the existence of the treasure in the hands of the Russians will finally put the young woman's fanciful tale to rest.

Excerpt from

Two Graves

A Kesle City Homicide Novel
By D.A. Graystone

Available July 2011

Before you embark on a journey of revenge, dig two graves.

- Chinese Proverb

Chapter 1

The boy lunged. "Out of the way, loser!" he yelled.

Preston stumbled backwards off the sidewalk and plopped onto the damp grass. His butt hit hard; his hands barely stopped him from going flat on his back. He snapped an arm over his face, turning away from his attackers. But the four teenagers were already continuing down the sidewalk.

He was already forgotten.

Embarrassment flooded his system. The heat on his face contrasted with the cold of his ass as the dampness from the grass soaked through the seat of his pants. Struggling to his feet, he pulled at his jacket, hoping it would cover the wet stain. The red in his mottled cheeks deepened as he watched his would-be attackers saunter down the street.

The boys wore matching brown leather vests with a white crest painted on the back. They moved together – a pack of animals ready to take on anyone who crossed their path. Their laughter cut through him. Laughter directed at him – the geek, lard butt, weirdo, jerk, and tub. He was used to that. People had been laughing at him for forty years. He checked the retreating figures once more before turning away. He shuddered.

"Little bastards," he said to the night. "Just lucky I wasn't more prepared. Kick that dick into next week."

He *should* have done something to the delinquents, he thought. But, he had been outnumbered. Yet again, his subconscious had registered the unbalanced odds and stopped him.

"You got lucky this time," he said down the street after the retreating punks. He kept his voice pitched low – no need to disturb the neighborhood.

He looked down at his shaking hands. He shoved them deep in his jacket pockets, fixed his eyes on the sidewalk just ahead of his Hush Puppies and started toward the store again.

He had always walked this way. Concentrating on his feet, trying to will them straight. Duck feet. How many times had the other kids teased him about his splayed walk? His footprints in the snow prompted the comment, "Hey, at least one duck stayed for the winter!"

He envied the others with their cocky walks. They always stared straight ahead, welcoming, even *daring*, eye contact but not him. Too much risk, too much pain resulted from the briefest eye contact.

His life had been one long walk through terror.

He had been the brunt of every joke, on the receiving end of some form of terrorism all his life. Laughter, taunting, teasing or worse.

So very often, it was so much worse – bruises, cuts, broken bones. If he inventoried his body, he could remember each injury, each moment of pain, each humiliation.

Yes, he knew fear. He knew it intimately. He knew every heart pounding, sweaty moment of true terror.

Fear dominated his life. Stalking him, it was his constant companion.

Fear kept him safe. Fear was his protector but not his friend.

No, it was the other, darker emotion that he reveled in.

Rage.

Fear kept him safe but rage kept him sane.

At the store, he took a carton of orange juice up to the counter and felt the anger build. He let it grow, develop. He felt the heat form in his belly instead of his cheeks.

"Is that everything?" the young clerk asked.

"Obviously," he answered tersely, relishing the spill of anger.

If I wanted more, I'd put it on the Goddamn counter!

His mind played the entire conversation out as he tapped the counter, impatiently waiting for his change. He snatched the juice without waiting for a bag.

"You're welcome," came the sarcastic voice from behind him.

Mumbling obscenities through the closed door, he started for home. He felt the rage seething and roiling in his body. His pace quickened, his body hunched over, his eyes unseeing. His blood boiled with the rage.

Sweet, sweet rage.

His mind whirled with what he might have done to those boys. He imagined the satisfying crack of bone, the whoosh of air, the whimpering and the begging. And then there would be the blood. And that smart mouth clerk. He pictured how a few sharp staples would take care of him and his *you're welcome*!

He kicked at a stone, sending it into the side of a car. The small thud wasn't satisfying. He needed to hit, crush and inflict pain. His mind flicked to his neighbor's cat. The feel of the tiny bones under the heavy mat of fur, the slow squeeze...

"Hey!" He froze in mid stride, his head snapping up, suddenly face to face with the boy.

The rage drained instantly from his body, threatening to take his suddenly too full bladder with it. All-consuming fear instantly replaced the rage. Sweat clamped his shirt to his back and ran down his spine and into the crack of his ass. His palms grew slippery against the carton of juice. He felt his bowels suddenly loosen as he searched for safety.

The boy stood alone at a bus stop beside an all night gas station, an unlit cigarette dangling between his lips. He made no move to get out of the way. He just stood, waiting.

He fought the urge to run. His eyes flicked toward the station but the attendant was playing a guitar, paying no attention as the world went on around him. No cars were at the pumps and nothing but empty cars on the street and in the lot. He was alone.

✳ ✳ ✳ ✳ ✳

Luis Gabel watched the blood drain from the fat cheeks of the loser in front of him and smiled. He couldn't believe his luck when he saw the blub waddling toward him.

This was the same wimp that had fallen on his ass when he scared him earlier. What a geek, Gabel thought as he watched the guy push his glasses back on his nose. God, the guy was sweating like a pig. There was actually steam coming off him.

This porker was ripe and Gabel was going to pick him clean. One glimpse of his blade and he'd be handing over his wallet. Gabel knew the type. He'd be too scared of him and his crew to ever call the cops.

"Christ man, you look like you gonna piss your pants," the boy said, putting his ace into his vest pocket. "We need to talk about a toll on my sidewalk."

The blub never looked him in the eye but tried to step around like some peasant avoiding the King. Gabel stepped onto the grass and grabbed his arm. The carton slipped and hit the ground. Orange juice shot up the Gabel's boots and jeans. In the half-light, it looked like he had wet himself. And then, the asshole actually laughed.

"Look watcha did to my boots! They're fucked. Now you are really gonna pay. Gonna shove my boot right up your ass!"

As he planted his foot to kick out, Gabel stepped on the half-empty carton. His foot went out from under him and he sailed into the air. Unprepared, he went down hard in the small garden on the boulevard, his breath rushing out of him.

Preston took one look at the prone figure and ran. He crossed the street and looked over his shoulder. Expecting to see the kid right behind him, the empty street surprised him and he stumbled into a parked car. Prepared for a ruse, he was ready to bolt at the first sign of movement. But there was nothing.

Seeing the helpless figure dispelled the fear. Rage flowed into the void. Checking left and right, he cautiously went back.

"Were you going to give me some of this?" he asked, pulling his foot back. The toe of his shoe connected just below the teenager's rib cage. The tentative kick barely moved him. Stumbling backwards, Preston saw no reaction, not even a moan. Bravado surged in him, giving flight to his rage.

"I can do better than that!" he said.

Taking a step, he slammed his foot into the boy's side. The force of the kick rolled him onto his stomach.

In the spill of the gas station lights, he could see blood, so dark it was almost black. It had soaked into the boy's stringy blond hair.

He had killed the little scum sucker.

RUN, his brain screamed at him. They're going to blame you.

He wiped his sweaty palms on his jeans and swallowed the bile rising in his throat.

THINK. You know they will blame this on you. You won't last in jail, not even for a single night.

Fighting the rising panic, he looked around. The kid in the booth still had his back to him, headphones on his ears and a guitar in his lap. None of the houses had direct line of sight because of the trees. Suddenly, he was relieved for the empty street.

RUN.

Car.

"Turn, turn," he said, willing the car to turn down one of the side streets. "Damn," he said, unaware he was talking aloud.

The lights were getting close.

No time to run. Think, damn it.

He grabbed the boy by the vest and propped him against the bus sign. The punk fell over; his head sounded like a ripe melon when it hit the sidewalk. Preston started to giggle and fought for control. The second time, he got the body balanced against the sign. With seconds to spare, he stood facing away from the car and waited. The car didn't even slow as it passed.

Genius. God damn genius. Now RUN!

Ya, run, genius. Great idea. How many bodies do you think turn up at the side of this street? Did the driver get a good look at you? How much would he remember? You do stand out.

Hide the body. The longer it takes to find, the less chance of the driver making a connection. But where? He couldn't carry the kid very far.

A small sliver of light showed along the crack in the partially open door of the station restroom. "What better place for a piece of crap?" he said aloud and another giggle escaped.

He picked up the boy and wrapped an arm under his armpits. He felt the blood soaking into the sleeve of his jacket. He toted the teenager over to the washroom, just one friend helping another. The boots made the only sound as they bounced along the asphalt. Panting, he pushed the door open all the way and grunted as he pulled him over the lip of the threshold. He staggered and let the body drop just clear of the door.

He shut the door as quietly as possible and caught his breath. Dragging the boy across the floor, Preston pulled him up on the toilet seat. He pushed his head against the wall. The skull met the tiles with a satisfying, dull thud.

He grabbed a handful of hair and slammed the head against the wall again. This time, he heard a squishy crunch and smiled. Pounding the head against the wall in a primal rhythm, he spoke in a low voice.

"See what you made me do? All of you, always pushing, pushing,

pushing! Never satisfied. You laugh at me, make jokes about me. Hurt me. Well, you pushed too far, didn't you? Now, you paid the price." In his mind, he could see all those who had terrorized him in the past.

Not conscious of his actions, he continued to pound the head against the wall until the skull was a chipped pulp. Suddenly, he realized how much noise he was making. Frightened, he released the hair. The body slumped forward off the toilet seat. He listened and could barely make out the chords of the guitar. He took several deep breaths to calm himself. He pulled the boy back up to the toilet seat.

Grabbing a wad of paper towels, he carefully wiped down the leather vest. CSI wouldn't get anything.

Turning to leave, his foot kicked something, sending it across the floor in a metallic skitter. Bending under the sink, he picked up a knife. He pressed the small button on the black and red handle and a six-inch blade sprang into view. The knife must have fallen from the boy's pocket when he fell off the toilet. Preston closed the knife and slipped it into his pant's pocket.

Standing in the bushes by the bathroom door, he scanned the area. The neighborhood was quiet. He took several deep breaths and started across the station lot.

As he passed, he picked up the empty juice carton. He tossed it and his bloody jacket into the garbage bin at the Chinese food place near his home. Smiling, he was confident he had left no clues.

✳   ✳   ✳   ✳   ✳

Dan set his guitar down and stretched, rolling his head to relax his neck. Less than three hours and his shift would be over. He hated the 11 to 7 but at least he could practice his guitar. He stretched again and grabbed the key for the washroom. Carefully locking the door to the booth, he went around the building.

He opened the washroom door and immediately stepped back.

"Sorry man, didn't know you were in here. Hey, you okay, man?" Then he saw the blood, the matted hair and splintered skull. "Jesus Christ!" was all he got out before he threw up all over the crime scene.

Before you embark on a journey of revenge, dig . . .

DG

Two Graves

A Kesle City Homicide Novel

D.A. Graystone

Available July 2011
http://www.dagraystone.com

www.ingramcontent.com/pod-product-compliance
Lightning Source LLC
Chambersburg PA
CBHW060801120626
46557CB00001B/60